MURDER AT
ALDWYCH STATION

By Jim Eldridge

LONDON UNDERGROUND STATION MYSTERIES SERIES

Murder at Aldwych Station
Murder at Down Street Station

MUSEUM MYSTERIES SERIES

Murder at the Fitzwilliam
Murder at the British Museum
Murder at the Ashmolean
Murder at the Manchester Museum
Murder at the Natural History Museum
Murder at Madame Tussauds
Murder at the National Gallery
Murder at the Victoria and Albert Museum
Murder at the Tower of London

HOTEL MYSTERIES SERIES

Murder at the Ritz
Murder at the Savoy
Murder at Claridge's

a&b

MURDER AT ALDWYCH STATION

JIM ELDRIDGE

Allison & Busby Limited
11 Wardour Mews
London W1F 8AN
allisonandbusby.com

First published in Great Britain by Allison & Busby in 2022.
This paperback edition published by Allison & Busby in 2023.

Copyright © 2022 by JIM ELDRIDGE

10 9 8 7 6 5 4 3 2 1

ISBN 978-0-7490-2843-5

Typeset in 11/16 pt Sabon LT Pro by
Allison & Busby Ltd.

Printed and bound by
CPI Group (UK) Ltd, Croydon, CR0 4YY

To Lynne, without whom there'd be nothing.

CHAPTER ONE

Tuesday 3rd December 1940. 1 a.m.

Bombs rained down on London from the fleet of German bombers, pounding the city and sending flames of destruction across it, just as the Luftwaffe had done for the past three months. It was estimated that about fifteen thousand Londoners had been killed since the start of the Blitz in September, with another twenty-five thousand seriously injured. Much of London had been razed to the ground, whole streets flattened.

Deep below ground beneath central London, two figures emerged from the entrance to a narrow tunnel into the larger one where the Underground railway line ran between Aldwych and Holborn stations. The electric current to this section of the line had been switched off. The two carried the body of a young man. Between them, they headed towards Aldwych station until they came to a barrier that had been set up across the tracks, protecting the treasures from the British Museum stored there. They laid the young man's body across the railway tracks, then made their way back to the smaller tunnel from where they'd come and vanished into the darkness.

CHAPTER TWO

Tuesday 3rd December 1940. 6 a.m.

The shrill wail of the all-clear sounded across the city, signifying the night raid by the Luftwaffe was over. There were no more German bombers headed for London, at least for now. In Knightsbridge Underground station, those who'd taken shelter from the bombing began to make their way to the surface. Among them were retired former general Cedric Walters and his wife, Phyllis. Although Phyllis had been able to fall asleep on a rug on the platform, General Walters had spent most of the night awake, as he did most nights, bitterly regretting that because of his age he couldn't enlist and take an active part in the war. He remembered his time in the trenches during the First War. Yes, he'd been wounded, but he'd survived, unlike many of his comrades. For him, his time at war had been glorious, every emotion heightened, facing the enemy and the prospect of dying every day. This business of spending his nights skulking like everyone else below ground galled him, but he had little chance of doing anything else if he was going to keep Phyllis safe. She wouldn't go down to the Underground for shelter if he didn't.

'We've been together for forty years,' she told him. 'I couldn't be with you in the trenches but I'm with you now, and we're going to stay together. I won't allow it that you get killed on your own. If you die, we both die.'

And so, every night, when the air raid warning sounded, they sought shelter on the platform of Knightsbridge station, among other locals, many of whom had become friends – or at least people to talk to – as they sheltered here during the past three months, until the all-clear told them it was safe to return to the streets above them.

Each time, they wondered what those streets, the city itself, would look like. How much would have been destroyed during the night's raid? Would their home be standing, or would it have been flattened like so many others?

When the general and his wife approached the small block of flats where they lived, their own flat being on the top floor, they saw that the building had indeed been hit. It was still standing, but it looked as if the roof had been struck. A fire engine was parked outside the block of flats and there were pools of water flooding across the road and pavement. Thick fire hoses ran from the engine up the steps to the entrance of the flats, and continued onwards up the concrete staircase.

Walters and Phyllis hurried up the stairs until they reached the top. They saw at once that the door to their home had been broken open so the fire crew could gain access.

Inside their flat, four men in fire crew uniforms switched off the valves on the fire hoses and laid them down, then stood, surveying the damage.

'What happened?' demanded Walters.

The four men turned and looked at the couple warily. 'Who are you?' asked one of the men.

'We're the owners,' said Walters. 'This is our flat.'

The man pointed towards a hole in the ceiling and said, 'The explosion tore off part of the roof and set the rafters alight. Luckily we got here in time or you'd have lost the lot.'

Phyllis looked with dismay at the state of the flat, every piece of furniture drenched in water. The carpet was so waterlogged it was like walking across a shallow stream.

'Everything's ruined,' said Phyllis, upset.

The man shrugged. 'That's water for you. That's what it does. It's either that or flames. Most people prefer it wet like this than burnt to ashes.'

General Walters suddenly spotted that the door of his safe was hanging open.

'What's happened there?' he demanded, pointing.

'What?' asked the man, and the other three began to drag the fire hoses out of the flat.

'My safe,' said Walters, outraged. 'It's been broken open!'

'Well, don't look at us,' said the man. 'We haven't touched it. That must have been done before we got here. Or maybe you left it unlocked?'

'No, I locked it before we went out,' said Walters firmly. 'I check every time we leave the flat.'

He went to the broken safe and opened the door wider. 'They're gone!' he said, shocked. He turned to the four men. 'My wife's jewels. My medals. And cash.'

'Like I said, nothing to do with us,' said the man curtly. He turned to the other three and said, 'Get those hoses out into the street and back on the engine.'

'Oh no you don't!' barked Walters, and he stood between the men and the door, barring their way. 'My safe has been robbed and you're the only people who've been in here. I insist on searching each of you.'

The men stared at him, indignant.

'You what!' shouted one, the biggest and burliest. He dropped the hose he was holding and advanced on Walters. 'Are you accusing us of nicking the stuff from your safe?'

'As you ask, yes I am!' retorted Walters. 'You can prove your innocence by allowing me to search you all.'

The men stared at one another, outrage writ large on their faces. The burly man scowled and turned back to Walters. 'You've got a bloody cheek!' he barked, and suddenly his fist flew out and struck the general hard on the side of the face, sending him down to the squelching carpet. 'We risk our lives saving your bloody flat, and this is the thanks we get!' He bent down over the fallen general, bringing his fist back to strike another blow.

'Hold it, Joe!' said the man in charge. 'He's learnt his lesson.' As the man called Joe stepped back, still scowling, the man who'd stopped him glared at the general and at Phyllis. 'Don't think we won't remember this,' he said angrily. 'Next time we get a call out here, you can handle it yourselves.'

With that the four men left, dragging the hoses with them. General Walters pushed himself to his feet.

'The thieving swine!' he said. 'They're not going to get away with this. I'm going after them.'

'No, Cedric!' said Phyllis, and she grabbed him by the arm, pulling him back from the door. 'There are four of them. You wouldn't have a chance against them. Let the police handle it.'

'The police!' said Walters scornfully. 'They're not going to do anything. They're too busy going around arresting people for breaking the blackout and other petty things.'

'Breaking the blackout isn't petty,' said Phyllis. 'It leads to loss of lives.'

'Yes, alright,' admitted Walters grumpily. He put his hand to the side of his face where a bruise was showing. 'But they won't do anything about this. They'll just say there's a war on and they've got more important things to deal with.' He gave a vengeful scowl towards the stairs where the men had vanished. 'But I know someone who'll get something done about this. Those thieving scum won't get away with it!'

CHAPTER THREE

Tuesday 3rd December 1940. 10 a.m.

Detective Chief Inspector Edgar Walter Septimus Saxe-Coburg, accompanied by his detective sergeant, Ted Lampson, walked along the currently disused railway track of the Aldwych Underground station, deeper into the tunnel. Just three months before, this branch of the Piccadilly line to Holborn had been an active part of the London Underground system, but the Blitz in September changed all that.

The Blitz had begun in early September, the intensive bombing by the Luftwaffe of London and Britain's other major cities, but primarily London. Before that there'd been daytime bombing raids by the Luftwaffe, but the small Spitfires and Hurricanes from the airfields in Kent and Essex had kept most of them at bay during the period from mid-July until early September that became known as the Battle of Britain. The death toll had been high during the Battle of Britain, especially among the young fighter pilots who'd been sent up day after day to confront the giant German bombers and engage in aerial battles with their German fighter Messerschmitt escorts, but the death toll for the Germans had been even higher. Finally, the Germans had to admit that the RAF had defeated the Luftwaffe in these daytime attacks, so the Germans had switched to night-time attacks, when the small fighter planes could not defend the city.

The docks in the East End had been among the first to suffer, the whole area ablaze, and then more and more of London had become a target. On 10th September, Buckingham Palace itself had been hit by a German bomb, proving that no one and nowhere was safe. The block of flats in Hampstead where Coburg and his wife, Rosa, had lived had been completely demolished during a raid. Fortunately for the couple, they had been out when it happened, but everyone else in the block who'd sought safety in an Anderson shelter in the grounds had been killed.

Coburg and Rosa had relocated to another flat in central London, this time ensuring that it had a strong shelter in the basement.

Coburg's sergeant, Ted Lampson, a widower in his early thirties, lived in Somers Town, a major target area for the Luftwaffe because it was right next to Euston, St Pancras and King's Cross stations, all main railway termini. For him and his ten-year-old son, Terry, Euston Square Underground station was their nearest shelter.

At first there had been panic among Londoners

when the Blitz began, then, as it went on night after night, and occasionally during the day, a kind of unhappy acceptance had settled in. Daylight raids were less frequent because the RAF were still battling in the skies above Kent, downing the giant German bombers when they could, while at the same time engaging in aerial dogfights with the German bombers' Messerschmitt fighter escorts. Now, in early December, the bombing had been going on for fourteen weeks, with no apparent let-up. And life in the capital went on. Shops were open, although in the case of butchers' and some grocers', with limited supplies due to rationing. People still went to work. Coburg's wife, Rosa, a well-known pianist and jazz singer, also worked part-time driving an ambulance for St John Ambulance. Nearly everyone volunteered to help the war effort as air raid wardens and auxiliary firemen to battle the blazes from the bombing. Many former soldiers and retired people joined the Home Guard, ready to resist the Germans when they invaded, as everyone expected them to do. Reports of German troopships and landing craft moored off the French coast just twenty-five miles from the Kent coast were common knowledge. It was not *if* the Germans launched their invasion, but when.

Crime also carried on in the capital. The black market thrived in these days of rationing: sugar, bacon and especially petrol, along with many other products that were not freely available without coupons restricting how much anyone could buy at any one time: a limit of four ounces of bacon per person, and eight ounces each for sugar, butter and cheese, with meat purchases restricted to one shilling's worth. As a result, butchers' shops and warehouses had become prime targets for thieves.

Murder, also, seemed to Coburg as bad as ever. Along with the daily count of dead bodies from the bombing came reports of dead bodies found in places where the bombs couldn't reach. Like now, with the report of the body of a dead man discovered deep in one of the tunnels at Aldwych station, close to where the famous Elgin Marbles were being stored, following their removal from the British Museum.

Although the electric current had been cut to the rails, it still powered the overhead and side lights in the walls of the tunnel, but the lighting was dim and they had to walk carefully to avoid stumbling over the rails and sleepers. Finally, they came to a long, low flatbed wagon on the tracks, on which lay a massive length of carved marble. Beyond that was a second identical flatbed wagon containing another length of marble, and then another, and another, each of them covered with a length of cloth.

'The Elgin Marbles,' said Coburg. 'Or, more properly, the Parthenon Sculptures.'

'Bloody hell,' said Lampson, impressed. 'They're

enormous! How many of them are there?'

'The whole thing is 246 feet long, when laid end to end,' said Coburg. 'Didn't you see them when they were on display at the British Museum?'

'I've never been to the British Museum,' admitted Lampson.

'Ted, I'm shocked,' said Coburg. 'It's one of the greatest museums in the world, and you live within walking distance of it.'

'Yeh, well, museums were never my thing,' said Lampson. 'They reminded me too much of school, which I was never fond of. If I had an afternoon off, I went to football. White Hart Lane.' He looked at the lengths of carved marble. 'They must be bloody heavy.'

'A hundred tons, I'm told,' said Coburg. 'They were moved here at the start of September.'

'How?' asked Lampson.

'A low-loader lorry from the British Museum to the London Transport depot at Lillie Bridge in Kensington, then transferred to rail wagons, and then here. It's not the first time this station's been used for hiding valuable treasures to keep them safe. In September 1917, because of the threat of German air raids during the First War, the National Gallery sent most of its paintings here to be stored, and they were kept here until December 1918.'

'All this stuff's more important than people, is it?'

said Lampson sourly. 'I remember the scenes of people clamouring to get into the Tube stations when the Blitz started to try and get somewhere safe from the bombing, and the gates were locked and the people were actually beaten back to stop them coming in.'

'I was told that was because the government were worried that once people came below ground to seek refuge, they wouldn't go up top again, which would mean no workers,' said Coburg. 'No firemen, no plumbers, no bus drivers, no one to keep the city operating.'

It had been the invasion of the Savoy Hotel by angry East Enders on 14th September that had changed things, reflected Coburg. Furious that the people of the East End were being killed in their hundreds by the German blitzkrieg because the public were barred from seeking safety in the Underground stations, but instead had been left to go to the street-level brick public shelters, which invariably collapsed when a bomb went off near one of them, a crowd of people from Stepney had descended on the Savoy, brought by the Savoy's advertising campaign in which it boasted of its basement air raid shelter, extolling its virtues, its luxury, the guarantee of safety. The Savoy's Swiss night manager, Willy Hofflin, had allowed them in and they spent the night in the hotel shelter. This invasion by the proletariat sent ripples of unease through the ruling classes, many of whom were at the Savoy that night, and shortly afterwards the government relented and allowed London's Underground stations to be used as shelters.

Aldwych station had been closed down as a passenger station early in September and electricity to the line disconnected to allow safe storage of the British Museum's valuables, not just the Elgin Marbles but part of the British Museum's collection of rare books and some oriental antiquities. Towards the end of the month, it had been handed over to the local authority, Westminster City Council, for use as a public air raid shelter, with people using the platforms and for 320 yards into the tunnel towards Holborn. It was estimated that two thousand, five hundred people sheltered in it. Most of them went back to the surface during the day, but there had still been a few people on the platforms when Coburg and Lampson arrived, surrounding themselves with chairs, mattresses and small tables, creating subterranean homes from home. A uniformed constable stood behind a barrier that had been placed in front of the wagons. Next to him was a man in the uniform of a British Museum attendant. The constable saluted when he recognised Coburg.

'PC Thompson, sir,' he said. 'I've been here keeping guard since I got the call about the body.'

'Where is it?' asked Coburg.

The constable pointed along the line of wagons. 'It's at the end of these wagons,' he said. 'There's a bloke from the British Museum along there, checking these marble slabs in case any of them had got damaged. It was him who found the body. I've also alerted the duty doctor.'

Coburg nodded, then he and Lampson made their way past the wagons. They were halfway along when they came upon a man in his late forties in a long white coat who had pushed back the cloth cover of one of the wagons and was examining the marble sculpture beneath. The man turned towards them and held up his hand in greeting.

'Chief Inspector!' He smiled.

'Sir John,' responded Coburg. He gestured towards Lampson. 'This is my sergeant, Ted Lampson. Sergeant, this is Sir John Petersham, the man responsible for the safety of the Parthenon Sculptures.'

'And a complete headache that is,' sighed Petersham. 'As if the bombing wasn't bad enough, now we have this.'

'The constable said you found the body.'

'Yes. I haven't touched it. I know you policemen like to examine the scene of the crime in as undisturbed a state as possible. I'll show you where it is.'

Petersham led the way past the remaining wagons and stopped by the last one. Beyond that was a wooden barrier, and by the barrier the body of a young man lay between the tracks. He looked to be in his late teenage years, possibly eighteen or nineteen, smartly dressed in formal evening clothes, complete with bow tie. His shoes were missing, and his socks had holes through which his toes poked.

'Interesting,' murmured Coburg. 'Did he walk here like that or was he carried?'

'Yes, I noticed that,' said Petersham. 'Which do you think it was? And if he walked, what happened to his shoes?'

Coburg looked back along the line of wagons. 'Walking along there, which is quite narrow with the wagons in the way, wouldn't be easy if someone was carrying a body.' Petersham shook his head.

'That's the sort of puzzle that's beyond my sphere of knowledge,' he said. 'More your sort of thing. I remember you were always a bit of a clever clogs when it came to puzzles. Wasn't it Jefferies who called you the brainbox of the Oppidans?'

'An exaggeration, like many of Jefferies's utterances,' said Coburg.

He knelt down and peeled the jacket away from the front of the body.

'No obvious wounds,' he said. With Lampson's help, he rolled the body onto its front and lifted the back of the jacket. 'No obvious wounds there, either.' He stood up. 'How long ago did you find the body?'

'About an hour ago. I was here with my assistant, Wellington Porter, and we were walking along checking the sculptures, something we do regularly since they've been down here in case there's any damage to them.

We've put up a barrier manned by attendants from the museum who keep guard over them, but we still get people coming along trying to look at them. Or, in some cases, looking for somewhere private to do whatever they want to do. I always come to the end of the line first and then make my way back, and that's when I saw him lying there, just as you see him. I sent Wellington to find a policeman, and once the constable arrived, I sent Wellington off.' He gave a rueful look. 'The poor chap was quite overcome. Never seen a dead body before. Sensitive sort of chap.' He nodded approvingly towards the distant point where PC Thompson was still standing guard. 'Good man, that constable. He's arranged for the doctor to come, got a message to Scotland Yard to alert you, and he's been rock solid at keeping people from coming down here. I believe other officers are on their way to relieve him, and also remove the body when the doctor's finished giving it the once-over. Very efficient, especially with everything else that's going on up top.'

Coburg then checked the dead man's pockets, looking for a wallet or any form of identification, but found nothing. Petersham looked along the line of wagons and said, 'Ah, here come the medicos!'

Coburg looked up and saw Dr Welbourne from University College Hospital approaching, accompanied by two ambulance men carrying a stretcher.

'Chief Inspector Coburg! Sergeant Lampson!' Welbourne greeted them. 'Here we are again, gathered together over an unfortunate corpse.' Welbourne looked down at the body of the young man. 'How did he die? Shot? Stabbed? All I was told was someone had been murdered down here.'

'That's what we're hoping you'll be able to tell us, Doctor,' said Coburg.

Welbourne knelt down beside the body. 'Anyone checked him for wounds?' he asked.

'Yes,' said Coburg. 'Front and back. Nothing, as far as I can see.'

Welbourne examined the young man's face, felt his neck, checked his wrists and arms for rigor mortis, then opened the dead man's jacket.

'No wounds on the front of the body,' he confirmed. He gestured to the ambulance men. 'Can you help me turn him over?'

With help from the ambulance men, Welbourne turned the young man over and peeled his jacket off him.

'No wounds in the back,' he said. He began to examine the man's scalp closely. 'No wounds to the head, so he wasn't knocked unconscious.'

He gestured to the ambulance men and they rolled the young man on his back again. Welbourne leant forward and sniffed at the young man's mouth.

'Poison is my guess,' he said. 'But I'll be able to tell

24

you more once I've taken a proper look at him.' He looked around. 'There's no trace of a bottle near the body, so he didn't do it to himself.'

'When do you think he died?'

'At a guess, some time during the night.' He looked at his watch. 'It's half past ten now. Say nine hours ago, give or take an hour either side.'

'So, about one in the morning,' said Coburg. 'When the platform of the station would have been packed.'

Welbourne lifted the man's left hand and examined the fingers.

'This is interesting,' he said. He showed Coburg the grooves in the man's fingertips, along with the hard, calloused skin. 'I think he may have been a guitarist.'

'A guitarist?' asked Coburg. 'Or possibly a violinist? They press down on the strings of the instrument. So do banjo players.'

Welbourne shook his head. 'When I've seen grooves like these before they're usually the result of steel strings. Violins use gut, as do Spanish guitars. I think you'll find that our friend here used to play in a jazz group. The giveaway is his clothes. If he'd played country and western guitar he'd be dressed as a cowboy.'

'You should have been a detective,' said Coburg. 'But then, you already are, deducing cause of death from the evidence presented. Although this deduction of him being a jazz guitarist goes one better.'

Welbourne got to his feet and gestured to the ambulance men. 'Take him to UCH,' he said.

The ambulance men put the dead man on the stretcher and then, with some difficulty, made their way along the railway tracks past the wagons loaded with the massive Elgin Marbles.

Welbourne looked at the Parthenon Sculptures and commented, 'It must have been some job to get this lot here.'

'It was indeed,' said Petersham.

'Dr Welbourne, this is Sir John Petersham from the British Museum. He's the one who found the body. Sir John, this is Dr Andrew Welbourne from UCH.'

The two men shook hands.

'Very impressive, that business of him being a jazz guitarist,' complimented Petersham.

'Personal experience. I used to play guitar at university,' said Welbourne. 'Spanish guitar, that is. Steel strings were too much for me.'

'Can you arrange for a photograph to be taken of him at the hospital?' asked Coburg. 'At the moment we have no idea who he is.'

'No problem,' said Welbourne. 'I'll have it ready for you this afternoon. At the same time, I should be able to give you more of an idea about what killed him.'

CHAPTER FOUR

Tuesday 3rd December 1940

Coburg and Lampson walked back towards the platforms at Aldwych station. Once they passed the barriers and the security people from the British Museum who were keeping watch over the Parthenon Sculptures, they came to the people camping in the now defunct railway tracks. Some sat on the rails, some lay curled up between the rails, asleep, but most seemed to have moved back to the platforms now the crowds there had thinned out.

They asked those who were resting between the rails and were awake if they'd seen anyone answering the dead man's description walking into the tunnels.

'A young man in his teens, wearing a dark suit, white shirt and bow tie, and he had no shoes on.'

Everyone they asked shook their head. 'No,' was the general answer, 'no one like that.' Most of them also added, 'Lots of people walk into the tunnel at night because it's nearer than the platforms if they need to go to the toilet. Especially because there's only a couple of Elsan portable toilets there, and they get full up.'

The response was the same from the people who were camping on the platforms. Many of them had recreated their homes there as best they could, with tables and chairs and mattresses to sleep on. Some had brought camping stoves. At one end of the platform, as distant as they could be from the Elsan toilets hidden behind hanging blankets, was a refreshment table set up by the Women's Royal Voluntary Service, with tea urns kept hot on portable stoves and some slices of bread skimmed with margarine.

Everyone they spoke to agreed that the description of the young man meant he would have been noticeable, but no one had seen him on the platform or walking along the railway tracks into the tunnels.

They returned to the barrier and the two British Museum security guards, one of whom had been on duty the night before.

'No,' he assured the two policemen. 'No one like that came this way.'

'And someone's here at the barrier twenty-four hours a day?' asked Coburg.

'Absolutely,' said the man firmly. He gestured back towards the wagons with the marble sculptures. 'This lot are too valuable to leave unguarded. They may be too heavy for people to nick, though I wouldn't put it past people, but there's always the danger of some young whelp coming along and carving his name in one of them for fun.'

'If he didn't come through Aldwych, the only way he could have got to where he was found is if he was brought from Holborn station and carried along the tracks,' observed Lampson. 'But that would take two people.'

Coburg turned back to the British Museum guard and asked, 'Is there a maintenance man who services the station? I know it's shut, but there's usually someone on duty.'

The guard nodded. 'Percy Wenlock,' he said. 'He's got a little place further in the tunnel, a room with a kettle and everything. Keep going and it's the first door you come to on the left.'

'Are there many of these rooms inside the tunnels?' asked Coburg.

'There are a few,' said the man, 'but I only know the one where Percy is. We take turns to go and have a cuppa with him, and he's usually got some biscuits as well.'

Coburg and Lampson walked past the wagons with the Elgin Marbles on, then to the place where the young man had been found, and then continued on into the tunnel. The lighting set into the walls of the tunnel had been left on, though it was dimmed. Here, away from the people on the platform and camping between the rails, away from the loaded wagons, it was spookier, emptier, the sound of their shoes crunching on the thin layer of gravel between the rails echoing back at them as they walked.

They found the wooden door and knocked at it, and it was opened by a man in his fifties wearing a pair of overalls. They introduced themselves, and he introduced himself as Percy Wenlock and invited them in.

It was a small room, with tools of different sorts hanging from hooks in the wall, and pieces of equipment on the shelves. There was a bare wooden table and two chairs. In one corner was a portable paraffin heater, atop which sat a kettle. A teapot and cups, and a bottle of milk, were on one of the shelves.

'Terrible, what happened,' said Wenlock. 'The dead man.'

'When did you find out about it?' sked Coburg.

'When I came on shift about an hour ago. The guard at the barrier told me. Can I offer you both a cup of tea?'

'That would be very nice, thank you,' said Coburg.

They stood as Wenlock poured water from the kettle into the teapot.

'Sit yourselves down,' he said.

'Thanks, but we won't take your chair,' said Coburg. 'That wouldn't be fair.'

Wenlock pulled a wooden crate from the wall and placed it by the table. 'This'll do me,' he told them.

They sat down while Wenlock poured the tea for them, and then opened a small tin. 'Biscuit?' he asked.

'Thank you,' said Coburg. 'Very much appreciated.' They each took a biscuit from the tin, as did Wenlock. 'We're wondering where the dead man could have come from,' explained Coburg. 'He didn't come through Aldwych. This track goes to Holborn, so we're wondering if he was brought here from there.'

'It's possible,' said Wenlock. 'But there's other places he could have come from.'

Coburg frowned, puzzled. 'Are you saying there are other places between Holborn station and here where someone can gain access to the line?'

Wenlock chuckled. 'Oh, bless you, yes!'

'So there's another tunnel that connects with this one?'

'Not just one. This whole place is a maze of tunnels. When they were digging the Kingsway tram tunnel that runs parallel to this one, there were all manner of connections made. Then there's the old post office line. It operates between the sorting office at Paddington and runs to Whitechapel delivery office. What's fascinating about it is it uses driverless trains, so the trains and carriages that carry the mail don't have to be very tall. It serves seven stations between the two end ones, and the one at New Oxford Street ain't far from here. Again, while they were building it, they sank all manner of shafts and dug service tunnels criss-crossing between other existing tunnels.'

'Where were the existing tunnels built?' asked Coburg. 'Is there a plan of them, showing where they are?'

'Some,' said Wenlock, 'but only the recent ones.

Mainly the tunnels that were dug for cables and such. Not the old ones. Remember, this city's been here since Roman times, and the Romans dug tunnels under it. Then later on people built on top of what the Romans built, making other tunnels, making a series of cut-and-cover tunnels. Then you've got the rivers that run under London with their own tunnels. And the sewers. And the catacombs.'

'The catacombs?' asked Lampson. 'Burial chambers,' interpreted Coburg.

'That's them.' Wenlock nodded. 'And not just places where people were interred. One of the biggest catacombs in London that's known is in Camden, near the canal. They were originally used as stables for horses and pit ponies working on the railways. There's even an underground pool for canal boats.'

'What about around here?' asked Coburg.

Wenlock shrugged. 'Sure to be. After all, there's been enough churches around this area. They was always digging tunnels beneath 'em. And whenever a tunnel was being dug, like for the Underground railway, many's the time they crossed one of the old catacombs.'

'So this young man could have arrived here from almost anywhere?'

Wenlock nodded. 'That's about right,' he said. 'But whoever brought him here would have had to know their way around the tunnels.'

CHAPTER FIVE

Tuesday 3rd December 1940

As they made their way back to Scotland Yard, with Lampson driving, Lampson asked, 'What was all this *Oppidan* stuff that museum bloke was going on about? What's an Oppidan?'

'Sir John and I were at Eton at the same time, although he was a couple of years above me,' explained Coburg. 'There are two sorts of scholars at Eton: King's Scholars or Oppidans. King's Scholars attend on scholarships awarded by examination each year. The name goes back to the original school, which was founded by Henry VI in 1440. The original school consisted of seventy scholars who were educated and boarded at the foundation's expense. As the school grew, other students came in who paid their own fees and lived in boarding houses in the town of Eton. They were known as Oppidans from the Latin *oppidum*, meaning town.'

'And who was this Jefferies bloke he mentioned?'

'Our housemaster.'

Lampson shook his head, amazed. 'You old

Etonians get everywhere. Have you noticed that nearly every case we get drawn into, there's usually another of your old schoolmates involved?'

'That's because the powers-that-be at Scotland Yard seem to think just because of my name, and the fact I went to Eton, that these people will talk to me.'

'A member of the royal family.' Lampson grinned.

'I am not a member of the royal family,' said Coburg firmly. 'The original name of the royal family before they changed their name to Windsor was Saxe-Coburg-Gotha. There may be some distant connection, but very distant. I repeat, I am not part of the royal family.'

'Maybe not, but you're titled,' said Lampson.

'My brother, Magnus, is titled,' Coburg corrected him. 'He's the Earl of Dawlish, because he inherited the title from our late father. I am *not* titled.'

'You will be when your brother falls off the perch,' said Lampson. 'He's got no kids. So it'll be you as the earl, and your missus as Lady Dawlish.'

'Magnus is not going to fall off the perch any time soon,' said Coburg. 'And, if he did, it would be my brother Charles who'd inherit. He's the second son.'

'And he's currently in a German POW camp,' said Lampson. 'So you're in with a chance.'

'I am not in with a chance,' insisted Coburg. 'I do not *want* to be in with a chance.'

'Oh come on, guv.' Lampson chuckled. 'Just

think of it, a detective in our department who the superintendents and even the commissioner will have to call sir, or Your Grace, or whatever it is.'

'I refuse to have this conversation any more,' said Coburg. 'We have a dead body in a tunnel. That's what we should be concentrating on.' Then, thoughtfully, he added, 'Dr Welbourne said that jazz guitarists use steel strings. Maybe Rosa might know who our dead man is.'

Rosa, at that moment, was up to her elbows in grease, making sure that all the moving parts of the ambulance were in working order and wouldn't let them down when they were out on an emergency call. Her co-driver, Doris Gibbs, a nurse in her fifties who worked at Paddington Hospital and volunteered with St John Ambulance in her time off, was washing the outside of the ambulance using a sponge and a bucket of hot soapy water. Rosa had volunteered to be responsible for the mechanical side of the ambulance, including the intricacies of the engine. 'When I was a kid in Edinburgh, my dad had a vegetable business and he taught me to drive his lorries, and along with that, I watched him as he did the servicing, and then helped him.' She shut the bonnet of the ambulance. 'I never thought I'd be using what he taught me this way.'

She plunged her hands and arms into the bucket of soapy water and began to scrub the grease off.

'Right,' said Doris, 'shall we make sure it's working okay? If you get behind the wheel, I'll turn it over with the starting handle.'

They'd been given one of the older ambulances that had been out of service for a while to get it back into proper working order and cleaned. The more modern ambulance they'd been using with pull-switch ignition to fire it up had been badly damaged in a night call when it had been hit by a bus during the blackout. Fortunately for both Rosa and Doris, another crew had been driving it at the time of the accident. The two men who'd been the crew had escaped with minor cuts and bruises, but the front of the vehicle had been crushed and it had been towed away to a garage for repairs.

'Careful with that starting handle,' warned Rosa. 'If it kicks back, it'll break your thumb.'

Doris chuckled. 'Don't you worry about me, Rosa,' she said. 'My old man's car only started with the handle. Doing this is second nature to me.'

She took the starting handle from the cab and pushed it into its slot beneath the radiator grille.

'Ready!' she called.

Rosa pulled the lever to start enough fuel flowing for ignition, then shut it off and raised a thumb to let Doris know it was ready. Doris cranked the handle sharply, keeping a tight grip on it: once, twice, then on the third crank the engine fired up. Doris pulled the starting handle out and Rosa opened the fuel flow, revving it up. She was just about to turn the engine off when she saw their supervisor, Chesney Warren, running towards them, a piece of paper in his hand. 'Looks like a shout!' she said loudly, over the noise of the engine.

Doris turned and saw Warren, who handed her the piece of paper, then backed off and hurried back to the single-storey brick building that was his office.

Doris climbed into the cab and settled herself in the passenger seat.

'What have we got?' asked Rosa.

'Woman and a baby hit by a car in Lisson Grove,' Doris told her, looking at the details on the paper Warren had given her.

'Right, get the bell going,' said Rosa, and she put the ambulance into gear and drove across the yard towards the entrance to the main road, while Doris pulled the rope that set the bell clanging, warning other drivers and pedestrians that they were on an emergency call and wouldn't be stopping.

CHAPTER SIX

Tuesday 3rd December 1940

Dr Welbourne had a head-and-shoulders image of the dead man ready when Coburg and Lampson arrived at the mortuary at University College Hospital.

'We didn't have time to use make-up to make him look more alive,' he said.

'Even with make-up, dead people tend to still look dead in photos,' said Coburg, pocketing the picture. 'The main thing is he's recognisable. Thanks for that.'

'And as to the cause of death, it was strychnine poisoning. I've had it confirmed by our Mrs Mallowan.' He smiled as he added, 'And if anyone would recognise the symptoms of strychnine poisoning, it's her.'

Coburg returned his knowing smile. Mrs Mallowan was better known as Agatha Christie, the crime novelist, who was currently working in the pharmacy department at UCH, doing her part for the war effort.

'Yes,' said Coburg. 'It does seem to occur in quite a few of her books. *The Mysterious Affair at Styles*; "How Does Your Garden Grow?"; "The Coming of Mr Quin".'

'You are obviously a fan of hers, Chief Inspector,' said Welbourne.

'I am,' said Coburg.

'Out of curiosity . . . as a policeman, do you always work out who the murderer is in her books?'

'No,' Coburg admitted. 'Have you any idea how it was administered?'

'I'm afraid not. Either it was added to a drink or some food, or it was forced down his throat. The fact that there was partly digested food in his stomach and intestines suggested he didn't vomit it up. You know how strychnine works?'

'Sadly, yes,' said Coburg. 'Death comes any time after ten minutes, and can be as long as three hours, depending on the circumstances. If medical aid is given, for example. And depending on the amount of strychnine used. Death is from asphyxiation or inner tissue paralysis.'

'A textbook definition,' said Welbourne.

'And that's exactly where it came from,' said Coburg. 'The amount of murders committed that way meant I needed to read up about it. Anything else about the victim?'

'I assume you mean were there any drugs in his system because of the suggestion that he was a jazz musician?'

Coburg gave a rueful smile. 'I know it's an archetype, but I'm wondering how he came to be poisoned. Was he overpowered while he was under the influence of something?'

'If so, it certainly wasn't drugs,' said Welbourne. 'He hadn't eaten anything for some time before he died. There were small traces of whisky in his system, but nothing that would have rendered him drunk and incapable.'

That evening at their flat, over a supper of Spam and mashed potatoes, Coburg and Rosa related the events of their separate days' high spots and low spots.

'The high spot was a shout we had about a woman and a baby being hit by a car. We thought the worst, but fortunately we were able to patch them up and get them to the hospital. The baby was actually unharmed, the mother had managed to push the pram out of the way, but she suffered a broken leg and arm. The real casualty was the driver of the car. He was dead. Heart attack, though whether it had happened before the crash and been the cause of it, or afterwards because he was shocked at what had happened, we don't know. What about you? How was your day fighting crime?'

'A strange one,' said Coburg. 'A body was found in the tunnels leading from Aldwych station. The line's out of use at the moment, so the station and the tunnel to it are used as an air raid shelter, and also for storing important items from the British Museum. The body seems to be of a very young man. He was dressed in evening clothes, but without shoes. The doctor who examined him reckons he was a jazz guitarist from the grooves in his fingers.'

'A jazz guitarist?' said Rosa. 'Who is he? I might know him.'

'We don't know.' He took the photo of the young man from his pocket and pushed it across the table to her. 'The same thought about you possibly recognising him struck me.'

Rosa looked at the photograph, then said, 'Oh my God, it's Benny Martin. I played with him.' She gave the photograph back to Coburg. 'This is awful! A real tragedy! How did he die?'

'Poisoned with strychnine.'

'But . . . why? Who'd do something like that?'

'That's what we're trying to find out. Now you've given us his name you've made our job a whole lot easier. What do you know about him?'

'He was nice. Good guitarist, not like some of them who can get a bit precious.'

'Precious?'

'Resentful of other musicians who they think get a bigger profile. You know, saxophone players. Trumpet. Drums. They're the big instruments that the major people play. Guitarists are often seen as just supporting players. But Benny wasn't like that. He didn't crave fame like some people; he just loved playing with other musicians, good musicians.' She gave an unhappy look at Coburg. 'He was only nineteen. He was waiting to be called up.

41

He was so eager to get into uniform and fight.'

'Where did he play?'

'Everywhere he got a chance to sit in. He had a great ear so he could pick up whatever the group were doing, or whoever he was playing with, and just take it.'

'Where did you play with him?'

'At the Buttonhole Club in Frith Street. It wasn't a formal gig, more of an impromptu jam session after I'd done my set. That often happens after a gig: whoever's about comes up and joins you onstage, if you're happy to do that.'

'And you are?'

'Indeed I am. You often pick up new tunes, and meet talented people you wouldn't otherwise know about. Like Benny.'

'You haven't worked with him since?'

'Seen him, but not worked with him. About five months ago I went to the Pink Parrot, a jazz club in Soho, to talk to the owner about doing a gig there, and Benny was playing there with this quartet. So I stayed and listened.'

'You didn't talk to him?'

She shook her head. 'No, it was already late by the time his group came on, and I needed to get some sleep. I doubt if he even knew I was there.'

'Do you know where he lived?'

'No, but the owner of the Pink Parrot will know. His name's Gerry Matthews.'

CHAPTER SEVEN

Wednesday 4th December 1940. 10 a.m.

Lord Colin Cuddington came down the steps of the Reform Club and hailed a cab to take him home. Sitting in the back of the cab, he reflected on the awkward interview he'd just had with Sir Horace Percy, chairman of International and Domestic Commodities, one of the companies on which Lord Cuddington had a seat on the board. Sir Horace had arranged a private room for the interview, which had struck Cuddington as ominous. He'd met with Sir Horace often at the Reform, but usually in the lounge or the bar, but for some reason Sir Horace wanted this to be a private discussion. Cuddington soon found out the reason why.

'There have been rumours, Cuddington,' Sir Horace said. Sir Horace invariably had a fierce and grim expression on his face, particularly during board meetings, but today he looked grimmer than ever.

'Rumours?' repeated Cuddington, putting as much innocent puzzlement into his voice as he could. Inside, fear surged through him. What had they found out? He felt sick, but he fought to keep the nausea from rising into his mouth. As far as he knew, no other members of the board had any idea of his activities. True, he'd taken chances, and one of two of them had skated on fairly thin ice, but he'd managed to handle them without anything being discovered. At least, as far as he knew.

'About your wife,' said Sir Horace.

Immediately, Cuddington felt a sense of relief wash over him. The rumours weren't about him, but about Pamela. Thank God for that!

'My wife, Sir Horace?' he asked, again putting on a puzzled expression.

'Is your marriage . . . in good form?' asked Sir Horace.

What a funny way to put it, thought Cuddington. *No, it's not. It's never been in good form.*

Aloud, he said, 'You say there are rumours about my wife?'

'About her . . . activities.' Sir Horace fixed Cuddington with an intense and fierce gimlet gaze. 'A cousin of my wife occasionally frequents some of London's jazz clubs. Miranda James. Do you know her?'

'No, Sir Horace, I can't say that I do.'

'Miranda told my wife she's seen your wife at some of these places. Now there's nothing wrong with that. I enjoy some of that music myself. The melodic sort, you understand, not this wild discordant noise you get from some of them.'

'Yes, Sir Horace. I know exactly what you mean.'

'The thing is, Lady Cuddington wasn't alone at the clubs, according to Miranda. She was with a young man, a musician. He was appearing there, playing the guitar.'

Cuddington nodded and put on a look of polite interest as he waited for what he knew would be coming next. Sir Horace leant forward.

'According to Miranda, on both occasions she saw them together in this club, they were involved in what could only be described as sexual activity.'

Cuddington looked shocked. 'Sexual activity? My wife with this musician? In front of people?'

'Not exactly in front of the others,' amended Sir Horace. 'Inside the actual club, they were simply affectionate to one another, but Miranda had occasion to visit the conveniences and discovered your wife and this musician *in flagrante* on the floor of the ladies' toilets.'

Cuddington stared at Sir Horace with what he hoped was shock and bewilderment.

'*In flagrante*?' he repeated.

'On both occasions.' Sir Horace nodded. 'That particular time in the ladies' toilets, and then on another occasion in a passageway leading to a rear exit.'

Cuddington continued to stare at Sir Horace in horror, his mouth open. Then he shut his mouth and said, 'I had no idea! Pamela said she was going to a jazz club with a lady friend of hers who was an aficionado of that sort of music. Are you sure about this, Sir Horace?'

'Absolutely,' said Sir Horace. 'Miranda is not the sort of person to make things like that up.' He leant forward and said with firm intensity, 'You have to deal with this, Cuddington. If word gets out it will reflect badly on you, and therefore badly on you as a member of the Board of International and Domestic Commodities. We cannot afford scandals of any sort. Bring her to heel, Cuddington. If you can't bring her to heel, find out who this musician is and buy him off. Men like that only understand money, or a beating. Gigolos. You have to stop this, Cuddington. Nip it in the bud now, before it gets out of hand.'

'I will, Sir Horace,' said Cuddington. 'And thank you for giving me this information. As you can imagine, I'm absolutely shocked. I really believed that Pamela and I had a solid marriage, but it seems I was wrong. I may have spent too much time on my commitments to the company, doing my duty for International and Domestic, which may have led to Pamela feeling neglected. I shall deal with this immediately and bring her back into the fold.'

As he sat in the taxi, heading for home, he thought with grim satisfaction: *It's already been dealt with.*

The Pink Parrot was a small subterranean club in Carlisle Street, one of many such establishments in Soho, although most of the others seemed to specialise in exotic dancers, which usually meant striptease and nudes. At this time of the morning when Coburg and Lampson walked in, the club was empty of customers, just staff clearing up the debris from the night before. Gerry Matthews was a short, tubby man in his fifties, dressed down in shirtsleeves and braces as he supervised the empty bottles being removed, and the glasses being collected.

'Late night?' asked Coburg, showing his warrant card.

'We're a jazz club,' said Matthews. 'Jazzers play better late at night and the early hours of the morning, and that suits our customers who'd rather seek shelter here than in one of the public places. One of the advantages of being a private club, licensing laws don't apply.' He looked enquiringly at the two policemen. 'So, what can I do for you?'

'We're here about a young man called Benny Martin, a guitarist. We understand he's played here.'

'Yes. Nice guy. Good musician a well.' He regarded them warily. 'Is he in some sort of trouble?'

'The worst kind there is,' said Coburg. 'He's dead.

He was poisoned. We're trying to find out who his family are, his next of kin, and anything you can tell us about him.'

Matthews looked at them, shocked. 'Poisoned? Accidental?'

'It looks like he was murdered. His body was dumped in the tunnel at Aldwych Tube station.'

'What was he doing there?' asked Matthews, bewildered. 'That's what we're trying to find out. Do you have an address for him?'

'Yes. He lived in Swiss Cottage, one of those big houses that's been turned into bedsits.'

'Did you ever go there?'

Matthews shook his head. 'No, I stay here in Soho. I heard him talking about it, complaining about his neighbours in the house. If you come to the office, I'll get the address for you.'

As the two police officers began to follow him towards his office, Matthews stopped, then asked Coburg awkwardly, 'Actually, Mr Coburg, can we have a word in private?'

Coburg was about to say no, when Lampson spoke up. 'I'll wait in the car, guv.'

As Lampson walked out of the club, Coburg asked, 'What's so private you can't mention it in front of my sergeant?'

Matthews gestured for Coburg to follow him to his office. Once they were inside it and the door was shut, he said, 'The thing is, Benny had a lady friend who was very involved with him. Very. She's quite a bit older than he was, married, and with a title. I mention it because she was here one night with Benny when her husband arrived and started having a go at her, calling her a slut and all manner of other stuff.

'Benny stood up for her, went for the guy and they got into a bit of a fight. The husband was dragged off Benny, but as he left he told Benny he'd finish him. He tried to drag his wife out with him, but she wasn't having any of it.'

'Who's the lady, and who is her husband?'

'He's Lord Cuddington. She's Lady Pamela Cuddington.' He looked enquiringly at Coburg. 'She was here one night when we saw in the newspapers about you and Rosa getting married, and she said, "I was engaged to him once."'

'Engaged?' said Coburg, taken aback. 'Never!'

'She said it was years ago, long before she married Cuddington. She used to be called Pamela Westbrook.'

Coburg stared at Matthews. 'Good God,' he said, stunned.

'So, I guess the lady was telling the truth,' said Matthews. 'It was a long time ago,' said Coburg. 'We were just kids.'

'Anyway, I was the only one around when she saw the bit in the paper. I haven't told anyone else.'

Coburg nodded. 'Thanks, Mr Matthews. It looks

like I might have some explaining to do to Rosa in case it comes out. I'd rather she heard it from me than saw it in the papers.'

'That may not be necessary,' said Matthews. 'There's no reason it should come out.'

'There's no reason, but once Benny's death is reported in the papers, it's possible that Lady Pamela may surface. And, if she does, so will this nugget of information.'

The address Matthews gave them for Benny Martin was a house in Frognal in Swiss Cottage. The front door was unlocked, giving access to a narrow four-storey house that had been turned into bedsitters. They found the room Martin had called home on the second floor. Coburg swore when he tried the door.

'Locked,' he said. 'I should have thought of that.' He went to the next room and knocked on the door. There was no answer. It was the same with the rest of the rooms along the corridor. Coburg looked at Lampson.

'I don't suppose you happen to have some of your tools with you?' he asked hopefully.

Lampson grinned and pulled a lockpick from his pocket. 'Never go anywhere without it,' he said cheerfully, and he set to work on the lock. It took just a few seconds before they heard the click of the lock mechanism, then Lampson pushed the door open.

'It's that easy to burgle somewhere?' asked Coburg as he and Lampson walked into the small room.

'Depends on the lock,' said Lampson. 'A place like this, the landlord won't be bothered to spend money on good secure locks.'

There wasn't much in the room: a few comics and a piece of sheet music on top of the dressing table. In the drawers they discovered an ID card, a ration book, and letters and cards from his mother in Nazeing, a village in Epping Forest, Essex. There was also a press cutting from a local Essex paper about Benny Martin appearing at a concert in Woodford Green.

'Right,' said Coburg. 'It looks like a trip to Epping Forest is our next move. Do you fancy driving?'

CHAPTER EIGHT

Wednesday 4th December 1940

The members of Auxiliary Fire Service Crew 127 sat in Ernie Morris's garden shed and watched as Dan Reeves divvied up the money, counting the bank notes into four equal piles. One pile for Ernie Morris, one for Joe Barker, one for Billy Dodds, and one for Reeves himself.

'There,' said Reeves when he'd finished.

'It ain't much,' commented Barker sourly. 'There was some good jewellery there.'

'It's all I could get off him,' said Reeves defensively.

The way it worked, whatever was lifted from the properties they went to on a call was shared equally. The cash was divided up among them straight away. The jewellery and any precious pieces Dan Reeves took to his fence, where he haggled and got the best possible price for them, and then shared that money with the others.

'You sure your fence ain't ripping you off?' demanded Barker.

Reeves shrugged. 'If any of you can do better, I'm happy for you to try.'

'You know the rest of us haven't got those sort of contacts, Dan,' said Dodds.

'I don't mind if anyone wants to look around,' said Reeves airily. 'The trouble is, the people in that kind of business, fencing stolen jewels, are dangerous and secretive. They protect themselves. If you challenge 'em too much they can get upset. And when they get upset, they get worried. And a worried fence means trouble.' He shrugged. 'But if anyone wants to take it on, by all means. It'll take the heat off me. And I only get the same share as the rest of you, so I'm the one who's putting himself in the line of danger.'

'That's alright,' said Morris reassuringly. 'You carry on, Dan. We know you're doing your best for us. We don't want to make it difficult for you.' He took the pile of notes in front of him and stuffed them in his wallet. 'After all, whatever we get is extra to the cash.' He grinned as he added, 'So long as we keep getting called out to posh places where they've got plenty of loose money and some precious stuff lying around, you won't get any arguments from me.'

Coburg knew that Lampson was pleased to take any opportunity to get behind the steering wheel of a car, not having one of his own, and Coburg was just as happy to take the role of navigator for the journey to Essex and look at the countryside they passed through.

'Have you ever been to Epping Forest, Ted?' asked Coburg.

'Not me, guv,' replied Lampson, with such vehemence in his voice that Coburg looked at him, puzzled.

'Something bad happen there?' he asked.

'No, but it might do if I went there.'

'I don't understand,' said Coburg.

'That's because, for you and other upper-class folks, London is a place you visit and stroll around in, even if you live there. There's no barriers for you. But for working-class Londoners, London isn't territorial, it's tribal. A North Londoner would never go over the Thames to South London, not unless he was weaponed up and mob-handed. And the same's true for South Londoners about going north of the Thames. Now Epping Forest is where East Enders go, and East Enders are a different tribe to North Londoners. There's barriers between them. Unseen, maybe, but still barriers to be watched out for. For a North Londoner, the border's Bethnal Green and the eastern bits of Hackney. Past them and you're into Leyton and Poplar, definitely East End tribal lands. Beyond that, West and East Ham, where no North Londoner will go.'

'But you came with me when we went to Stepney,' pointed out Coburg.

'Yes, but that was on police business,' said Lampson. 'That's different.'

I don't understand, thought Coburg. And then he realised that he did. He and his family, and his class, the aristocrats, were tribal, too: separate from the working class, only really meeting on a work level.

We're all human, but *we're all separate*, realised Coburg. *This war is just another tribal fight*. Someone had described the First War as a family dispute: two of Queen Victoria's grandsons, the English King George V and the German Kaiser Wilhelm, squabbling, and causing the deaths of millions. Was this war the same – one branch of the Anglo-Saxon family fighting another?

The address they'd got for Mrs Martin turned out to be a small cottage on the outskirts of the village of Nazeing. The woman who opened the door to their knock was small, thin and nervous. Her face had a tired look and the dark rings around her eyes suggested she hadn't had much sleep lately.

'Mrs Martin?' asked Coburg.

The woman looked anxious. 'Yes?' she said.

Coburg produced his warrant card and showed it to her. 'Detective Chief Inspector Coburg from Scotland Yard.'

'Scotland Yard?' said the woman in alarm. 'What's up? It's not Alice, is it?'

'Alice?'

'My daughter. She lives in London.' Then, awkwardly and embarrassed, she added, 'She's been in trouble a couple of times with the police. Nothing big, shoplifting, but times are hard with rationing.'

'No, it's not about your daughter. I'm afraid it's about your son, Benny.'

She looked puzzled. 'Benny? He's not in trouble, is he? He's a good boy.'

'Do you mind if we come in?' asked Coburg.

She stood back from the door and let them enter, then showed them into a small kitchen and gestured for them to sit at the table.

'What about Benny?' she asked anxiously.

'Mrs Martin, I'm very sorry to have to tell you that Benny is dead. He appears to have been murdered. Poisoned.'

She stared at the two policemen, her mouth opening and closing nervously, but no sound came out. At last, she said, in a hoarse voice, 'No.'

'I'm afraid so.' He produced the photograph and held it out to her. 'If this is him. And if he was a jazz guitarist.'

She took the photo and stared at it, uncomprehending. 'Yes, that's him. He's dead, isn't he,' she said numbly. 'My dad looked just like that when he died.' She stared at them, bewildered. 'But how? Where? When? Who did it?'

'That's what we're trying to find out. Can you think of anyone who would want to harm him?'

'No. Everyone liked him.'

'How long had he been living in London?'

'He moved there about eight months ago. April, it was. He wanted to see if he could make it as a musician before he joined up. He'll be . . .' She stopped, choked, then corrected herself: 'He'd have been twenty in February. He wanted to go into the air force.'

'Was he happy in London?'

'He seemed to be. He wrote me letters saying what he was doing, and how he was playing in this club or that one, and who he was playing with. Not that the names meant anything to me.'

'When did his sister move to London?'

'Just before Benny did. February.'

'Is she older or younger than Benny?'

'Two years older.'

Coburg looked around the room and saw a photograph of a man in his forties in uniform on the dresser.

'Forgive my asking, but is that your husband?'

Mrs Martin nodded. 'He's somewhere abroad with the army. They say he's not allowed to tell anyone where he is.'

'Do you know if Benny and Alice saw much of one another?'

'Not as far as I know. Benny never mentioned seeing her in his letters. And as for Alice, she doesn't write. I've written to her, sent her a birthday card, but

I've never heard anything back from her.'

'I'm afraid we need an identification from a relative. Can I suggest, to save you coming all the way to London, that we ask his sister Alice to do it?'

'Yes, that would be good. If she's still at the same address, that is. Like I say, I haven't heard from her. I'll give you the address I've got for her.'

'Is she on the phone?'

'I don't think so. If she is, she never let me know. But then, I haven't got a telephone anyway. Can't afford it.'

'Very well. We'll call on Alice and see if she agrees to do it. We'll write and let you know what she says.'

Mrs Martin nodded and wrote Alice's address on a piece of paper, which she gave to Coburg.

'I'll also give you my sister's address in Waltham Abbey,' she said, writing some more. 'I'm going to leave here and stay with her.' She gave a groan as she added, 'I can't stand it here any more with the bombing at night.'

'Bombing?' queried Coburg. 'In Epping Forest?'

'It's because of the airfield.'

Coburg frowned. 'I thought the nearest airfield was some miles away from here. RAF North Weald Bassett.'

'That's the proper airfield.' Mrs Martin nodded. 'But they built this pretend one here at Nazeing so the Germans would bomb that rather than the proper

RAF one. They call it a decoy.'

Coburg looked at Lampson and asked, 'Did you know about this?'

Lampson shook his head. 'News to me, guv. But then, there's a lot going on we don't know about.'

Before they left the house, Coburg asked Mrs Martin for directions to the decoy airfield she'd talked about, and when they were back in the car he navigated Lampson towards it. Lampson didn't say anything, but he gave Coburg a surprised look as he followed the chief inspector's directions.

They arrived at a pair of tall double gates set in an equally long high hedge. There was no sign outside it to identify it, but there was a sentry box and two armed soldiers on duty who looked at the police car suspiciously as it pulled up outside the gates. One of the soldiers approached the car, his rifle levelled at them. Coburg wound down his window and held out his warrant card to the soldier.

'DCI Coburg from Scotland Yard. Can I see your commanding officer?'

'What's it to do with?' demanded the sentry.

'A murder.'

'A murder? What, here?'

'In London, but the victim was from Nazeing, which is why we're making enquiries locally.'

The sentry hesitated, then said, 'Wait here.' He

called to the other sentry: 'Watch 'em, Chalky', then walked into the sentry box. Coburg and Lampson saw him pick up the telephone and press a button, then have a brief conversation before hanging up the receiver and returning. He nodded at his pal, who proceeded to raise the security barrier.

'Follow the tarmacked road,' he instructed Lampson. 'First building you come to on your right. Report to Wing Commander Albertson.'

Coburg nodded. Lampson let in the clutch and they proceeded along the road until they came to a single-storey wooden building. During the drive, Coburg took in the other buildings, which included a proper control tower and radio masts, along with grass runways. There were also Hurricane fighter planes parked up.

'If this is a pretend airfield, it's unbelievable,' said the impressed Lampson. 'They've got real planes here! And a control tower!' He looked enquiringly at Coburg. 'What are we going to ask this wing commander?' he asked.

'I'll think of something,' said Coburg.

'This is just so you could come and take a look at this place, ennit,' said Lampson accusingly.

'Don't the things that are being done to protect the country interest you?' asked Coburg. 'Especially the secret stuff, these sort of subterfuges.'

'We shouldn't be poking our noses into it,' said

Lampson disapprovingly. 'That's why they're secret.'

'I'm not going to tell anyone,' said Coburg. 'Are you?'

'Of course I'm not,' said Lampson. 'But I still say it's wrong.'

'Then we can agree to disagree,' said Coburg. 'And if that's how you feel, perhaps it might be better if you stay in the car while I talk to the wing commander. Your expression might give away your disapproval.'

'I don't disapprove of this,' said Lampson indignantly. 'I reckon it's brilliant. I just don't think we should be nosing around it.'

'So you won't come in?'

'Try and stop me,' said Lampson. He pulled the car to a halt. 'This is too interesting to miss.'

Wing Commander Albertson was in his mid-twenties. He stood up as they entered the wooden hut and as he limped forwards to greet them, they heard the familiar clicking of metal. 'Lost it during a dogfight,' he said ruefully as he patted his left leg. 'Still, this keeps me moving, but I'm afraid I'm now ground-based. What can I do for you? The sentry said something about a murder.'

Coburg and Lampson showed him their warrant cards.

He studied them, then handed them back.

'Scotland Yard,' he said. 'Not local police.'

'No. The victim was murdered in central London,

but we've discovered he came from Nazeing, so we've come here to make enquiries about him to see if anyone knew him and can throw any light on why anyone would want to murder him. His name's Benny Martin. We've just come from his mother's house. I don't know if you know the family?'

Albertson shook his head. 'No, we're a bit of a haven to ourselves here,' he said. 'We get some local provisions delivered here, of course, within our rations. But we don't really socialise. Security.'

'I understand,' said Coburg. 'We've been told this is actually a decoy airfield.'

Albertson gave a rueful smile. 'Local gossip. You can't stop it, despite all these posters warning everyone that careless talk costs lives.'

'It's very impressive,' complimented Coburg. 'The control tower. The planes.'

'Fakes. Plywood and cloth.' Albertson smiled. 'Good, though. From a distance they look real enough to fool the Nazis, especially from the air.'

'Isn't it dangerous for you?' asked Coburg. 'I mean, you're inviting to be bombed with no real defences.'

'We have underground shelters,' said Albertson. 'And away from the control tower, by the outer fence. It's from there we do the illusions.'

'The illusions?'

'Start small fires to make it look as if we've already been hit. An airfield that's already been hit always looks attractive to Jerry. They're in trenches dotted around the airfield. We even added lights along one of the grass runways to make it more inviting. Half-concealed, of course.' He gave a happy smile. 'These arty types who set it up know what they're doing. Most of them worked in films before the war, building sets and things.'

They listened as he stood by the window and pointed out various features of the decoy airfield, obviously with great pride. Finally, he said, 'Well, I'm sorry I couldn't help you with your investigation. I hope you find your murderer. What was the name of the victim again?'

'Benny Martin. Aged nineteen. Played the guitar professionally. He's the son of Mrs Martin who lives in the village.'

'Well, if I hear anything that might be useful, I'll get in touch with you at Scotland Yard.'

'Whitehall 1212,' Coburg told him. 'Ask for DCI Coburg or Sergeant Lampson.'

As they climbed back into their car, Coburg looked at Lampson with amusement. 'It was exactly as I said it would be,' said Coburg. 'The whole time your face had a look of serious disapproval.'

'I wasn't disapproving of us,' snorted Lampson. 'It was that wing commander, talking like that, telling us all about it. The place is supposed to be secret, for heaven's sake. We could have been anyone. German spies, fifth columnists.'

'We showed him our warrant cards.'

'Easily forged,' said Lampson.

'We are driving a police vehicle, with the word "POLICE" in big letters and blue lights on it.'

'Anyone can botch up a vehicle to look like something else,' grunted Lampson, not appeased. 'If they can fake fighter planes, they can do it with police cars.'

CHAPTER NINE

Wednesday 4th December 1940

Auxiliary Fire Service Crew 127 pulled up outside the large, white detached house in Ennismore Gardens in Knightsbridge.

'You sure no one's going to be in?' asked Billy Dodds nervously.

'I had it on good authority from the postman that the family have gone away to their house in the country,' said Joe Barker.

'But say someone comes and asks what we're doing here?' persisted Dodds, obviously anxious.

'We tell 'em we had a call-out,' said Dan Reeves.

'But there's not even a sign of a fire,' protested Dodds. 'We're putting our heads in a noose.'

'You worry too much, Doddsy,' said Reeves. 'If anyone asks, we say we had a call about a suspected incendiary bomb that had come through the roof of the house and could go off at any moment.' He looked intently at Dodds and said, 'This could be a big one for us. The postman told me a jeweller and his family live here. There's bound to be a safe.' He lifted the heavy pointed hammer from where he'd put it behind his seat in the cab. 'Come on, lads.'

Reeves led the way, followed by Barker and Dodds, with Ernie Morris, the team's official leader, bringing up the rear. They reached the front door and Reeves rang the bell, saying, 'Just in case,' to the others. When there was no answer, Reeves lifted his hammer and smashed it into the lock on the front door, sending the lock flying and the door swinging inwards.

'Emergency situations call for emergency action.' Reeves grinned at the others.

Leaving Dodds to keep watch by the front door, the other three entered the house. While Morris and Barker searched the downstairs rooms, Reeves made for the bedrooms.

'Found it!' he called.

Morris and Barker hurried up the stairs and joined him in the bedroom, where Reeves was standing proudly in front of a safe that protruded from one of the walls. The painting behind which the safe had been hidden was now leaning against a wall.

The safe had a big wheel with levers attached in the centre of its front casing. Reeves examined it and chuckled. 'Look at it, all that fancy mechanics, but the hinges are still sticking out.' He smiled.

He hefted the hammer, brought it back over his head, then brought it crashing down on the top hinge. It took another seven blows before the top hinge buckled and then fell off.

Reeves attacked the bottom hinge, and when that, too, buckled, he began smashing the side of the door, and soon there was enough space for him to reach his hand inside the safe.

The others saw his expression change from one of delight to one of stunned disappointment.

'The bastard's taken it all with him!' he snarled.

Joe Barker pushed Reeves aside and shone his torch into the gap where the broken door hung, revealing that the safe was empty.

'The bastard!' Barker echoed angrily. 'Honestly, you can't trust anyone these days.'

It was the middle of the afternoon by the time Coburg and Lampson returned to London. They drove to the address Mrs Martin had given them for her daughter, Alice. Similar to her brother's residence, it was an old house that had been turned into rooms to let, as could be seen by the list of names fixed to the doorpost, each name beside a bell push.

'She could be out at work at this time,' said Lampson.

'Depends what she works at,' said Coburg. 'If there's no answer, we'll try again.'

They rang the bell marked 'A Martin', and after a while the street door opened and a woman in her early twenties peered out at them warily through the crack in the partly opened door.

'Yes?' she asked.

'Miss Alice Martin?' asked Coburg.

'Who wants to know?' she asked, suspicious.

Coburg and Lampson produced their warrant cards and showed them to her.

'DCI Coburg and Sergeant Lampson. We're from Scotland Yard. Can we have a word with you?'

'What about?' she asked, still suspicious.

'It's about your brother, Benny. Can we talk inside?' She hesitated, then opened the door and let them in.

'I'm on the first floor,' she said.

They followed her up the stairs to a door in the first landing marked with the number three. She unlocked the door and let them in, then joined them, sliding the inside bolt closed.

'You have to be careful all the time around here,' she told them. 'People breaking in.'

The room was sparsely furnished, none of the table and chairs matching; they'd obviously been provided as the cheapest possible option by the landlord. The single bed at one side of the room beside the window looked rumpled, a bedspread pulled up to cover it. The fact that Alice Martin was wearing a dressing gown and slippers suggested she'd just got up from it. She must have seen the quizzical looks the two policemen exchanged, because she said in a defiant tone, 'I've been ill. Being down the Tube station shelter at night with all them people who've got colds and such, it's unsanitary.' She gestured them to sit in the chairs at the table and joined them. 'What's Benny been up to?' she asked.

'We're sorry to tell you that he's dead,' said Coburg gently.

She looked at them suspiciously. There was no trace of shock or grief. Instead, she asked, 'How? In the bombing?'

'No, I'm afraid to tell you he was murdered. Poisoned.'

She looked at them, bewildered. 'Poisoned? How? Who by?'

'That's what we're trying to find out. His body was discovered in a disused railway tunnel at Aldwych Underground station.'

'What was he doing there?'

'Again, that's what we're trying to find out. Did you see much of your brother?'

She shook her head. 'No.'

'You didn't get on?'

'It wasn't that. We moved in different worlds. He had his interests and I had mine. He played the guitar in jazz clubs.'

'Yes, so we understand. Did you ever go to see him play?' She shook her head. 'Jazz ain't my thing.'

'What is?' asked Coburg.

'At the moment, staying alive,' she said sourly. 'We're all gonna die, ain't we.'

'I hope not,' said Coburg. 'What do you do?'

'What do you mean?' she asked, again her tone suspicious.

'Workwise.'

She shrugged. 'At the moment I'm between jobs. I was working at a shop, but then it got bombed out.' She looked at them, wary again. 'How did you find out about me?'

'From your mother.'

'You've seen her?'

'Yes,' said Coburg. 'It was she who gave us your address.'

'Why?'

'Two reasons: one, in case you'd seen anything of Benny and could tell us something about him. His lifestyle here in London, who he mixed with. And the other reason is because we have to have a relative identify him officially. We hoped that you'd do it rather than have to drag your mother all the way to London from Nazeing.'

She hesitated, thinking it over, then asked, 'What do I have to do?'

'Just come with us to University College Hospital where his body is and say it either is or isn't him.'

'When?' she asked.

'It would be helpful if you could do that with us now,'

said Coburg. 'Then we can put the paperwork to rest.'

'Alright,' she said. 'If you wait downstairs, I'll get dressed and join you.'

They stood up and made for the door, then Lampson stopped.

'That's a very attractive box,' he said, pointing at an ornamental box on the sideboard. 'Do you mind if I take a look at it? Only I'm thinking of getting something like that for my mum for Christmas.'

Alice hesitated, then nodded. 'Help yourself.'

Lampson picked up the box and examined the ornate carving on the lid and round the sides, along with the sparkling stones that had been inlaid.

'Beautiful,' he said, putting it back. 'Forgive my asking but was it expensive?'

'No idea,' she said. 'It was a present.'

'Well, it's a beautifully made piece of work,' said Lampson.

Coburg waited until the two policemen were outside in the street to wait for Alice before he asked, 'What was all that about the jewellery box?'

'It's an expensive piece,' said Lampson. 'It's also pretty full; I could feel the weight when I picked it up. What does that tell you? She's living in a cheap bedsit and not working, but she's got an expensive jewellery box, and I bet you a pound to a penny that if we opened it we'd find some good stuff inside it. You noticed it was locked and she didn't offer the key?'

'I did,' said Coburg. 'So what do you think? She's on the game?'

'If she was, she'd be living in a better place than that,' said Lampson. 'No, I reckon it's nicked.'

'You may be doing her a disservice,' said Coburg. 'It could be a present from someone, just like she said.'

'The sort of bloke who can afford to give her something as good as that would have her in a better place than that.'

'Not necessarily,' countered Coburg. 'A married man, maybe?'

Alice appeared from the house, now dressed, and they took her to the mortuary in the basement of University College Hospital, where she was shown the body of the young man. Coburg peeled the sheet back from the young man's face. Alice nodded.

'Yeah, that's Benny,' she said. She gave an unhappy sigh. 'Poor bastard.'

Coburg looked at her. The unhappy sigh was the only expression of emotion; there were no tears, no wringing of hands or biting of her lip like he usually saw in the bereaved.

'Thank you, Miss Martin,' he said. 'We'll take you home.'

* * *

They dropped Alice Martin off outside her house. She mounted the stairs to her room where she discovered her boyfriend, Dan Reeves, sitting on the bed. Reeves was a tall, muscular man in his early thirties. He got to his feet as Alice came into the room and walked towards her, a look of deep suspicion on his face.

'What was all that?' he demanded. 'With the police? I was coming to see you when I saw you getting in the car with them and driving off.'

'They wanted me to identify Benny,' she told him.

'Where?'

'At University College Hospital.'

'What did they say about him?'

'That he'd been murdered. Poisoned. His body was discovered in the tunnels at Aldwych station. They wanted to know if I knew what he'd been up to and who he hung around with.'

'And what did you tell them?'

'Nothing. I told them I didn't have anything to do with him.'

'And they believed you?'

'Why wouldn't they?'

Reeves pointed at the jewellery box on the dresser and scowled. 'Was that there when they came?'

'No,' she lied. 'I took it out when I changed, before I went down to join them. They were waiting for me outside in the street. If you saw, you know that already.'

'Why did you get the box out?' he demanded.

'Because I like looking at it.' She smiled coyly at him. 'I look at it and know that that's going to be our way out of this hole.'

'Well, keep it locked away. We don't want people seeing it. Especially if any of my crewmates come round here.'

'Why would they?' she asked.

'They might be looking for me, and if they see that we'll be in big trouble.' Then he corrected it to: '*You'll* be in big trouble.'

'Even if they saw it, they wouldn't know what was in it. It's locked.'

'Of course they would, you stupid cow. That box came out of one of the safes we did. They'd know it's jewels, and I'm supposed to have sold all the jewels we got.'

'You do sell some.'

'Of course I do, because if I didn't they'd know something was up.' He gripped her firmly by the upper arms and looked at her grimly as he said, 'I've told you before, the way it works is I take most of the jewels to my fence, but some I keep back, and they go in the box.'

'You're hurting me,' Alice complained.

Reeves loosened his grip on Alice's arms, but kept talking, his tone firm.

'It's only fair; it's my share to pay me for taking the risk in dealing with the fence.'

He didn't tell her that he also kept some of the money he got from the fence back for himself. That was his money. Not his and Alice's but *his*. Payment for the extra risks he took.

'*Our* share,' said Alice pointedly.

'Our share,' agreed Reeves, releasing Alice. 'Our way out of all this. But no one must know. So long as I'm picking up money for some of the jewels and sharing it out, the others won't query it. Well, they will, but they won't do anything about it. That's why you've got to keep that box out of sight. Hidden.'

'It's safe,' she assured him.

'Make sure it is,' he said firmly.

'Are you coming back tonight?' she asked.

'No, we're on call,' he said. Then he grinned. 'More pickings for us!'

CHAPTER TEN

Wednesday 4th December 1940

As Coburg and Lampson drove to Scotland Yard, they discussed Alice's apparent cold response to the sight of her dead brother.

'She didn't look one bit upset,' commented Lampson.

'It's a time when so many people are dying, some seem to have become immune to reacting when they're seeing it so often,' said Coburg.

'Yes, but this was her brother,' said Lampson. 'You'd expect something.'

'True,' agreed Coburg. 'Trouble is we never know for sure what goes on in families. At least we've got a name to go on. Benny Martin, a teenager who played jazz guitar in different places. He was dressed in formal clothes when he was found, suggesting he'd been playing somewhere the night before. So what we need to find out is where he was playing that night, and who was with him. I suggest we start by getting as many copies of the photo of him that we can and distributing it to the stations that cover central

London, especially Soho. The local beat bobbies will know their local jazz clubs. They're to visit each one and ask if Benny Martin was playing there on the night of Monday 2nd December. Just in case he was sitting in and didn't give his name, that's where the photo comes in.'

'It's a lot of beat-pounding, guv,' said Lampson doubtfully. 'I'm not sure if we'll get anything. You know what the clubs are like, especially the ones in Soho. They don't like talking to the police. Oh, they're polite enough, smile and make all the right noises, but it ain't easy to get genuine information out of them. They always seem to think we're trying to bust 'em for something. Drugs. Bootleg booze. And once they hear that this bloke was murdered, they'll know we're looking for the people he was with that night, and they'll just give the old smile and polite look with a regretful shake of the head. "Sorry, Officer, I don't know him."'

'True, but at the moment that's all we've got. We've got to try.'

When they entered their office at Scotland Yard, they found Superintendent Allison sitting at Coburg's desk, writing on a small piece of paper. He stopped when he saw them and screwed the paper up and dropped it in the waste basket.

'I was just leaving you a note asking you to call to see me when you got back,' he explained. 'But luckily you're here.'

'Yes, sir,' said Coburg. 'What did you want to see us about?'

'There's an assault that needs to be looked into.'

Coburg frowned. 'An assault, sir?' he queried. 'Surely that's a case for uniforms?'

'Usually, but unfortunately the victim is an old friend of the police commissioner, a General Walters.'

'General?'

'Retired. He's in his sixties. It seems that his block of flats in Knightsbridge was bombed during a raid. He and his wife sought shelter, and when they returned they found their safe had been opened and money, his medals and his wife's jewels taken. He discovered an Auxiliary Fire crew at the flat who'd been involved in putting out the blaze and he challenged them, accusing them of taking the money and his wife's jewels. The leader of the crew became belligerent and told him he should be grateful they'd risked their lives to save his flat. He denied they'd taken anything. When General Walters said he was going to search them, one of the firemen reacted angrily and struck him, knocking him to the ground. The fire crew then left.'

'It still doesn't sound like a job for us, sir.'

'I'm afraid the commissioner insists. Apparently there have been quite a few reports of looting going on during and after air raids.' He handed Coburg a piece of paper. 'This is where you can get hold of the general. At the moment, he and his wife are staying at The Dorchester while they see if they can sort out their damaged flat, or else find somewhere else to live.'

'How soon do you want us to make contact with him? We've got this murder at Aldwych to look into.'

'Yes, I know, but that man's dead and won't be making any complaints to the commissioner, unlike General Walters. Let me know how you get on.'

With that Allison left.

Coburg looked at the address the superintendent had left him, The Dorchester hotel, and scowled.

'I thought we were supposed to be servants of the public, not the commissioner's friends,' complained Coburg.

'Yeah, but maybe this *is* one for us,' said Lampson guardedly.

Coburg looked at his sergeant inquisitively. 'What do you know that I don't?' he asked.

'Well, I've got this mate who's an auxiliary fireman, and he was telling me that some of the crews are a bit iffy. Rotten apples, if you get my meaning.'

'Looting the properties they've gone to protect?'

'Yeah, in a word. They're only a minority; most of 'em are dead genuine. Like my mate Archie. But the ones who are on the nick are bringing down the reputation of the good ones.'

'How widespread is it?' asked Coburg.

'I can only speak for the area my mate Archie looks after. According to Archie, and he should know, the Auxiliary Fire Service in London is twenty-three thousand strong, all volunteers, unlike the London Fire Brigade, who are paid professionals. The AFS has got three hundred Auxiliary Fire Service substations. The London Fire Brigade has got fifty-nine stations, plus river stations on the Thames. So, as you can see, the AFS is the bigger by far and so gets most of the call-outs. Now when they started calling for volunteers, most who signed up were like my mate, Archie, set on doing something for the war effort: protecting property and saving lives. But once the Blitz started, some blokes signed up because they saw it as a way of lining their pockets.'

'Looting?'

Lampson nodded. 'Some councils appointed salvage officers to oversee the recovery of properties that had been bombed and quite a few of those rotten apples ended up in court. There was even one mob that used gelignite to blow open safes at wealthy-looking places they went to put the fires out.'

'Places like the block of flats where this General Walters lives.'

Lampson nodded. 'Anyone who can afford to stay at The Dorchester has got to be worth a few bob. And when you think about it, guv, the fire service is the same as any big organisation. Twenty-three thousand on the force – if only five per cent are crooked, that's still over a thousand.'

'So this assault case might turn out to be something bigger?'

'If what Archie says is true, and I don't have any reason to doubt him.'

'I must say it's not something I've thought of,' admitted Coburg. 'In effect, I'm like most people: we assume the people in uniform whose job is to protect us are doing just that. The RAF, the army, nurses, the police. But we both know there are corrupt police officers taking bribes to look the other way, and when I was in the army, in every regiment there was always someone who stole army property and sold it, usually working with a corrupt quartermaster.'

'And how many of them got jail time?' asked Lampson pointedly.

'Hardly any,' admitted Coburg. 'It's about protecting the reputation of the organisation. So anyone caught with their fingers in the till – or worse – is usually allowed to resign. No charges filed.'

'Which looks to be the same with some of the auxiliaries,' said Lampson. 'So even if they're doing it, we might not get the charges to stick. Morale of the organisation, and that sort of thing.'

'We'll do what we can,' said Coburg. 'I suggest we start by calling on General Walters.'

CHAPTER ELEVEN

Wednesday 4th December 1940

Pamela Cuddington picked up the ringing telephone in the hallway of the house she shared reluctantly with her husband, Lord Colin Cuddington.

'Cuddington,' she said.

'Pam-baby,' said a man's deep voice, and even in those few words she could hear sadness in his voice.

'Alexis,' she said.

'I got some bad news for you, baby. Benny's dead.'

She stood, momentarily silent, then slumped into the small chair beside the telephone table with a little whimper.

'Pam?' she heard Alexis say, apprehensive.

'How . . . how?' she forced herself to ask, and already she could feel the tears rolling down her cheeks.

'He was poisoned is what I heard,' said Alexis. 'They found him in the Underground tunnel at Aldwych station. I wanted to let you know before you saw it in the papers. Although they may not even put it in at all.' He fell silent, but he must have heard her weeping because he said, 'I'm sorry, Pam. It's really bad. If I hear anything more, I'll let you know.'

Pamela replaced the telephone and gave herself to grief, her howls of anguish echoing through the large house. Her howls had subsided into sobbing as the front door opened and her husband walked in.

'What are you snivelling about?' he demanded.

'Benny's dead!' she managed to utter, before lapsing back into tears.

'Benny?' asked Colin Cuddington. Then he remembered, and a smile crossed his face. 'Oh, *him*,' he said scornfully. When Pamela looked at him, pain writ large on her face, Cuddington smirked and said, 'I warned him what would happen.'

'*You* did it?!' burst out Pamela, aghast.

'Let that be a lesson, Pam,' said Cuddington. 'Don't cross me.'

He walked past her and made for the stairs. 'I shall be out this evening,' he said. 'No need to wait up for me.'

As Coburg and Lampson walked up the steps of The Dorchester towards the main entrance, the sergeant commented, 'I suppose this is another place where you know half the staff and they know you. Not to mention the guests.' Three of the previous cases Coburg and Lampson had been involved in had occurred at The Ritz, The Savoy and Claridge's, three of the most luxurious hotels in London. Now, with this visit to The Dorchester, their set was complete. Like the other five-star luxury hotels in London, The Dorchester had been built to withstand bombing and earthquakes, with the result that the wealthiest Londoners had flocked to it once the Blitz began.

Lampson was proved correct when they approached the reception desk and the concierge, resplendent in a purple frock coat adorned with gold braid, greeted them with: 'Mr Coburg! What a pleasure to see you again!'

'See?' grunted Lampson in a whisper.

'Good afternoon, William,' said Coburg. 'Is General Walters available, do you know?'

William cast a look at the rows of keys behind him, then nodded.

'His key is out, so I assume he's in. Although I saw Mrs Walters leave the hotel not long ago.'

'That's alright, it's the general we need to see. Can you ring his room and tell him DCI Coburg and Sergeant Lampson from Scotland Yard are here to see him?'

'Of course.' William smiled. He dialled a number, then said, 'General? It's reception. DCI Saxe-Coburg and Sergeant Lampson from Scotland Yard are here to see you.' He nodded. 'Thank you. I'll send them up.'

He put down the phone and said, 'It's room 354.

And my apologies for expanding to your full name, but it helps to differentiate between you and some other Coburg.'

Coburg nodded, and then headed for the lifts. 'Are there many Coburgs, then?' asked Lampson.

'One or two, I believe,' said Coburg. 'Mostly in central Europe.'

'Germans?'

'And Hungarians, so I'm told.'

General Walters was a tall man in his sixties, well dressed, with neatly barbered white hair and a grey military moustache. The only blot on his otherwise immaculate image was a purple bruise around his left eye. He welcomed them into the hotel room.

'Thank you for coming. It's just me, I'm afraid. The *memsahib*'s gone out to do some shopping.' He looked quizzically at Coburg. 'Saxe-Coburg,' he mused. 'Any relation to Magnus Saxe-Coburg?'

'He's my eldest brother,' said Coburg.

'Good chap,' said the general. 'We were in the trenches together in the first lot. You were in that, too, I believe. Shot and wounded just before the armistice, so Magnus told me.'

'Yes,' said Coburg.

'There's your brother Charles, as well,' said the general. 'I bumped into Magnus a couple of months ago. He told me that Charles is in a PoW camp in Germany. Taken prisoner at Dunkirk.'

'That's right,' said Coburg. 'But, with respect, sir, we're here to learn about the robbery you experienced.'

'Those damned auxiliary firemen!' Walters scowled. 'Bunch of gangsters! Punched me in the face!'

'How sure are you that they were responsible?'

'Very sure. When the air raid warning sounded, Phyllis and I gathered everything up. We keep a couple of bags ready by the door. Before we left the flat, I checked the safe, as I always do. It was shut and locked.'

'Where was the key?'

'In my pocket. I always keep it with me. When the all-clear sounded, we came out of the shelter and went back to the block of flats. Our flat is on the top floor, and unfortunately we'd taken a hit. Roof gone. The fire service was there, auxiliaries, not regular. There was a fire engine parked in the street and it was pretty obvious they'd doused the building; there was water everywhere. We went up to our flat and saw they'd broken in, smashed the door down. To be honest, I was niggled at that, but not unduly upset. It struck me they might have had to break in to put out any fire, but although there was a hole in the roof there didn't seem to be any sign of fire damage inside the flat. But there was water everywhere, ruining everything. The furniture, the carpets, everything. And then I noticed my safe was open. The door was hanging off its hinges.

'The fire crew who were in the flat asked what we were doing there. I told them we were the owners and we'd come to see what damage there was. I pointed the safe out to the one in charge and demanded to know what had happened to it. He said he had no idea. I then told him it was empty, all my wife's jewellery had gone, along with my medals and the cash we kept in it. He said it was nothing to do with them.

'Well, I could tell he was lying. He looked shifty. He had the same look I used to see on the faces of men in the army when they were caught doing something they shouldn't. I challenged him. Demanded to look in their pockets and bags. It was then that the bastard punched me. Outrageous behaviour! Then they left.

'I was going to go after them, face them down, but Phyllis held on to me, told me they might be dangerous. I could get hurt. I told her, in the trenches we were always in danger and I got hurt often enough then; I wasn't going to be frightened off by a bunch of crooks.

'Eventually I managed to persuade her to let go of me, I didn't want to push her, one doesn't do that to one's wife, but by the time I got downstairs they and their fire engine had gone.'

'Did you get the number of the fire engine?' asked Coburg.

'I'm afraid not,' said the general. 'I thought of going to the AFS HQ and asking which fire crew would have been here, but then I thought it would only alert them and they'd have their excuses and alibis worked out. So I decided that letting the police handle it was the best way forward.'

'It might be useful if we could look at the scene,' said Coburg. 'Would you mind accompanying us to your flat?'

'Delighted to,' said the general. 'I'm glad that someone's doing something.'

Coburg and Lampson accompanied General Walters to his block of flats in Knightsbridge. Pools of water were still evident on the pavement outside the block, and all the way up the concrete stairs.

'There's a lift,' said the general, 'but we've avoided using it in case the electrics were damaged. Last thing we want is to get trapped.'

The door to the flat had been smashed in so that the fire crew could gain access. Inside, everything had been soaked with water. Although there was a hole in the ceiling, there didn't seem to be much in the way of fire damage inside the flat.

The general led them to the safe, the door of which was hanging open on the lower hinge; the top hinge had been smashed off.

'It's been hammered,' said Lampson. 'Heavy hammers, with a pointed side. Like a cross between a sledgehammer and a tree splitter.'

'So the fire crew did it,' said Walters.

'Not necessarily,' said Coburg. 'Someone could have seen you and your wife leave, come in, broken into the safe and then run off before the bomb hit.'

'It's a bit unlikely' said Walters doubtfully.

'In this war, anything's possible,' said Coburg. 'What we'll do is have a word with the auxiliary fire crew who attended. There'll be a record of which crew it was. In the meantime, I'd advise you to get on to the block's management company and get them to fix the roof and the door.'

'I've done that,' said the general. 'They've said they'll have it done as soon as they can. It seems they've got the same issues at their other blocks.'

They took General Walters back to The Dorchester, then made for Scotland Yard.

'I suppose the next thing is to track down the crew who attended the fire,' said Lampson.

'We'll do that tomorrow, after we've got back doing what we were planning before this robbery business came up,' said Coburg. 'Getting the stations in Soho to check the clubs and find out which one Benny Martin was playing at the night he died. I want to dig into Benny Martin's murder before the trail goes cold.'

CHAPTER TWELVE

Wednesday 4th December 1940

That evening, Coburg filled Rosa in on their meetings with Benny's mother and his sister, Alice.

'Neither were much help, to be honest,' he said. 'We're going to check all the clubs in Soho to find out where Benny was playing the night he died, but Sergeant Lampson is doubtful if it will yield much in the way of information.'

'What about his guitar?' asked Rosa.

'His guitar?' asked Coburg, puzzled.

'If Benny was dressed to perform, he must have left his guitar somewhere. Find the guitar and you'll find out where he was.'

'Surely a guitar's just a guitar,' said Coburg. 'How will we know if it was his?'

'Because Benny had stuck his initials in pearl letters on the front: BM.'

'That's good,' said Coburg thoughtfully. 'I'll pass that on to the squads tomorrow.' He looked at Rosa and said, 'By the way, something came up today you need to know about.'

'Oh?'

'Yes. Your friend Gerry Matthews at the Pink Parrot club.'

'Was he able to help?'

'Very much. It was he who gave us Benny's address in London, and from there we got the addresses of his mother and sister.'

Rosa grinned. 'Gerry's always been a fount of information.'

'Yes. He also told me something else, something I haven't shared with anyone else for the moment.'

'Oh? Why?'

'I'm weighing up where to go with it. It seems that Benny had a lady friend. Lady Pamela Cuddington.'

Rosa frowned. 'So that's who it was.'

'You've seen her?'

'She was in the audience at a gig where Benny and his band were playing, and when he came offstage he went to the table where she was sitting and she was all over him. At first I thought she might be his mother, she looked old enough, but the way she acted – wow! – that was no mother expressing her affection for her son. Luckily the lights were low, but as it was one of the waiters had to go and have a discreet word with them. Mainly with her. I thought that Benny looked embarrassed. Anyway, they left soon after.' Rosa looked inquisitively at Coburg. 'So, what's so secret you haven't shared it with anyone? Not even Ted?'

'Not even Ted,' said Coburg. 'But I will because it could affect the case. The thing is, Gerry Matthews told me that Lady Pamela told him that she and I were once engaged to be married.'

Rosa stared at him, stunned. 'Engaged? You and her?'

'Yes, although she was Pamela Westbrook then.'

'My God,' chuckled Rosa. 'Was she like that then? All over you? She must have worn you out!'

Coburg shook his head. 'There was nothing like that. We were both young. I was seventeen and she was sixteen. We'd been introduced by a mutual friend, and we started going out together. Just a couple of kids. And one day her father asked me what my intentions were towards his daughter. He was a very severe man, quite intimidating. I thought it was the right thing to do. It's what our class did then. The decent thing. So we got engaged. A few months after that, I got my papers to go to war. I'd applied to go, but the paperwork took time. The tide had begun to turn in the war and there were lots of young men about my age applying for a commission.'

'A commission?'

'I was the son of an earl. It was expected that I would go in as an officer. I'd done officer training at Eton, along with almost everybody else. So, January 1918 saw me go to France and take charge of a battalion of the 2nd Sussex, even though I was younger than everyone else in it.' He fell silent for a thoughtful moment, then said unhappily, 'It was a dreadful time. The slaughter on both sides. Cutting a long and painful story short, I managed to stay alive for the rest of the year, just a few minor injuries occurring. But then came the 4th of November and I led a charge of the Sussex at the Sambre–Oise Canal, along with the 2nd Manchester and the Lancashire Fusiliers. It was meant to be the final assault that would end the war. In fact, the war ended just a week later with the German surrender and the armistice.'

'That's where you were badly wounded,' said Rosa.

Coburg nodded. 'For some time they thought I wouldn't pull through. The machine guns we were up against had ripped most of the men to shreds. I was lucky, although I lost a lung.

'Anyway, I spent the next six months in a convalescent hospital in England, being rebuilt. Pamela had written to say she'd visit, but she never did. Finally, a letter arrived from her father to say that it was with regret the family had decided the marriage could not go ahead, due to my medical condition. It was felt that, as an invalid, I would not be able to provide for her. So that was that.'

'How did you feel?' asked Rosa.

'In a way, relieved,' said Coburg. 'Mr Westbrook's letter was only putting into words what was already in my mind. I'd already realised that I'd have to call it off. Westbrook's letter saved me the embarrassment and humiliation of doing that.'

'Did you ever see her again?'

'No. When I was fully recovered, I applied to join the police force, and that's where I've been ever since. Gerry Matthews told me that Pamela married Lord Cuddington, although if his and your accounts of her behaviour with Benny are right, it doesn't sound like a happy and contented marriage.'

He smiled at her. 'So that's it. Something from my long-ago past. In truth, I haven't thought about her at all during the last almost twenty years. But now this has come up, I'm expecting some journalist to write about her relationship with Benny and hint that it may have been a motive in his murder.'

'The angry jealous husband, Lord Cuddington?'

'Or perhaps the lady herself, if Benny threw her over.'

'You think that's likely?'

'I think I'd better find out.'

They were interrupted by the telephone ringing. Coburg picked it up and heard the voice of his eldest brother, Magnus, the Earl of Dawlish. 'Can I come and see you? I'm in London at the flat.'

'Certainly. When?'

'I'll be there in half an hour. I've got something to tell you.'

'You sound worried,' said Coburg. 'Can't you tell me now?'

'No. Rather do it face to face.'

With that, Magnus hung up.

Rosa looked enquiringly at Coburg. 'That was very short,' she said.

Coburg frowned, puzzled and concerned. 'He says he's got something to tell me. Something he'd rather say face to face.' He pondered. 'He sounded worried, so whatever it is isn't good news. It could be something he's picked up about the war. Something hush-hush he can't talk about on the phone.'

'Of course, he's old friends with Churchill, isn't he,' said Rosa.

'Yes, but if it was something that Churchill had sworn him to secrecy about, he wouldn't tell me.' He frowned. 'I wonder what it is?'

Magnus arrived half an hour later, carrying a briefcase. Coburg looked at his brother, trying to find a clue to what Magnus was concerned about, but his eldest brother's face gave nothing away.

After the usual greetings, including a brotherly kiss for Rosa, Rosa said, 'I'll leave you two to talk,' and made for the kitchen, but she was stopped by Magnus saying, 'No, this concerns you as well, Rosa. After all, you were his sister-in-law.'

'Were?' said Coburg, darkly and immediately

alert. Magnus gave a rueful sigh.

'Yes, sorry about that,' he apologised. 'Charles is dead. He was shot trying to escape from that damned PoW camp he was interned in.'

'Dead?' repeated Coburg, shocked. 'But . . . but . . .' He fell silent, stunned. Rosa put her arm around him.

'I'm so sorry,' she whispered.

'Are you sure?' asked Coburg.

'I'm afraid so,' said Magnus. 'A chum at the War Office told me. They've had it confirmed by the German authorities.'

Coburg sank onto an armchair. 'How did it happen?' he asked.

'It seems that Charles and a few other chaps had either got hold of some wire cutters, or more likely made them, and cut a section of fence one night, and went through. They were spotted by guards patrolling the perimeter. They didn't give them a chance to surrender, just shot them. A policy of warning anyone else who might be thinking of doing the same.' He sighed. 'Poor Charles.'

Coburg sat on the settee in a stunned and unhappy silence, Rosa sitting next to him with her arm around him.

Magnus opened the briefcase and took out a bottle of brandy.

'This is a special bottle. I thought if we were going to drink a toast to Charles it should be done with something he'd approve of.' He tuned to Rosa and explained, 'Our brother was a bit of a bon vivant, a gourmet when it came to food and drink. He had taste in that, and everything he did. Even his last act was one of defiance against the Germans.'

Magnus opened the bottle and poured three glasses.

'I know your taste is for Irish whiskey,' he said to Rosa. 'So, please, feel free to pour yourself a glass of that.'

'No,' said Rosa, picking up one of the glasses. 'This is for Charles. I wish I'd met him.'

'I wish you had,' said Coburg. 'He'd have liked you.'

Coburg and Magnus lifted their glasses, and the three clinked them together.

'To Charles,' said Magnus, and Coburg and Rosa responded with 'To Charles.'

CHAPTER THIRTEEN

Thursday 5th December 1940. 2 a.m.

That night, Rosa woke and saw that Coburg's side of the bed was empty. The clock showed 2 a.m.

She got up and went to the living room, and found Coburg sitting in the dark.

'You should have woken me,' she said.

'I'm sorry,' said Coburg. 'I woke up and couldn't stop thinking about Charles. Not just getting killed, but when we were boys growing up.' He shook his head. 'He was so alive. I can't believe he's gone.'

Rosa sat down next to him and put her arm around him. 'It's alright to cry,' she said. 'It's not an unmanly thing to do.'

'I'm not in the mood for crying,' he said. 'I'm too angry. The bastards, shooting him like that.'

'You were in the last war,' said Rosa. 'It's what people do. You got shot.'

'But I was armed. I doubt if Charles or his pals had any weapons on them.'

She cuddled him closer to her. 'I'm so sorry, Edgar,' she whispered.

* * *

The next morning, Coburg and Lampson telephoned the stations in the Soho area with instructions. 'Check all the jazz clubs and find out if a young guitarist called Benny Martin was playing there on the night of Monday 2nd December. If they say no, check the premises for a guitar with the letters BM on the front in pearl. If you find it, let us know and we'll make a visit.'

That done, they set off for the local headquarters of the Auxiliary Fire Service to find out which crew had attended the fire at General Walters's block of flats. They learnt that it was Crew 127, led by a man called Ernie Morris, whose day job was as a mechanic at a car repair shop in Paddington.

Morris was in his forties, a broad-shouldered, muscular man who regarded the two Scotland Yard detectives with suspicion.

'What's all this about?' he demanded after they'd introduced themselves and shown him their warrant cards. 'You and Crew 127 were on a shout at a block of flats in Knightsbridge a couple of nights ago.'

'What of it? We're always out on calls.'

'This one was at a flat owned by a General Walters and his wife. General Walters says there was an altercation and that one of your men punched him in the face.'

'He did, and it was understandable. He was provoked. Here we are, putting our lives on the line and doing our best to save this bloke's flat, when he turns up with his missus and accuses us of nicking stuff from his safe. It's no wonder Joe got upset.'

'What's Joe's other name?'

'Why?'

'We need to talk to him.'

'Barker,' said Morris reluctantly. 'And where can we find him?'

'He's a plumber with the local council,' said Morris. 'He works out of the depot at Bishop's Bridge Road. But he didn't do anything wrong.'

'He assaulted someone.'

'Because he was making false accusation against us, I told you.'

'We saw the general's safe. It had been broken open using a heavy hammer. One with a pointed edge.'

'So what?'

'Do you use heavy hammers?'

'Of course we do. Some of the dangerous situations we find ourselves in, the only thing to do is smash our way in. And out. Loads of people use heavy hammers.'

'Did you or any of your crew break the safe open when you were in the general's flat?'

Morris glared at Coburg, angry. 'I'll tell you the same thing we told that old general. No, we did not. We did not break open his safe.'

'You were there when the general got back to his flat.'

'So?'

'Was the safe open when you arrived at the flat?'

'I have no idea. Weren't looking at the safe. We went in because there were reports of the roof being on fire and it spreading to the flat below. When we went in there was a big hole in the ceiling and there was smouldering on the floor and some of the furniture, so we doused it. We stopped it getting hold. If we hadn't done that, the whole place could have gone up, not just that general's flat but the other flats there. We saved his property. We didn't take anything, and we certainly never busted his bloody safe open.'

When Rosa arrived at the St John Ambulance station at Paddington, she discovered that the ambulance she and Doris had been using had been badly damaged during the night.

'The night crew took it out,' Chesney Warren told her and Doris. 'In the blackout, it dropped into a bomb crater. We managed to get it dragged out and taken to a garage, but at the moment we haven't got a vehicle for you. I'm having to divert calls to other stations.'

'When will it be back on the road?' asked Doris.

'Hopefully, tomorrow,' said Warren. 'There's filing to be done, if you're free.'

'Okay,' said Doris. 'It's better than sitting around at home, moping. And you never know, one of the other crews might need help.' She looked at Rosa.

'What about you, Rosa? Fancy filing?'

'Actually, there's something else I need to do,' said Rosa. 'But I'll call back later in case there's any change.'

She left the ambulance station and caught a bus to Charing Cross Road. The business of Benny Martin's guitar bothered her. No musician would willingly abandon his or her instrument. She'd heard of saxophone players who'd pawned their instrument for money to buy drugs, but Benny hadn't been on drugs as far as she knew. So where was his guitar? There was a possibility that Edgar and the police might find it at one of the clubs, but her guess was whoever had killed Benny wouldn't have left it lying around. The chances were they would have sold it, and the music shops that offered the best prices for second-hand instruments in London were in the northern part of Charing Cross Road and round the corner in Denmark Street.

She went to all the music shops she knew, looking in the windows at the instruments for sale, and going in them and checking out the guitars. She found Benny's guitar in Izzy Morrant's shop in Denmark Street. The shop was busy with musicians trying out the various instruments for sale, as well as others flicking through the racks of sheet music.

'Rosa!' Morrant greeted her. 'Looking for sheet music?'

'Not at the moment,' she said. 'I'm curious about

the guitar you've got in the window. The one with BM on it.'

'Ah yes,' said Morrant. 'It just came in just the other day. A lovely instrument.'

'Who brought it in?'

'Chuck Wheeler. He works for Pat Riley at the Riff Club. He said that one of the house band at the club needed money, so he was selling it. It's got a lovely tone.' He regarded her curiously. 'You're not thinking of changing instruments?'

Rosa laughed. 'No. The piano's the one for me. Did Chuck say who was selling it?'

'No, and I didn't ask. You don't want to embarrass people.'

'Not to mention that if word gets around that you talk about what people are up to, they stop doing business with you.'

Morrant chuckled. 'There's that, too.'

So, thought Rosa as she left the shop, *Pat Riley at the Riff Club*. That was her next port of call.

CHAPTER FOURTEEN

Thursday 5th December 1940

Coburg and Lampson found Joe Barker at the Bishop's Bridge Road depot. Just as Morris had done, he regarded them with suspicion as they showed him their warrant cards.

'What's this about?' he demanded.

'You're part of Crew 127 with the AFS,' said Coburg. 'I am,' said Barker, 'and proud to be doing something for the war effort. The blokes who are fighting overseas need to know that someone's looking after their families back home.'

'You and Crew 127 were on a call at a block of flats in Knightsbridge,' said Coburg. 'You encountered a tenant of one of the flats, a General Walters and his wife, and got into an altercation with him.'

Barker eyed them warily. 'Who said?'

'General Walter, and your own team leader, Ernie Morris. According to both of them, you punched General Walters in the face.'

Barker hesitated, then said defiantly, 'I was provoked. He accused me of nicking his stuff. Me, who was there risking his life to save that bastard's belongings.'

'His safe had been broken open and his wife's jewels taken,' said Coburg.

'That may be, but it wasn't me who done it. Nor any of my mates.' And Barker stuck resolutely to this answer during the rest of the time Coburg and Lampson talked to him.

'What do you think?' asked Coburg as he and Lampson walked to their car.

'I think there's something there,' said Lampson.

'So do I,' agreed Coburg. 'I think we need to look at Crew 127's call-outs and see if anyone else had the same problem with safes being broken into and jewellery missing. Let's go back to AFSD HQ and make a list of places they've been sent to lately.'

Rosa made her way along Wardour Mews, a narrow backwater in the centre of Soho, and in through the entrance to the Riff Club, then downstairs to the club itself. At this time of day there was no one around except a barman replacing bottles on the shelves.

'Is Pat around?' Rosa asked.

'In his office,' said the barman.

Rosa made her way to the office at the back of the club and knocked on the door, opening it at Riley's call of 'Yeah?'

Riley's face split into a grin as he saw who his visitor

was. 'Rosa! How are you? Still driving ambulances?'

'Still behind the wheel.'

'When are you going to come and do a session for me here?'

'When you want me.'

Riley grinned. 'Excellent! Let's have a look in the diary and see when you're free.'

As Riley opened the large bookings diary on his desk, Rosa said, 'Actually, Pat, I'm here because of Benny Martin.'

'Oh?'

'Yes. You know he died. Poisoned.'

'Yeah.' He shook his head, stunned. 'I still can't believe it. He was here the night he must have died. He was playing with the Johnny Kepple Trio.'

'I was in Izzy Morrant's shop and I saw Benny's guitar there.'

Riley nodded, unhappy.

'I sold it to him,' he said. 'It was tragic. As I say, Benny was here that night and he was in desperate trouble. He told me he owed money to some people. Fifty quid. Money that he didn't have, and these people were real heavies.'

'Who were they?'

'He didn't tell me and I didn't ask. It doesn't do to know too much about certain people; they have ways of finding out and then you're in trouble. He said he knew someone who'd lend him the money, but he couldn't get hold of them right at that moment, and he was desperate. I could see he was scared stiff. I really liked the kid, so I gave him the fifty quid. He insisted on leaving his guitar with me as security.

'It was next day someone told me he'd been found dead. I guess the heavies who were after him caught up with him, and even though he had the money to pay, it looks like they killed him.' He gave a rueful shrug. 'I guess they were making an example of him to let others know what would happen if they didn't cough up. So, sadly, I sent my man, Chuck, to Denmark Street to sell Benny's guitar on. He only got thirty quid for it, so I'm down twenty, but that's a small price to pay compared to what it cost Benny. I only wish he'd come to me earlier; I might have been able to help him.'

'And you don't know who these heavies were who Benny was meeting with?'

'No, and I didn't want to know. As I said, such people are dangerous, and I don't like being around dangerous people.'

Rosa left Wardour Mews and was walking along Oxford Street, approaching Tottenham Court Road Underground station, when she felt something hard press into her ribs. Annoyed, she turned and saw a tall man was walking very close beside her, and she realised he was holding something against her side.

'This is a gun,' muttered the man. 'Scream or try and run and I'll shoot you.'

Rosa stopped, bewildered. 'What the hell . . .' she began.

'Do what we say,' came another voice on the other side of her. She turned and found herself face to face a with a short man. 'Just keep walking. Cross over Tottenham Court Road and keep going.'

CHAPTER FIFTEEN

Thursday 5th December 1940

'What's all this about?' demanded Rosa.

'Later,' grunted the short man. The tall man shoved the gun harder into her side.

'Walk,' he ordered.

Rosa looked around at the crowds, looking to see if she could spot a police helmet. They surely wouldn't shoot her if the police were near. But there was no sign of any police, or any sort of help. Reluctantly, she began to walk, all too aware of the gun being thrust into her side. They crossed Tottenham Court Road then walked along New Oxford Street. *Am I being kidnapped, or are they going to kill me?* wondered Rosa.

It had to be connected with the fact she'd been asking questions about Benny's guitar, and as Benny had been murdered, the likelihood was they were going to kill her to stop her asking more questions.

The two men stopped by a parked car. The one without the gun walked to the driver's side, opened the door and got behind the steering wheel. The one with the gun opened the rear door and jerked the gun at Rosa.

'In,' he said.

Rosa fell against the side of the car, her fall half-closing the car door. The man scowled in irritation and grabbed the edge of the door to open it again, and as he did Rosa smashed the door shut, crushing his fingers against the door frame. The man screamed in pain. Immediately, Rosa swung her foot up and kicked him hard in the groin, eliciting another scream of pain. He dropped the gun, but Rosa didn't stop to pick it up from the pavement; she was already running back towards Tottenham Court Road where the crowds were. She saw the other man climb out of the driver's seat, but she didn't stop to see if he had a gun. She just ran. When she reached the corner of Tottenham Court Road, she ran down the stairs into the Tube station. She saw a uniformed police constable standing near the ticket office and ran to him.

'Constable,' she blurted out. 'I'm the wife of DCI Coburg of Scotland Yard. Two men have just tried to abduct me at gunpoint. I managed to get away. Their car is round the corner in New Oxford Street.'

'Show me,' snapped the constable.

Rosa ran back up the stairs to the street, the constable close behind her. He followed her to where the car had been parked, but there was no sign of it.

'It was here,' she said. 'They've driven off.'

'DCI Coburg, you said?' the constable asked.

'Yes.'

'Follow me,' said the constable. She followed him back to the junction and then over New Oxford Street towards a familiar blue police phone box. The constable opened the door and picked up the phone, while Rosa stayed outside, watching out in case the car with the two men returned.

The constable came out of the blue box. 'DCI Coburg has been alerted,' he said. 'I'm to wait here with you until he arrives.'

It was barely fifteen minutes later that Coburg and Lampson pulled up outside the blue box, blue lights flashing and the alarm bell ringing. Coburg leapt out.

'Are you alright?' he asked.

'I am now,' said Rosa. She turned to the constable. 'Thank you, constable.'

'Yes, thank you, constable,' added Coburg.

'My pleasure, sir,' said the constable. He gave them a salute, then walked off.

'Get in the car. We'll talk on the way to the Yard,' said Coburg.

Rosa slid into the rear seats, where Coburg joined her. As soon as the doors were shut, Lampson put the car in motion, but this time without the flashing lights and bell.

In short, urgent phrases, Rosa told them what had happened: being taken at gunpoint to the parked car, then managing to slam the man's hand in the car door and running off.

'Did they tell you what it was all about?' asked Coburg.

'No, but I've got an idea. This all happened after I went in search of Benny Martin's guitar, and found it at Izzy Morrant's music shop in Denmark Street. Izzy told me it had been brought in by a bloke who worked for Pat Riley, who owns the Riff Club in Soho. I've done gigs there and know Pat, so I went to ask him about it. He told me that Benny had been there the night he must have been killed. He was desperate for money because some heavies were after him. He needed fifty pounds. Pat gave him the fifty and Benny left him the guitar as security, saying he'd pay back the loan as soon as he managed to see some people he knew who'd help him.

'When Pat learnt that Benny had been killed, he sent one of his blokes to Izzy's music shop in Denmark Street with the guitar. Izzy gave him thirty pounds for it. My guess is that someone either overheard me asking Izzy about the guitar in his shop, or someone got nervous when they saw me going to the Riff Club.'

'What about this Pat Riley? Could he have been behind you being abducted?'

Rosa looked doubtful. 'I can't see it,' she said. 'I've known Pat for some years. He's always struck me as straight. Well, straight-ish for a jazz club owner.'

'What about the music shop owner?'

'Izzy?' She shook her head. 'No way.'

'You need to get out of London for a bit,' he said.

'Why?' she demanded.

'Because it looks like someone wants to kill you.'

'Maybe they were just taking me somewhere to question me,' said Rosa.

'If this is connected with Benny's death, then they're either murderers themselves, or connected with murderers. They would have killed you after they'd quizzed you. I suggest I contact Magnus and see if you can stay for a few days at Dawlish Hall. You should be safe there.'

Rosa looked at him thoughtfully. 'I don't want to, but I suppose it's the best way at the moment.'

'It is,' Coburg told her firmly. 'If whoever was behind it tries again, the only way I can stop them is by staying with you to protect you. And that'll mean I can't start digging into whoever's behind this.'

'It must be because someone thinks I've found out something about Benny's murder,' she said. 'The trouble is, I didn't.'

'You found out where he was the night he was murdered,' said Coburg.

'Yes, but not who these people were that he owed money to. It looks like it was them who killed him.'

'Leave that to me,' said Coburg. 'The first thing to do is arrange things with Magnus.'

* * *

113

When they got back to Scotland Yard, Coburg made a telephone call to Magnus's flat.

'Let's hope he's there,' he said,

They heard the voice of Magnus's valet and general factotum, Malcolm, who answered the phone and passed it to Magnus when Coburg asked to speak to his brother.

'Magnus, I'm phoning to ask a favour,' said Coburg. 'If there's anything I can do, just ask.'

'We're investigating a murder, and Rosa decided to play her part by asking questions around Soho about a vital piece of evidence that she found belonging to the victim. As a result, she was kidnapped. I think the men who did it intended to kill her.'

'Kill her?' exclaimed Magnus, shocked. 'My God!'

'Luckily she managed to escape.'

'How?'

'I'll tell you the details later. Right now I'd like to get her out of town because it's likely she's still in danger. Possibly even more than she was before, because she can identify the men who grabbed her. Would you mind if she took refuge at Dawlish Hall?'

'You don't even have to ask, Edgar. Of course. Where is she?'

'She's here with me at Scotland Yard at the moment.'

'Tell her to stay there. I'll sort some things out here, then Malcolm and I will call and collect her.'

'She'll need to pack some things to take with her.

I need to take her to our flat so she can get the things she wants, but first we've got to put together some information here on the men who abducted her. I'll phone you when we're ready and stay with her at the flat until you arrive. Will that be alright?'

'Of course.'

'I know it'll put you out . . .' Coburg began to apologise, but his brother cut him short.

'Nonsense. I was intending to head back to the Hall tomorrow with Malcolm. This just brings it forward. We'll see you at the flat.'

'Thanks, Magnus,' said Coburg. He hung up and looked at Rosa.

'Magnus is coming to collect you at the flat,' he told her.

'Yes, I heard,' said Rosa.

'I'll be taking Rosa there,' Coburg told Lampson. 'Can you hold the fort? You can tell the superintendent where I am if he wants to know.'

'No problem, guv.'

Coburg turned to Rosa. 'But before we do, I want you to draw pictures of what these two men looked like.'

'I'm not very good at art,' said Rosa doubtfully.

'You don't have to be,' said Coburg. 'Do a drawing of each that shows up any identifying marks, scars, what their hair looked like, that sort of thing. Then we'll get one of our artists to do a version from your sketches, and you can work with the artist to put them into shape. That'll give us something to show around. My guess is these guys are based somewhere in Soho, so we'll issue the pictures to the stations covering Soho.' He took some sheets of paper and a pencil from his desk, which he gave to Rosa. 'See what you can do.'

Rosa looked at the blank sheets of paper, doing her best to remember what the two men had looked like. The tall one had a scar on his left cheek, she remembered. And the short one had a twisted ear.

She set to work, the pencil moving across the paper. 'I'll have to phone Mr Warren at St John Ambulance and tell him I'm going to be away for a few days,' she said.

'Alright, but don't tell him where,' said Coburg. He stood over her, watching as the images of the two men came alive on the sheets of paper. She'd done images of each man's face, along with separate drawings showing the height and build of each man, along with good representations of the clothes they were wearing.

'These are good,' said Coburg. 'You've got a good eye, and a great memory.'

'I was with these goons for some while, being ushered along Oxford Street at gunpoint,' said Rosa. 'Believe me, what they looked like is burnt into my brain.'

She finished and sat back. Lampson picked up the two drawings.

'I'm not even sure if we need a police artist,' he said. 'In my opinion, you've got everything we need to find them, Mrs Coburg: scars, hair styles, shape, that twisted ear on the short one. These are great. I'll get them copied.'

Lampson left the office.

'Right,' said Coburg. 'Let's go to the flat and get you packed. And once you're safely on your way to Dawlish, I'm going to find the bastards who snatched you.' As they walked down the stairs from the office towards reception, Coburg asked, 'You say it happened after you'd been to see this Pat Riley at the Riff Club?'

'Yes.'

'Which makes me think he was behind it.'

Rosa looked doubtful. 'I don't like to think that, Edgar. As I said, I've known Pat a while. He's always struck me as a good guy. Same with Izzy Morrant, the music shop owner who told me about the guitar.'

'What's this Morrant like?'

'As I said, as with Riley, a good guy. There were other people in the shop when I was talking to him about the guitar. Maybe it was one of them.'

'I'll have a word with both Riley and Morrant,' said Coburg. He looked grim. 'Whoever was behind it has crossed the line and is going to suffer very seriously.'

CHAPTER SIXTEEN

Thursday 5th December 1940

The crew members of Auxiliary Fire Service Crew 127 sat in the public bar of the Rose and Crown pub, pints of beer in hand, and looked at their leader, Ernie Morris, with unhappy frowns on their faces.

'Say that again,' said Joe Barker.

'I said we'd better take a break from busting the safes,' repeated Morris. 'That general bloke you belted has brought the law in. Scotland Yard.'

'The bastard!' exploded Dan Reeves.

'We'll just have to content ourselves with picking up what's lying around,' said Morris.

'The best stuff is in the safe! That's why these toffs have them,' said Reeves, angry.

'It's too risky, Dan,' said Morris. 'Just till the law stops sniffing around.' He looked thoughtful, then added reluctantly, 'Actually, it might be a good idea to even let the loose stuff alone for a while. It's a DCI from Scotland Yard who's on the case, not just some local plod. We don't want to ruin a good thing and land ourselves in jail.'

'Or worse,' muttered Billy Dodds, usually the silent member of the crew. 'There's talk about hanging looters.'

'Rubbish!' snorted Reeves.

'No, Billy's right,' said Barker. 'I heard that, too. I reckon Ernie's right, we'd better take a break for a while, until they back off.'

'Sod that!' said the angry Reeves. 'This is the best chance I've ever had in my life to make some proper money. I'm not giving it up now.'

'Then you're off the crew, Dan,' said Morris. 'I'm not taking a chance on you bringing us all down.'

Reeves glared angrily at the other four. 'If you feel like that, good riddance. I'll find another crew that'll take me. There's enough of 'em around.'

'Yeh, but not all of 'em dipping their hands in.'

Reeves snorted. 'Don't you worry about me. I know what I'm doing. And I'll be living it up while you sorry bastards are still scratching around for pennies.'

He finished his drink, slammed the glass down on the table, then left. The remaining three men exchanged concerned looks.

'We ought to do something about him,' said Barker. 'If he gets caught, he'll grass about us to try and get off lightly. And he *will* get caught.'

The others nodded.

'So, what are we going to do?' asked Dodds.

'The first thing we do is get back the money he stole from us,' said Barker. 'Then after that, we'll take steps.'

Morris looked at him, concerned.

'You don't know he stole from us,' he said. 'He's one of us.'

'He's one of us who's in it for himself,' countered Barker angrily.

'You agreed that he should be the one to get rid of the jewellery,' pointed out Dodds.

'Because he was the one who had the contacts,' said Barker. 'Like you, I trusted him. But after the last lot he handled, I had my doubts. There was a good three grands' worth there, and he came back with nine hundred nicker.'

'He said that's all he got for 'em,' said Morris.

'Yes, well, I had my doubts even before he went. So I followed him to find out who his fence was. And yesterday I went to see the fence myself and asked him how much he'd given Reeves for the stuff.'

'And he told you?'

Barker gave a grim smile. 'He didn't have a lot of choice. I've still got a pistol my old man had in the last war. I stuck it in his ear and told him if he didn't want his brains all over the place to tell me straight how much he'd given Reeves the last time. One and a half grand, he told me. So Reeves has stiffed us for six hundred.'

'You didn't say anything to him just now,' Morris pointed out.

'No, because I know what a lying toerag he is. He'd just deny it and walk out. Well, now he's walked out properly, so I say we go and get the money he owes us off him. Six hundred quid. And that's without what else he's short-changed us on. And then, when we've got our money, we deal with him.'

'When you say "deal" . . . ?' asked Dodds apprehensively.

'You know what I mean,' snapped Barker. 'He's cheated us. His supposed mates. That's treason, that is. And we know what they do to traitors.'

Coburg stood on the pavement, waving goodbye with a feeling of relief as Magnus's Bentley, with Malcolm, Magnus's factotum, at the wheel and Rosa and Magnus together in the rear, drove off. Rosa would be safe at Dawlish Hall. Magnus and Malcolm would make sure of that. Now Coburg needed to uncover who was behind the attempt on Rosa's life. It wouldn't be safe for Rosa to return to London until that person and his henchmen had been neutralised.

Coburg returned to their flat and phoned Lampson at Scotland Yard.

'Rosa's left,' he told him. 'I'm coming to pick you up and we can start digging.'

As Lampson drove them to Soho, Coburg told him about Pamela Cuddington's name coming up. 'It seems she was having an affair with Benny Martin. I can't imagine that went down well with her husband, Lord Cuddington.'

'So he might be in the frame for it,' said Lampson. 'Shall we bring them in?'

'We'll have to,' said Coburg, 'but there's a piece of information that I'm going to share with you, but I'd appreciate it if you keep it to yourself for the moment. I was engaged to her about twenty years ago.'

'Twenty years!' exclaimed Lampson. 'So she's about your age? Forty?'

'Thirty-eight, I think.'

'And she was having it off with Benny Martin and he was – what – nineteen?'

'If the reports I've heard are true,' said Coburg. 'The problem is, if the superintendent gets to hear that Pamela and I were engaged once, even though it was a long time ago, he might insist I give up the case because of a conflict of interest, especially if she or her husband are suspects.'

'That's rubbish, guv,' snorted Lampson. 'You're the most impartial bloke I know. You'd nick your own missus if she broke the law.'

'I'm not sure about that,' admitted Coburg. 'The thing is I want to stay on this case and find out who the swine was who wanted Rosa killed.'

'No problem for me, guv,' said Lampson. 'As far as I'm concerned, you and this Pamela Cuddington have nothing to do with one another.'

'Appreciated,' said Coburg. 'Let's see if this Pat Riley can throw any light on anything.'

Pat Riley was in his office when Coburg and Lampson walked into the club. Riley stood up to greet them, smiling. 'Mr Coburg!' He beamed. 'This is a small world. Your missus was in here earlier.'

'Yes, so I understand,' said Coburg. 'She came to ask you about Benny Martin's guitar.'

'She did,' said Riley, gesturing for them both to sit. 'She saw it in Izzy Morrant's shop, and Izzy told her it had come from me.' He gave them a rueful look and said, 'I'll tell you exactly what I told her. Benny was here at the club the night before he died, playing with a trio: him on guitar, Johnny Kepple on sax and Sam Watson on drums. As it turned out, Benny had a problem. After the show he came to me and told me he needed money. He was heavily in debt, and one of these debts was to a couple of heavies who were leaning on him. He was terrified.'

'Did he say who these heavies were?'

Riley shook his head. 'No, and I didn't ask. Like I told Rosa, I don't want to get burdened with that kind of information. People find out you know things, and they come looking for you. The thing was Benny said he knew someone who could let him have the money, but he couldn't get hold of them until later the next day, the Tuesday, and he was supposed to see these heavies that night to settle up. The trouble was he didn't have the money to pay them. He had a tenner but he owed fifty.'

'Had he ever asked to borrow money before?'

'No, that's why I knew this was serious. So I said I'd lend him the fifty, and for him to pay me back when he'd got himself sorted out.'

'He didn't say who this other person was who he could get the money off?'

'No. And I didn't ask. Anyway, Benny insisted on my keeping his guitar, as some kind of security against the loan. I didn't want to, but his pride was at stake. So I gave him the fifty and took the guitar.

'Next day I heard he'd been found dead. I assumed these heavies had done him. You know, even though he paid up they must have given him a going-over to teach him a lesson, but it went too far. So, I sent one of my blokes to Denmark Street to see what he could get for the guitar. He got thirty for it, so I was out of pocket. But I was still better off than poor Benny.' He looked at them, curious. 'Rosa said Benny was poisoned. Is that right?'

'That's what we've been told,' said Coburg. 'Did you tell anyone about Rosa coming in to ask about the guitar?'

'No. Only you, just now. Why?'

'Because after she left your club she was abducted by two men who had orders to kill her.'

Riley stared at them, horrified.

'Kill her?' he echoed. 'Who?' Then, alarmed, he asked, 'She's alright, isn't she? I mean, the fact you're here says she is. What happened?'

'That's what we're trying to work out,' said Coburg. 'But yes, thankfully, she got away unharmed.'

'Where is she now?'

'Safe,' said Coburg. 'Getting back to Benny Martin, what time was it when he left the club on Monday night?'

'It must have been about midnight. Maybe half past eleven. I don't know, I wasn't checking the clock, I was just worried about the lad.'

Dan Reeves sat in the living room of his small terraced house in Paddington, a glass of beer in his hand, and fumed. The bastards! Ernie and the others pulling the plug on the looting racket, just when they were starting to make real money.

He looked at the photograph of himself and his late wife, Ellie, on the sideboard. It had been cancer that had taken her, four years before. She'd taken a long time to die, and in the end her passing had come as a relief to him, and – he was sure – to her. The last six months for her had been nothing but pain and morphine sleep.

125

'The only good thing is you never saw this war, love,' he murmured quietly. 'The bombing. The death and destruction. The irony is it's given me a chance to finally make some money.' He took a swig of beer. 'If we'd had money, would you have survived? Would there have been medicines we could have bought?' He gave a heavy sigh as he looked at the photograph. 'No, even the rich can't buy their way out of cancer.'

What was he going to do? He could ask around about joining another AFS crew, asking subtle questions that might hint about looting. Or perks, as they called it. But that could be dangerous. Someone might get suspicious and ask why he'd left his last crew.

The trouble was, he was short of money. He needed ready cash. The only answer was to trade in some of the jewels in the box. Alice wouldn't like it, but she'd see reason once he told her that if they didn't, she wouldn't have any money from him. She'd have to go out and get a job.

That should do the trick.

'You didn't show him the pictures of the two blokes who lifted Rosa,' said Lampson as he and Coburg walked out of the Riff Club into the street.

'No,' said Coburg. 'I must admit I get a feeling of something iffy about Mr Riley. He smiles too much. Rosa was lifted because of the guitar. The only two places she'd been were Izzy Morrant's music shop and Pat Riley's Riff Club. If Riley was behind what happened, showing him those drawings will put him on his guard. We'll see how things work out with some other people first before we show them to him.'

'What's our next move?' asked Lampson.

'We split up so we can move things along a bit. I'm going to see Izzy Morrant at his shop. You know the desk sergeant at the Soho nick, I believe.'

'Reg Dancy.' Lampson nodded. 'A good bloke.'

'Go and show him the drawings, see if he recognises them.'

'Where will we meet up?'

'There's a coffee house on the corner of Oxford Street and Tottenham Court Road. Eddie Rampton's.'

'I know it,' said Lampson.

'I'll see you there in about an hour.'

While Lampson made for the Soho police station, Coburg headed for Denmark Street and Izzy Morrant's shop. The shop had just a few customers, most tinkering with the instruments on display, others rummaging through the racks of sheet music. Coburg guessed that the small, bald, bespectacled man behind the counter was Izzy Morrant, and he walked to him.

'Mr Morrant?' asked Coburg.

Morrant beamed at him. 'Mr Coburg!' he exclaimed delightedly.

Coburg frowned, surprised. 'Have we met before?' he asked.

Morrant shook his head. 'I recognised you from the picture in the paper when you married Rosa.' He smiled. 'You've got a good one there! Such a talent!'

'Yes, she is,' agreed Coburg.

'What can I do for you?' asked Morrant.

Coburg looked at the small crowd of people in the shop, ostensibly sorting through sheet music or checking the various instruments for sale but obviously also eavesdropping on him and Morrant. *Information*, he realised. In Soho, any bit of information could be traded, for money or for a deal.

'Is there somewhere we can talk privately?' asked Coburg.

Morrant nodded. 'Rodney!' he called.

A young man who was playing a guitar quietly replaced the instrument in its rack on the wall and joined the two men.

'I need to talk to this gentleman in the office,' said Morrant. 'Can you keep an eye on the shop? If anyone needs me, tell them I'll be with them shortly. And don't sell anything without me being involved,' he added as a warning.

Morrant led the way to a small office at the back of the shop. 'Rodney's a nice kid. Too nice. If I'm not there, he'd virtually give away my stock for pennies.'

He opened the door marked 'office' and ushered Coburg in. The small room was filled with piles of sheet music and old gramophone records stacked up on top of one another. Morrant cleared a pile of records off one of the chairs and added them to the heap on the desk, then gestured Coburg to the now empty chair while he settled himself on the other. Morrant looked enquiringly at Coburg.

'Rosa came to see you this morning about a guitar,' said Coburg.

'She did.' Morrant nodded.

'You told her it had been brought in by someone who worked for Pat Riley, who owns the Riff Club.'

'Chuck Wheeler.' Morrant nodded again. 'He said one of the band needed to sell it.'

'Did you know the guitar belonged to Benny Martin?'

'No,' said Morrant. 'I know Benny, of course. He comes in here like all the musicians. But I didn't know the guitar was his.'

'After talking to you, Rosa went to see Pat Riley, and he told her Benny had left the guitar with him as security for a loan. That was on the night of Monday 2nd December. The next morning, Benny was found dead. He'd been poisoned.'

'Yes, I heard,' said Morrant. 'The music world is very small, especially in Soho. Everyone knows everyone else.'

'After Rosa left Pat Riley's club, she was grabbed by two armed men. We think they were going to kill her.'

Morrant stared at Coburg in horror, his eyes and mouth wide.

'K . . . kill her?' he echoed, shocked.

'Yes,' said Coburg. 'Now it must have been because someone thought she'd picked up something about Benny's murder and they decided to shut her up.'

'Kill her?' repeated Morrant, even more incredulous than before, his voice rising higher.

'Yes,' said Coburg. 'Now it can only be someone who heard you telling Rosa where the guitar came from, or someone who saw Rosa going into the Riff Club to see Pat Riley. Was there anyone here in your shop when you were talking to Rosa who might have overheard your conversation and passed it on to someone?'

'One of my customers did this?' exclaimed Morrant, shocked. 'Wanted to get Rosa killed?'

'We don't know if that was their aim. They may have just been asked to keep an eye on anyone asking about the guitar.'

Morrant fell into a thoughtful silence while he tried to remember the people who'd been in his shop at the same time as Rosa.

'Most of them were away from us,' he said, 'interested in what they were looking at. But there was one person, a woman, who I thought seemed to be listening. I just thought it was because of the way she was towards Rosa.'

'What do you mean?'

'She's a singer and she's always been jealous of Rosa. I've seen the looks she gives her. Not exactly hatred, but not friendly.'

'Who is this woman?'

'Bella Wilson. Technically she's not bad, she hits the right notes, but she doesn't have Rosa's way with a song, or with audiences. She hates it when she hears people praising Rosa. I've seen it when she's been in here and I've seen people pull out a record of Rosa's and talked about seeing her perform and how great she is, and Bella just gets sulkier and sulkier.' He looked perplexed. 'But I can't imagine Bella wanting to have anything to do with killing Rosa.'

'It's possible she didn't know that's what they planned. Where can I get hold of this Bella Wilson?'

Morrant looked at his watch. 'At this time of day you'll find her at the One Tun in Goodge Street.' He gave a sad smile. 'She drinks. I think she's trying to make her voice less good. You know, give her that Billie Holiday sound.' He shook his head. 'It's not just the voice, it's the heart of the music. Rosa has it, Bella doesn't.'

CHAPTER SEVENTEEN

Thursday 5th December 1940

Reg Dancy, the desk sergeant at the Soho police station, studied the two drawings that Lampson had given him.

'Any ideas, Reg?' asked Lampson.

'Yes,' said Dancy. 'Whoever did these is good. He's captured them dead right.'

'It was the boss's missus who drew 'em. You know them?'

Dancy nodded. He tapped the picture of the tall man. 'Henry Punt.' Then he tapped the one of the small man. 'Wally Maples.'

'Locals?'

'Well, they work locally.'

'Who do they work for?'

'Odds and ends. Mostly, they act as doormen for Pat Riley at the Riff Club and run errands for him.'

The One Tun in Goodge Street was about a hundred years old. Consequently, it had very small windows and was dark, even in daytime. The pub wasn't busy, just a few hardened drinkers, most of them sitting on their own. Coburg recognised Bella Wilson from Izzy Morrant's description of her having dyed red hair, a garish shade of henna that stood out from the other drinkers, mostly male.

She was sitting alone at a table, her hand gripping a glass of what looked like gin. He walked to the table and asked, 'Bella Wilson?'

She looked up at him, at first with curiosity, then her expression changed to one of disgust.

'What do you want?' she demanded.

'I'm Detective Chief Inspector Coburg from Scotland Yard,' he said, showing her his warrant card.

'I know who you are,' she said sourly.

Yes, she would, thought Coburg. *If she hates Rosa as much as Izzy Morrant believes, she'd know everything about her, including who she is married to.*

He sat down, and she scowled.

'I didn't say you could sit down?' she snapped.

'No, you didn't,' he said calmly. 'I've got some questions for you.'

'Well, I'm not answering any,' she said. 'So you can push off.'

'Unfortunately, I can't,' said Coburg. 'This is a murder enquiry, so if you refuse to talk to me here, I'll arrange for you to be taken to Scotland Yard and we can talk there, in an interview room under formal caution. It's up to you.'

Wilson looked at him with suspicion. Although she'd had quite a bit to drink, it wasn't enough to make her lose her wariness.

'Who's been murdered?' she asked.

'A young man called Benny Martin. A jazz guitarist. Did you know him?'

'I've seen him play,' she said. 'How did he die?'

'He was poisoned.'

'Who did it?'

'That's what we're trying to find out. We believe it's possibly the same people who tried to kill my wife earlier. I believe you know who she is.'

The anger on her face at the mention of Rosa showed there was no way she could deny it.

'What's any of this got to do with me?' she demanded.

'Rosa was in Izzy Morrant's shop at the same time as you. You were the only one close enough to hear her ask Izzy about Benny Martin's guitar.'

She shook her head. 'I don't know what you're talking about.'

Coburg sighed. 'Listen, Miss Wilson, I wasn't joking about taking you to Scotland Yard. And if I think you're still being obstructive when you're there, you'll be spending a long time in jail on remand while we continue our investigations.'

'What do you mean, on remand?' she blustered indignantly. 'On what charge?'

'Accessory to murder. Accessory to attempted murder. At this moment you're in a very difficult situation. We know you contacted someone after Rosa left Izzy's and told them that Rosa had discovered that Benny Martin's guitar had been sent to Izzy's shop from the Riff Club. Now all I need to know is who you told. Tell me that, and this is over for you. No charges. Refuse, and you're in the frame for conspiracy to commit murder.'

'I didn't know he intended to murder her!' burst out Wilson.

'Who?' asked Coburg.

Wilson hesitated, thinking it over, then she said in a voice that was almost a whisper, 'Henry Punt.'

'Who's Henry Punt?'

'He's a bloke who does odd jobs for people.'

'What sort of odd jobs?'

'Anything. He saw me heading for Izzy's shop and he stopped me and said for me to keep my ears open while I was in there. He said that if anyone came in and started asking about a guitar, to let him know. He said there'd be a fiver in it for me.'

'Did he describe the guitar?'

'Yes. He said it was a jazz guitar and it had the letters BM on the front.'

'Did he tell you where it came from?'

'No, he never said anything more about it, just that.'

'And you were in Izzy's shop when Rosa came in?'

She nodded.

'Where did you get hold of him? This Henry Punt?'

'I phoned and left a message for him.'

'Where did you phone?'

'At the Riff Club.'

'Pat Riley's place?'

'Yes.'

'Who took the message?'

'I don't know. Some bloke.'

'Not Pat Riley?'

'No, I'd have recognised his voice.'

'But you gave him the message.'

'I did.'

'What exactly did you say?'

'I said that Rosa Weeks was asking about the guitar, and I think she was going to the Riff Club to see Pat Riley.'

'What did he say to that?'

'He just said he'd pass it on to Henry.'

'Do you know if he did?'

She shook her head. 'No idea,' she said. Then she added with a scowl, 'If he did, I'm still waiting for my fiver the cheating bastard promised me.' She looked at Coburg, bewildered, and asked, 'Did someone really try and kill her?'

'Yes,' said Coburg. 'Fortunately, they didn't succeed.'

* * *

As Coburg drove the short distance from Goodge Street to the junction of Tottenham Court Road and Oxford Street, he thought over what he'd learnt from both Bella Wilson and Izzy Morrant. Wilson was jealous of Rosa and had reported her asking about the guitar to this Henry Punt with a phone call to him at Pat Riley's Riff Club. Wilson didn't care what happened to Rosa. Rosa had been abducted by two men immediately after leaving Pat Riley at his club. Everything pointed back to Pat Riley.

Coburg parked at the back of New Oxford Street and walked round the corner to Eddie Rampton's coffee house. It had been dressed up to look like one of the original London coffee houses from the eighteenth century, its large window made up of small, round glass panels set in a dark wooden frame, and the name Eddie Rampton's Original Coffee House in gold letters above it. It went against the fashion of the past few years for the coffee houses being given a modern look, mostly those that had been opened by the wave of Italian immigrants during the 1920s and '30s.

Lampson was already in Eddie Rampton's coffee bar when Coburg walked in. He ordered a coffee, then joined Lampson at his table.

'Sorry I'm late,' said Coburg. 'Talking to Izzy Morrant led me to another prospect. A woman called Bella Wilson.'

'Useful?'

'She was indeed. How did you get on?'

'I've got the inside track on the two blokes who grabbed Rosa,' said Lampson. 'Reg Dancy at the Soho nick recognised them from the drawings she did. Henry Punt and Wally Maples. Reg says they work for Pat Riley.'

Coburg gave a satisfied smile. 'And Bella Wilson told me that it was Henry Punt who saw her going towards Izzy Morrant's shop and asked her to keep an eye open for anyone asking about the guitar, and if they did she was to phone him at the Riff Club.'

'It all adds up,' said Lampson. 'It's Riley who was behind Benny Martin getting killed, and sending his blokes to kill Rosa.'

'That's the way it's looking,' agreed Coburg. 'We'll pull him in.' He smiled. 'It makes a change for a case to be open and shut.'

Lord Cuddington found the Honourable Jeremy Pike in the bar of the Royal Automobile Club in Pall Mall, and wryly wondered how many people assumed, wrongly, that the club was something to do with the motoring rescue organisation and telephoned it to ask for assistance when they'd broken down on the road. The Pall Mall Royal Automobile Club was a gentleman's private club, one of the most luxurious in London, and had been at its present site since 1911, when it moved from its previous location in Piccadilly into what had been the old War Office.

Pike was sitting at a table near the bar, a brandy in front of him. Cuddington dropped into the empty, sumptuously comfortable leather armchair at the table and produced an envelope from his inner pocket.

'Not here, dammit,' hissed Pike, casting apprehensive looks around. 'Downstairs, in the usual offices.'

With that, Pike drained the last of his brandy, put his glass down, then got up and strode towards the reception area.

For God's sake, thought Cuddington, irritated, *why do they play these cloak-and-dagger games?* This was the first time he'd got involved with Pike since being introduced to him by Justin Waterstone, who he'd dealt with successfully. Waterstone didn't go through all these ridiculous spy-like manoeuvres.

Cuddington rose and followed Pike through the reception area and the lobby and down to the conveniences. Pike was waiting for him inside the conveniences, and as Cuddington entered, Pike was just finishing checking that all the cubicles were unoccupied.

'Satisfied?' asked Cuddington.

Pike gave him a smile. 'I will be,' he said.

CHAPTER EIGHTEEN

Thursday 5th December 1940

Riley's face was a picture of bewilderment when Coburg and Lampson appeared in his office and told him they were taking him to Scotland Yard 'to help us with our enquiries'.

'What enquiries?' he asked.

'We'll tell you that when we get to Scotland Yard,' said Coburg.

'Oh come on, Mr Coburg! What's all this about?'

'It's an official enquiry, Mr Riley. We'll tell you that once we've issued the formal caution.'

'Formal caution?' Riley stared at them. 'What's this to do with?'

Coburg produced a pair of handcuffs. 'If you're going to be difficult, we'll have to put these on you.'

Riley shook his head. He stood up. 'I'm never difficult,' he said. He took his jacket from a peg on the wall and put it on. 'Let's go,' he said.

* * *

Inside the interview room, Riley sat across from Coburg and Lampson at the bare wooden table. A uniformed constable stood at one side, watching the proceedings. In front of Lampson was a pad and in his hand was a pencil to keep notes of the interview.

'Do I need a solicitor here with me?' asked Riley nervously.

'You can have one if you wish,' said Coburg. 'That's your right. If you feel you've got something to hide that you don't wish us to know about.'

'No, no,' Riley assured them. 'I've got nothing to hide.'

'In that case,' said Coburg, and he read Riley his rights, warning him that anything he said would be taken down and might be used as evidence against him. All the time, Riley stared at both detectives, incomprehension on his face. Finally, Coburg said, 'The two men who grabbed my wife with orders to kill her worked for you.'

Riley stared at Coburg, stunned. 'That's impossible,' he said.

'We've identified them,' he said. 'Henry Punt and Wally Maples.'

Coburg produced the copies of the drawings and laid them on the desk in front of Riley. 'Are these them?'

Riley stared at the pictures, then nodded, stunned. 'Yes, but . . . but . . . I don't believe it. Why?'

'Possibly because you gave them instructions?'

Riley looked at Coburg, a look of horror on his face. He gulped and blurted out, 'Mr Coburg, this is nothing to do with me. Henry and Wally will confirm that when you talk to them.'

'Where can I find them?'

'They've got a gaff off Charlotte Street. They rent a room there.'

'They live together?'

Riley nodded. Then he looked at Coburg defensively.

'It don't mean anything,' he said. 'They're not like that. Leastways, not as far as I know.'

Lampson pushed a sheet of paper and a pencil across the table to him.

'Write down the address,' he said.

Riley began to reach inside his jacket, but Coburg stopped him.

'What are you reaching for?' he asked.

'My book with the addresses and phone numbers of people,' said Riley. 'I can't carry them all around in my head.'

Coburg nodded and Riley pulled a small notebook from his pocket. He flicked through it and when he found the address for Henry Punt and Wally Maples, he wrote it down, then pushed the piece of paper back to Lampson before returning the address book to his inside pocket. Lampson folded the piece of paper up and put it in his pocket.

'Henry Punt got a phone message at your club this morning from a woman called Bella Wilson,' said Coburg.

'Not to my knowledge,' said Riley.

'But Henry Punt was there this morning?' Riley shook his head.

'No,' he said.

'Were you at your club all morning?'

'No,' admitted Riley. 'After Rosa left, I had to go and see a bloke about a drinks order we had in.'

'What about before she got here?'

'I was in, but in and out. I went round the corner for a coffee.'

'Don't you do coffee at the club?'

'Yeah, but not as good as what they serve round the corner. Italian coffee. I know most Italians are in jail or interred, but the family have still got their coffee shop. Di Angelo's in Berwick Street. I was there for about half an hour, drinking my coffee and reading the paper. You can check.'

'So when did you last actually see Henry and Wally?'

'Yesterday afternoon. I sent them on an errand.'

'What sort of errand?'

Riley hesitated, then said, 'To have a word with a bloke called Shelley Buttons.'

'Who's Shelley Buttons, and what sort of word were they to have with him?'

Riley looked very uncomfortable. 'He owns another club here in Soho, and for some time he's been leaning on me, trying to get me to sell. And at a knock-down price. Virtually giving it away. Well, I wasn't having that. So I sent Henry and Wally, to have a word with him.' He scowled. 'If what you say is true, I'm guessing they were stitching me up, working for Buttons as well. Buttons must have been behind them grabbing your missus.'

'Why would Buttons want to kidnap Rosa?' asked Coburg.

'It has to be something to do with Benny Martin being killed. Rosa told me she went looking for Benny's guitar, which is how she ended up asking me about it. My guess is you'll find Buttons was behind Benny being killed, so he got my two boys to grab her to silence her.'

'Rosa never mentioned Shelley Buttons. Just you,' said Coburg.

'Yeah, well, Shelley wouldn't know that. He's a very suspicious character; he doesn't take chances.'

'But why use two of your blokes instead of his own?'

'To put suspicion on me if it went wrong. Which it did.' He scowled. 'And I was fool enough to send Henry and Wally over to talk to him, warn him off. And all the time they were double-crossing me.'

Coburg regarded him thoughtfully, then asked, 'Was anyone with Benny that night at your club?'

'What do you mean?' asked Riley, puzzled.

'Lady Pamela Cuddington, for example?'

Riley gave a sour grin. 'Oh, her,' he snorted. 'No, thank God. We'd had enough trouble with her. Benny must have realised she was trouble because he gave her the elbow.'

'You know that for a fact?'

'Yes. I asked Benny about her and he said it was over between them. He said he couldn't cope with her tantrums. Said it was driving him mad.'

Coburg pushed another piece of paper to Riley. 'I suggest you get your address book out,' he said. 'We're going to need a list of everyone who was in your club the night Benny was killed.'

'Everybody?'

'We'll start with the performers, then your staff who were working that night.'

'Why?'

'Because we're investigating a murder that happened – by our reckoning – soon after Benny left your club.'

'I told you, he was going to meet these heavies about this money he owed. It must have been them.'

'Maybe, maybe not. We'll need to talk to everyone in case anyone saw something that might point to what actually happened.'

Riley gave a sigh, then took his address book out again and began to flick through it, then started writing down names and addresses, and some phone numbers.

'Johnny Kepple and Sam Watson,' he said. 'They were the ones playing with Benny that night. Kepple plays sax and Watson drums. They're not a regular group, just musicians who play together now and then, what you'd call a pick-up band. That night they were playing as the Johnny Kepple Trio. They were good.'

Riley flicked through his address book and added more names, with a description after each name: barman, storeman, door keeper, box office, stage manager. As the list got longer and longer, Coburg gave him another piece of paper.

'That's a large staff you've got there,' Coburg commented. 'It must be a big wages bill.'

'It is,' said Riley. He pushed the two sheets of paper across to Coburg. 'That's about it. I don't know who was in that night as far as customers went, but the staff will be able to tell you, I'm sure.'

Rosa got out of the Bentley and looked in awe at Dawlish Hall. The house was huge. It wasn't a house, it was a mansion, complete with ornamental Roman columns made of white marble at the front, framing the porch over the front door. Not that 'porch' was the right word for it, thought Rosa. She'd lived in places smaller than the so-called porch. And with its high windows, it looked like a smaller version of Buckingham Palace.

And the grounds were vast – the lawned area at the front of the house, separated from the house by the wide gravelled drive, was bigger than most farmers' fields: in truth, a small park, dotted with trees and with a paddock at one side, complete with stables.

The house was about two miles outside the small Buckinghamshire village of Dawlish, a village complete with a church, shops, blacksmith's and sundry other buildings that made it the perfect image of a Home Counties rural village. And Edgar had grown up here!

'It's magnificent,' she said as Magnus joined her, while Malcolm unloaded her bag from the boot of the car and took it to the house.

'It's not bad,' said Magnus. 'Not as big as some, but it suits us.' He looked wistful as he added, 'To be honest, it's a bit too large for us now, with the war on and the servants gone. Just Mrs Hilton, who comes in to cook and generally keep things tidy. But it's where I think of as home. And I hope Edgar does, too. And I hope you'll think of it like that.'

He headed for the house. 'We'll see if Mrs Hilton wants us to get anything from the village, and if not I'll get Malcolm to put the car in the garage. We don't really have much crime around here, but with so many strangers around these days, it's better to be safe than sorry.'

As Rosa followed Magnus towards the magnificent, imposing structure, she thought: *I have to bring Ma and Pa to see this and show them what I – the daughter of a man who sold fruit and vegetables from the back of a lorry – married into. They'd never believe it. I can't believe it!*

147

CHAPTER NINETEEN

Thursday 5th December 1940

'What do you think of Riley's story?' Coburg asked Lampson as they climbed the stairs to their office on the first floor. Riley had been taken to a custody suite in the basement.

'I've never heard such a load of old eyewash in my life,' snorted Lampson. 'He's the one who had Rosa lifted and he's trying to offload the blame on this bloke Buttons.'

'It certainly makes more sense than his convoluted story about Shelley Buttons,' said Coburg. 'The puzzle is that phone call of Bella Wilson's to the Riff Club. Pat Riley says he didn't take a phone call from her, she didn't recognise the man she spoke to. Riley says he hasn't seen Punt and Maples since yesterday. Bella would have recognised Punt's voice if it had been him who picked up the phone. If he's telling the truth, Riley was out at Di Angelo's, so it's possible that Punt and Maples were there at the club. Maples picks up the phone and takes the message.'

'Why doesn't Maples give the phone to Punt?'

'Maybe Punt wasn't there, but Maples was. We know that Punt must have got the message, because he and Maples then abducted Rosa.'

'It's still all a bit off, guv,' said Lampson. 'For me, everything still points to Riley being behind it.'

'Unless it's this Shelley Buttons, as Riley says. Do you know this Buttons character?'

'Not personally,' said Lampson. 'He's bound to have a record if he's the bad lad that Riley says he is.'

'I suggest we have a word with the Soho nick about Buttons, see what they say, before we talk to him. Then we'll see how he shapes up.'

'What are we going to do about Riley? Bang him up on remand?'

'Not for the moment,' said Coburg unhappily. 'I've got a feeling about him, but we've got no proof to nail him with. For the moment we'll have to release him, but before you do, line up a couple of detectives to follow him discreetly, see where he goes and who he meets with.'

Lampson looked at the chief inspector inquisitively and commented, 'According to Riley, Benny had dumped your old fiancée, Lady Pamela whatsername. Which might make her a bit upset.'

'She is not my old fiancée,' protested Coburg, before adding unhappily, 'Alright, she was, but that was twenty years ago. I haven't the faintest idea what sort of person she is now.'

'A bit of a slapper, by all accounts,' said Lampson. 'We're going to have to have words with them, you know, guv. Lady Pamela and her husband.'

'Yes, you're right,' sighed Coburg. 'We'll talk to them once we've dealt with Henry Punt and Wally Maples.'

There was no sign of Punt and Maples at the address in Charlotte Street that Coburg and Lampson had been given by Riley. Like many other large older houses, it had been turned into small flats and bedsits, and, knocking on the doors adjacent to Punt and Maples's room, they learnt there had been no sign nor sound of either of the men for at least a day and a night. It was the sound that was conclusive: 'They used to have their wireless on all the time,' said the man who lived directly next to them. 'I used to have to ask them to turn it down. Sometimes they did, sometimes they didn't. But there's been no sound of their wireless since early yesterday morning.'

'Since before they lifted Rosa,' observed Lampson as they left the house. 'Reckon they've done a runner, guv?'

'It's possible,' said Coburg. He checked his watch. 'I think that's us for the day,' he said. 'Tomorrow we'll look into this Shelley Buttons and talk to the people from the Riff Club, plus everything else. Do you want a lift home? I'm going back to the Yard to see if there's anything new, then I'm heading for home as well.'

'No, I'm fine. I'll walk from here,' said Lampson. 'If you speak to Rosa, give her my regards, guv. Tell her we'll have her back in the smoke in no time.'

'Thanks, Ted. Let's hope that's so.'

CHAPTER TWENTY

Thursday 5th December 1940

To Coburg, with Rosa away, the flat seemed hollow and empty. He missed her more than he could say. The key to all of it was to get hold of Henry Punt and Wally Maples. Once they'd told him who had hired them to grab Rosa and they'd arrested him, then it would be safe for Rosa to come back.

He was jolted out of his reverie by the phone ringing, and his first thought as he snatched up the receiver was that it would be Rosa.

It wasn't. Instead, he heard another woman's voice. 'Edgar,' she said. 'It's Pamela Cuddington. Pamela Westbrook, as was.'

'Pamela,' said Coburg. 'It's been a long time.'

'It has. I see you're married now. To Rosa Weeks.'

'I am,' said Coburg.

'Is she there with you?'

Coburg hesitated, then said, 'Not at the moment.'

'I wonder if I could come and see you?'

'I don't think that's advisable.'

'Because your wife might turn up?'

'No. Because I am investigating a murder, and your name has been mentioned in the context.'

There was a pause. Then the sound of a sob before she said, 'Poor Benny. Someone told me he'd been found in the tunnel at Aldwych station. He'd been poisoned. I asked around and was told you were in charge of the case.'

'I am,' said Coburg. 'And yes, I will need to talk to you, but it would not be appropriate for us to meet at my home. This is an official enquiry under the jurisdiction of Scotland Yard.'

'I will not go to Scotland Yard!' she said suddenly. Coburg was tempted to say, *You will if I say you will*. But then he remembered how stubborn she could be, and guessed she still was. If he wanted to get the truth out of her about her relationship with Benny Martin, and about the events that may have led to his death, then he needed to play it carefully. Not give her anything, certainly not give her an advantage, but he needed to get to the bottom of Benny's murder. Not least so that he could bring Rosa home.

'I have a suite at The Dorchester,' she said. 'We can meet there.'

'A private meeting between us in your hotel suite would also be inappropriate,' said Coburg. 'Recently I agreed to meet another lady in her hotel suite at The Savoy to talk about the murder of her husband. It was completely innocent, but the fact that we were in her suite without a chaperone led to my being suspended from duty.'

There was a pause, then she said, 'In that case, there is a tea room here at The Dorchester, separate from the restaurant, but open to the public. I can arrange a table there apart from any other guests. We'll be in sight of them, but out of earshot. Will that be acceptable?'

'That will be,' said Coburg. 'Thank you. When will be convenient?'

'If you're free, in half an hour?' she suggested.

'I'll see you in half an hour at The Dorchester,' said Coburg.

He hung up and sat looking at the telephone. Whether he liked it or not, a painful part of his past was surfacing and clawing at him.

Ted Lampson and his ten-year-old son, Terry, walked across the road from Petty's Pie and Mash shop to their terraced house, each clutching a small pudding basin filled with mashed potatoes and a portion of meat pie, the whole adorned with a generous ladling of parsley sauce, also known as 'liquor' in common parlance. The short walk meant there was little chance of the food cooling down, but when they got in, Lampson draped a tea towel over the basins after he'd put them on the kitchen table to keep the warmth in.

It was their regular Thursday treat. On Thursdays, Lampson's mum just made Terry a sandwich after she'd fetched him from school to 'keep him going', until his dad arrived to collect Terry, taking his school stuff and whatever he'd taken to his parents' back to their house. Once settled, they made the short trip across the road to Petty's.

Right from the start, Terry had elected to eat his pie and mash straight from the basin rather than pour it onto a plate, and Lampson had been happy to join in. Both elected to use a spoon rather than a knife and fork. It was a dish that didn't need cutting. The meat was minced so small as to be unidentifiable. Rumour had it that with the shortage of meat, a lot of meat products were actually made from horsemeat. After all, most racing had been abandoned with the threat of bombing and racehorses were expensive to keep.

'Right, we need to talk football,' said Lampson.

Lampson had recently started a boys' football team based around the boys at Terry's junior school, and gradually some of the boys' parents had begun to join in the activity. Lampson had every other Saturday off work, and he'd been able to arrange matches with other local schools or organisations, like the Boy Scouts, local churches or boys' clubs, on the Saturdays when he was free. On the Saturdays when Lampson was at work, other dads took part in football practices at the local park, along with

Terry's school teacher, Miss Eve Bradley, who was as enthusiastic as anyone.

At first, Terry had questioned Miss Bradley's involvement. 'She's my teacher,' he'd objected. 'And she's a woman.'

'So would you object if your teacher was a man?' asked Lampson.

'No,' said Terry. 'But women don't know anything about football.'

'Miss Bradley does,' Lampson had told him. 'Her dad played for West Ham and her mum played for West Ham Ladies during the First War.'

'Women's football?' said Terry scornfully.

'Listen, don't you criticise until you find out the facts. In the First War, with most of the men away, women played football to crowds of forty thousand. It was massive. You ask Miss Bradley about it. She knows as much as I do about football.' Then he paused and added, 'Well, almost as much, although hers is mainly about the Hammers.'

Since then, Miss Bradley was as much a part of the group behind the boys' team, along with Lampson's own parents, who were fierce and very vocal when they went to support their grandson's team every two weeks.

'Now, tomorrow week we've got a match against a team from the King's Cross Methodist Chapel. I've seen 'em in action and they're rough, so on Saturday

I want you all practising how to deal with rough shoulder charges and dodge getting kicked. They may be a churchy lot but they're no angels. How are you getting on with your shooting?'

'Good,' said Terry. 'Me and Tony Bennett practise in the playground at lunchtimes. We take turns to be in goal.' He gave a smug smile. 'Today I scored twelve goals and he only managed four.'

'Okay, but don't get overconfident,' warned his father. 'I've seen too many centre-forwards start to think they're the bees' knees, and suddenly they can't score a goal to save their life.'

Pamela Cuddington was waiting for him in the tea room at The Dorchester, sitting at a small table adorned with a pristine white tablecloth, an ornamental vase filled with flowers, and a glass of whisky. Coburg had wondered on his way to the hotel how he would feel when he saw her again after all these years, and he had to admit to a pang of deep affection in his heart when he saw her sitting at the table. She was older, but for Coburg that didn't matter – so was he – and Pamela still had that poise, that aura of beauty that she'd had when he'd first met her all those years ago.

She rose to her feet as her approached. He held out his hand to shake hers, and she used it to pull herself towards him and kiss him on the cheek before she sat down again.

'You look well,' she said.

'So do you,' returned Coburg, sitting down.

'Nonsense,' she said, almost spitting the word out. 'I look like what I am, an old and disillusioned hag.'

'You're not old,' said Coburg.

'But I am a hag.'

'No you're not,' said Coburg. 'You're as beautiful as when we first met.'

'Liar,' she said. 'My husband says I am. He calls me a slut and a hag.'

She waved at a waiter who'd appeared in the entrance to the tea room and he came over to their table.

'Another whisky,' said Pamela.

'The same for me,' ordered Coburg.

The waiter nodded, and left. Pamela looked Coburg firmly in the eye as she said, 'I keep a room here at The Dorchester to escape to when things get too bad between Colin and I, and I can't face being at the house with him. I hate him and my life with him.' Her expression softened as she said, 'I should have married you.' She gave him an apologetic look as she said, 'I was too much of a coward. I listened to my mother and father telling me you'd be an invalid for the rest of your life, unable to function as a husband. When my father said he wanted to write to you telling you it was off, I should have said no. Defied him. But I didn't.' She gave a rueful sigh. 'You had a lucky escape. It could have been you instead of Colin having me thrown out of places.' Then she looked thoughtful. 'No, it couldn't have been. I wouldn't have been able to treat you that way, because you wouldn't have treated me the way Colin does. He goes off with his nancy boyfriends and then expects me to share my body with him afterwards. He even wanted me to take him and one of them to bed. And when I refused, he beat me.' Her lip curled in distaste. 'He disgusts me.' She looked at him, and he could see the pain in her face. 'That's why I fell for poor young Benny. He was a pure soul.' She gave a wry chuckle. 'Well, not *that* pure, but there was nothing filthy about him. No deviousness.' She fell silent as the waiter returned with their drinks. When he'd gone, she asked, 'Do you know who killed him?'

'We're still looking into it,' said Coburg.

'Look into Colin,' she said vengefully. 'He hated Benny.' She hesitated, then said, 'He as good as admitted to me it was he who killed Benny. Or had him killed.'

'He actually said that?'

'His actual words, when I told him that Benny was dead, were "I warned him what would happen", and then he added, "Let that be a lesson, Pam. Don't cross me." And he's perfectly capable of murder. He killed one of his nancy boyfriends who tried to blackmail him. Strangled him when they were in bed together. He took great pride in telling me about it, letting me know

159

what was in store for me if I opposed him in any way.'

'Do you know the name of the man he killed?' asked Coburg.

She looked at him in surprise. 'You're not thinking of investigating it?'

'If a murder has been committed, it's my duty to investigate it.'

She laughed. 'My God, listen to yourself, Edgar. You sound so sanctimonious.' Then she looked serious as she said, 'But at least I suppose it means you'll look into Colin without fear or favour, unlike most policemen who get involved with him who are happy to let him go in return for some cash or other favours.'

'Why do you think he wanted to kill Benny?'

'Because Benny threatened to expose him for the filth he is. He told him as much when Colin came into one of the clubs I was in with Benny. Colin was drunk and started attacking me. Benny stepped in and told him to keep his hands off me. He said if he didn't, he'd expose him for the pervert he was and that would be the end of him because no one would want to do business with him.'

'What is Colin's business?'

'He sits on the boards of various companies, most of them very old-fashioned ones who'd hate a scandal. He's been able to keep his boyfriends a secret because of me, the dutiful wife. That is until I started playing away from home and rumours began to spread. He countered by blaming me, saying I was a nymphomaniac with a lust for teenage boys. It's not true, but the sort of people Colin is involved with prefer to believe that about me rather than the truth about him. So, as I say, if you want to know who killed Benny, look at Lord Colin Cuddington.'

She sipped at her whisky, and looked at Coburg with a soft, wistful smile. 'This is nice,' she said. 'I've missed you. I followed your career, you know. If I see anything in the papers about the aristocratic copper, as they sometimes call you, DCI Saxe-Coburg, I cut it out and keep it.' She laughed. 'It annoys Colin enormously. I think that's partly why I do it. He's jealous of you, you know.'

'Of me?' asked Coburg, surprised.

'Because he knows you were my first love, and my only love. I do so wish we'd gone to bed together, but it wasn't the done thing in those days.' She smiled. 'Although we had some lovely times when we could snatch them.' She looked at him intensely as she said in a low whisper, 'Often I can still feel your fingers stroking me. Do you remember how it felt that time at my uncle's farm when the family were out doing something and we had the house to ourselves?' She looked at him and said, 'It seems a pity to waste the room I've got here.' He shook his head.

'No,' he said. 'I'm flattered, but . . .'

'You've got the little woman waiting for you at home,' she said with a sigh.

'No,' he said. 'Rosa's away at the moment for a few days.' She smiled and her eyes lit up.

'Then why not?' she asked. 'It'll be our secret. And just this once.' She smiled again. 'Although, if we like it . . .'

'No,' he said. 'I don't play away from home, Pamela. I know what I've got with Rosa and I don't want to lose it.'

'But you won't lose it,' she said. 'If she's not at home, she won't know.'

'*I'll* know,' he said. He finished his whisky and stood up. 'Thanks for the information about your husband, and I will chase it up. It's been nice to see you again.'

She stood up and said, 'It could have been nicer. For me, at least.'

He reached out his hand, and this time she took it to hold, and then shake.

'If you change your mind, you can always find me,' she said.

'I'm sure we'll see one another again,' he said. 'After all, I'm investigating the murder of your boyfriend.'

'He wasn't my boyfriend,' she said with an air of defiance. 'He was my lover.'

'And someone murdered him,' said Coburg. 'And you say it was your husband.'

She looked at him, bitterness on her face.

'And now you're using that as an excuse for us not to have a bit of fun. The protocol of police procedures. Getting sexually involved with possible suspects,' she said with a sneer. 'Well listen, DCI Coburg, I've got news for you. I know plenty of high-level police officers who not only get sexually involved with some of their suspects, but they enjoy it.' She gave a smirk. 'I've been caught shoplifting, for various motoring offences, and drunkenness in a public place, among other things. But never charged. I enjoy sex and so did those officers.' She looked at Coburg appealingly. 'I didn't want to end up like this. If you and I had stayed together, I'd never do that sort of thing. It's Colin's fault.'

'You have my sympathy, Lady Cuddington,' said Coburg.

'Lady Cuddington?' she echoed, irritated.

'I think it's best if we keep it formal, don't you?' said Coburg. 'Twenty years ago, that was then. This is now.' He gave a slight bow, and left.

When Coburg got back to the flat, he telephoned Rosa at Dawlish Hall.

'I just wanted to say goodnight,' he said.

'I tried phoning you earlier, but you must have been out.'

'I was,' said Coburg.

'On the razzle while the wife's away?' chuckled Rosa.

'Absolutely not,' said Coburg. 'I had to go and see someone with some information about Benny's murder.'

'Which you can't tell me over the phone,' said Rosa.

'Correct,' said Coburg.

'But was it helpful? Are you any nearer who finding out who did it?'

'Maybe. It certainly suggests another suspect who wasn't in the frame before.'

'It sounds like a crowded frame,' commented Rosa.

'And getting more crowded by the minute,' sighed Coburg. 'I hope you get a good night's sleep.'

'I think I will,' said Rosa. 'No air raids out here, by all accounts. You ought to come out here. It's gorgeous.'

'I know,' said Coburg. 'I lived there. Goodnight, my love. Sleep tight. I love you.'

'I love you, too, my honey. Take care and keep safe.'

CHAPTER TWENTY-ONE

Friday 6th December 1940

The first thing Coburg did on getting up the next morning was telephone Dawlish Hall again to check on Rosa.

'She's here and safe and well, Master Edgar,' Malcolm informed him. 'Do you wish to speak to her?'

'Yes please, Malcolm.'

A short while later, he heard Rosa's voice.

'Edgar, I know it's only been one night apart, and I know we talked last night, but I do miss you.'

'I miss you, too, my love. Is everything alright there?'

'Everything's fine. Magnus and Malcolm have got guns of all sorts lying to hand around the place in case of an invasion by either the people who were after me, or – more likely – by any enemy soldiers who parachute down.'

'Do they think that likely?'

'It's what Magnus said he'd do if he were Hitler. Launch an attack from behind the front line.'

'Yes, he was always a good military commander.'

'How soon can I come back home?' asked Rosa.

'Yesterday you said it was gorgeous there,' said Coburg.

'It is, and I love it,' said Rosa. 'It's a beautiful place, the grounds are wonderful, and I'm being pampered by Magnus and Malcolm in a way you wouldn't believe.'

'Knowing Magnus and Malcolm, I believe it very easily. At the moment, although I'd love you to be here, I think it's safer for you to be there. Trust me, my darling, I don't want you away from me for any longer than is absolutely necessary.'

Coburg picked up Lampson at Somers Town, as usual, and they drove to Scotland Yard, where they found a report from the detectives tailing Riley waiting for them. 'Riley goes into his club in Wardour Mews and stays there most of the day,' Coburg read aloud to Lampson. 'He goes home, and later he goes back to the club and stays there until the early hours, then he goes home again. Because Wardour Mews is a dead end, there's no way he can come out without us seeing him.'

'Well, at least we know where he is,' said Lampson.

They made their way to Soho and Di Angelo's coffee shop in Berwick Street, round the corner from Wardour Mews and Riley's Riff Club. There, the woman who ran it, Julia di Angelo, confirmed that

Pat Riley had been in for his coffee and to read the newspaper at the time he said he'd been there. 'He was here for about half an hour,' she told them.

'Alibi confirmed,' grunted Lampson sourly as they left.

'You don't believe her?' asked Coburg.

'Do you?' asked Lampson.

'No,' admitted Coburg. 'It may be true; it may not be.' They walked to the Soho police station and sought out Sergeant Dancy.

'Two visits in two days.' Dancy grinned at them. 'Something must be up? Punt and Maples again?'

'Not this time, Reg,' said Lampson. He introduced Coburg to the sergeant and the two men shook hands.

'A pleasure to meet you, sir,' said the sergeant.

'And you, sergeant,' returned Coburg. 'We're here to pick your brains again, this time about another local. A man called Shelley Buttons.'

'Him!' snorted Dancy derisively.

'Have you had much to do with him?'

'Nothing we can nail him for,' said Dancy. 'Buttons is a relative new bloke to the area. He came down from Birmingham about three years ago and bought his first club, the Red Feather.'

'His first?'

Dancy nodded. 'He owns three now, along with the Red Feather he's got the Danube and Pete's Place, all in Soho, and I get the idea he's intending to widen his little empire even more.'

'He must be wealthy to be able to buy up that many clubs,' said Coburg.

'Yes, well, the word is that he doesn't pay the market price.'

'Extortion?' asked Coburg. 'Threats and menaces?'

'But there's no proof that's how he does it,' admitted Dancy ruefully. 'No one wants to talk. Certainly not the people he bought the clubs from. Not after one of them, Jake Pond, had an accident. That shut the others up.'

'What sort of accident?'

'He was found in a backstreet. He'd been run over. And not just once. It looked like he'd been run over at least three times, the car going backwards and forwards over him. The message was out, hence the silence over how he'd got the clubs in the first place.'

'Let me guess: fights breaking out, break-ins, burglary, a bit of arson? All very expensive.'

'And backed up by some very heavy people Buttons brought with him from Birmingham.'

'Has he ever been arrested?'

'Not in London, as far as I know,' said Dancy. 'But if you want my advice, it might be worth talking to Birmingham CID.'

'That's a good tip,' said Coburg. 'Thanks.'

* * *

168

Joe Barker and Ernie Morris turned away from the door of the small terraced house in Paddington where Dan Reeves lived. There'd been no answer to their repeated knocking, and Morris had been reluctant to agree with Barker's view that they kick the door in and search the place.

'He'll report it as a burglary,' Morris had said.

'No chance,' snorted Barker. 'He's a crook. He's not going to want to get involved with the police. He's got our money stashed in there.'

'Why would he take a chance like that?' asked Morris. 'Anyone could break in and snaffle it. He'll have it stashed away somewhere else.'

Ernie Morris hated violence, both to himself or to other people. That's why he'd been upset when Joe Barker had belted that general bloke. Not just because it meant that the law would get involved, but because it meant that Barker was unstable, on the edge, and likely to do dangerous things. Like that business of him sticking a gun in the fence's ear and threatening to blow his brains out. He knew that had really worried Billy Dodds. If Barker could do that to the fence, he could do it to any of them. Just like what he was intending to do to Dan Reeves once he'd got the money off him. Kill Reeves, that's what Barker was intending, and Morris wanted no part of it. The only reason he'd come along with Barker in search of Reeves was because he hoped to stop him killing him. Talk him out of it. As it turned out, there hadn't been any need of it because Reeves hadn't been in. But that hadn't satisfied Barker.

'I bet he's at that bird's place,' he said grimly. 'Alice Martin's. He spends most of his time round there. It wouldn't surprise me to find that's where he's got our money stashed, hidden somewhere in her place.'

'I don't know, Joe,' said Morris doubtfully. 'We don't want to involve someone like her in our business.'

'I bet she's already involved,' said Barker grimly. 'Are you coming, or not?'

Very aware of the pistol in Joe's pocket, and also aware that he was perfectly capable of using it, Morris reluctantly nodded.

'Alright. But no trouble, Joe. We just ask her where Reeves is.'

'And if he's there?'

'We tell him we know about the six hundred and we want it.'

'Right.' Barker nodded. He patted his pocket. 'And if he don't hand it over, I'll wave this bad boy in his face.'

When they got back to their office at Scotland Yard, Coburg put a phone call through to Birmingham CID. When he was connected, he introduced himself and asked to speak to a senior officer.

'How senior?' asked the man at the other end.

'A working inspector rather than a superintendent,' said Coburg. 'And someone who might have had experience of man called Shelley Buttons.'

'That'll be me,' said the man. 'DI Bill Rodgers at your service.' He paused, then asked, 'Coburg? Are you the DCI Saxe-Coburg who married Rosa Weeks?'

'I am,' said Coburg.

'Congratulations,' said Rodgers. 'We saw it in the paper. My wife and I have always been fans of hers, that's why she spotted it. We saw her a couple of years ago when she was appearing here in Birmingham. Pass on to her how much we like her singing and playing, and ask her when she's going to be on the wireless again.'

'I will,' said Coburg. 'She'll be very pleased.'

'But you want to know about Shelley Buttons,' said Rodgers. 'What do you want to know, exactly?'

'Anything you can tell me about him,' said Coburg. 'What sort of character he is.'

Rodgers gave a harsh mirthless laugh, then said, 'He's one of the most vicious characters I ever met.'

'Did he do time?'

'Only as a juvenile. Borstal.'

'What for?'

'Violence. As a teenager he was working as an enforcer for a loan shark here in Birmingham. He was caught using a razor on a bloke, cut him about the face. That was the last time he was behind bars. He learnt that if he wanted to stay out of jail it was necessary to intimidate his victims and any witnesses into silence. And that's what he did. Once people realised that there was a chance of them or their loved ones ending up in a canal, they shut up. You know what things are like; you can't protect everyone twenty-four hours a day.

'What we started to do, though, was pick up his lieutenants. Some we managed to put away; others we . . .' He hesitated then chuckled. 'Let's just say we neutralised them. They got as good as they gave out. The warning was clear to Buttons. We may not be able to get witnesses to put him away in jail, but he was still only human with bones that break. Which is why we think he decided to leave Birmingham and move down to London with his mob. How are you getting on with him? I assume, as you're phoning, he's causing trouble.'

'Possibly,' said Coburg. 'I was curious to learn a bit about him before I start talking to him, find out what sort of person he was.'

'Like I said, vicious. And aggressive. He's got a chip on his shoulder about something.'

'What?'

'No idea. To be honest, I'm not interested in trying to get in touch with his inner self and rehabilitate

172

him, like the psychiatrists tell us. I just wanted him out of Birmingham. The other thing is that he ran drugs here, and on a big scale.'

'What sort of drugs?'

'Everything. Morphine. Heroin. Cocaine. Marijuana. Pills. Whatever people wanted, he dealt. He had a nightclub up here where he used to deal them. We raided it when we could, but we only found drugs on the premises once. I think the other times he'd been tipped off his club was about to be raided.'

Coburg replaced the receiver, looked at Lampson and asked, 'Did you hear anything of that?'

Lampson grinned. 'I think they might have heard right along the corridor. These Brummies have got loud voices.'

'Not all of them,' said Coburg. He got up and took his outdoor coat from the peg. 'I think now's a good time to bring Mr Buttons in to answer a few questions.'

Alice regarded the two men on the doorstep with wariness. 'What do you want?' she asked.

'We're friends of Dan's,' said Barker. 'He's sent us to pick something up.'

'What?' she asked.

'That's between us and Dan,' said Barker menacingly.

Alice began to shut the door on them, but Barker shoved his boot in the gap.

'We're coming in either nicely, or the hard way,' he snapped.

He pushed the door open and he and Morris entered the passageway.

'First floor, as I remember,' said Barker, and he and Morris mounted the stairs, Alice following, feeling helpless. *Dan should be here*, she thought angrily.

She'd left the door to her room unlocked while she'd gone downstairs to answer the ring at her doorbell, and Barker and Morris just walked in and stood surveying the room.

'Where's Dan?' asked Barker.

'He's at work,' replied Alice.

'When will he be back?' asked Barker. 'I don't know,' said Alice.

Barker spotted the decorated jewellery box on the table. 'I recognise this!' he said, and he strode to the table and picked the box up.

'You can't touch that!' said Alice, alarmed. 'That's Dan's.'

'No it isn't, it's ours,' said Barker. 'I was there when we took it.' He tested the weight of it. 'Loads in here,' he said to Morris. 'It looks like Dan's been holding out on us.'

'That's ours!' exclaimed Alice. 'Mine and Dan's. It's our perks.'

'Shut up!' snarled Barker. 'Where's the key?'

'I haven't got it,' said Alice quickly.

'Lying bitch,' snorted Barker derisively. 'No problem. I've got a hammer that'll open it.'

He tucked the box under his arm and headed for the door. Morris, uncomfortable, moved to follow him.

'You can't take that!' shouted Alice desperately. 'I'll tell Dan!'

'You do that, and tell him that if he wants this back he'd better give us the cash he stole from us. Tell him Joe Barker said he'd spoken to Dan's fence, so I know how much he got for the last lot. He owes us six hundred quid and counting.'

With that, he left the room, Morris following him.

Alice stared after them for a moment, then slammed the door shut and fell on the bed, sobbing with tears of rage and loss, and panic about what Dan would do to her when he arrived.

Coburg and Lampson made their way down the wide staircase and were walking across the reception area when a call of 'Mr Coburg, sir!' from the reception desk stopped them. They walked to where the desk sergeant, Derek Whitten, was waiting for them, a concerned expression on his face.

'Sorry to call you, sir,' said Whitten, 'but you know those two blokes you gave the pictures out of. The drawings.'

'Yes, sergeant. And now we know who they are: Henry Punt and Wally Maples.'

'They're also dead, sir.'

Coburg looked at the sergeant in surprise. 'How?' he asked.

'Shot,' said Whitten. 'Their bodies were pulled out of the canal at King's Cross. They were only found because they got caught up in a barge going upriver.'

'When did this happen?'

'I got the report about fifteen minutes ago. I tried phoning you in your office, but your phone was engaged. I was just about to send a message up to you.'

'Thanks, Derek. Where are the bodies?'

'They were taken to UCH.'

'Can I use your phone?' asked Coburg.

Whitten nodded and handed it to Coburg, who asked to be put through to University College Hospital. Once through, Coburg left a message asking for photographs of the two men whose bodies had recently been brought in, found shot dead in the canal at King's Cross. 'Just the faces,' he said. 'When they're ready, can they be sent to Scotland Yard, marked for the attention of DCI Coburg. And I'd appreciate it if this can be treated as urgent.'

He hung up the phone, then turned to Lampson. 'I'm re-thinking pulling in Shelley Buttons. From what Riley told us, he gave the impression that

Buttons was behind Rosa being abducted by Punt and Maples. Now he may be lying, or there may be truth in it. Whichever way, I suggest we leave confronting Buttons until we've got the photos of Punt and Maples. I want to see his face when I show him the pictures.'

'Makes sense,' said Lampson. 'One thing's for sure, it can't have been Riley who shot them. He hasn't left his club except to go home. And we had him in for questioning yesterday after Rosa was freed.'

'Not straight away,' pointed out Coburg.

'You still like Riley for the shooting and having Rosa lifted?'

'He's certainly in the frame as far as I'm concerned,' said Coburg. 'But so's this Buttons character, *if* he was working with Punt and Maples, as Riley claims.'

One glance at the look of abject misery on Alice Martin's face when he walked into her room told Dan Reeves that something was seriously wrong.

'What's happened?' he asked.

'Two of the blokes you're on the fire crew with came here, looking for you.' And the thought of it brought tears to her eyes once more. 'They took the box with the jewels in.'

He stared at her, shocked. 'You left it out!' he raged.

'No,' she defended herself. 'They went through

the cupboards and things and found it.'

He stepped towards her, and she flinched and backed away from him.

'You stupid cow!' he snarled. 'I told you to keep it out of sight.'

'I did!' she protested.

He grabbed her roughly by the arm. 'Who were they?' he demanded.

'You're hurting me!' she said, trying to twist out of his grip, but he was too strong for her.

'I'll hurt you properly if you don't tell me who they were,' he snapped.

'The one who took the box said to tell you Joe Barker wanted the money you stole from them.'

'What money?'

'He said it was six hundred quid. He said he'd been to see your fence to find out how much he'd given you for the last lot.'

Reeves released Alice's arm. 'The bastard!' he muttered.

'What are we gonna do, Dan?' asked Alice. 'That box was our way out of this hole. You should have sold it and turned it into money before.'

'No,' said Reeves fiercely. 'Jewels go up in price. The longer we could hang on to them the better.' He paced the room, deep in thought. 'I'm gonna get them back. It was me and my hammer that opened those safes. I shared any cash with them,

178

but by rights those jewels are mine.'

'*Ours*, Dan,' Alice corrected him. 'You said they were for us.'

'And they are,' said Reeves. 'If Joe Barker took them, it means finding out where he's stashed them. He's cunning, is Joe. And dangerous. He carries a gun.' He looked thoughtful. 'I might have to lean on the other two, Ernie and Billy, to find out what Joe's done with the box. They ain't so dangerous as Joe.' He looked grimly at Alice. 'And when I find them, I'm gonna have to finish Joe off, otherwise he'll come after us.'

'How will you do that?'

'I'm gonna have to get me a gun. It's the only thing that will stop Joe.'

Coburg had the two musicians, Johnny Kepple and Sam Watson, who'd played with Benny Martin at the Riff Club on his last night alive, brought in to Scotland Yard. He knew that the Riff's regular employees, barmen, doormen and such, could be found at the club, but musicians were notoriously itinerant. Kepple and Watson lived in Notting Hill, each in a bedsitting room in two of the large and crumbling houses that proliferated in the area.

'We'll take them one at a time,' Coburg told Lampson. 'Then compare notes to see how their statements match up.' The first one brought into the interview room was the saxophone player, Johnny Kepple, a man in his late forties. 'How come you and Sam Watson and Benny Martin were playing together that night at the Riff Club?' asked Coburg.

'Actually, at first it was just going to be me and Sam,' said Kepple. 'Johnny and Sam, sax and drums. But around lunchtime, me and Sam were taking some refreshment in Archer Street. It's where all the guys tend to gather looking to pick up gigs. We bumped into Benny, who was there just hanging out. We know Benny from jamming with him. Benny asked if there was anything we knew happening, and Sam suggested he join us for the gig at the Riff Club that night. He's good on that guitar of his, doesn't try to take over like some of these kids, show off and that.'

'How did he seem to you?'

'What d'you mean?'

'Did he seem worried? About money?'

Kepple laughed. 'Man, we're all worried about money. But it don't do to dwell about it, just get out there and try and earn some.'

'Did he tell you he was worried because he was in debt to some heavy people? We heard he was looking to borrow some money to deal with it.'

Kepple shook his head. 'No, but then he wouldn't, not with me and Sam. He knows we're both broke. You talk to your boys who came to pick us up, ask us about the shitholes we're both living in. We wouldn't be living there if we had money.'

'How much did you get for the gig?'

'A tenner each for me and Sam, a fiver for Benny.'

'Did you see if Benny was with anyone? Did he go off with anyone after the gig ended?'

'I can't help you there,' said Kepple, and he grinned. 'There was this woman there in the audience who liked what I did and she invited me for a private performance at her place. I picked up our money from Pat Riley, gave Sam and Benny theirs, then me and this chick made for the outdoors.' He chuckled. 'It's one of the perks of being a featured player.'

After Kepple, Sam Watson was brought in. Watson was a pasty-faced, thin young man in his twenties, who chain-smoked throughout the interview. Coburg suspected from his nervous, edgy demeanour that the young man used drugs and it had been some time since his last fix.

'Would you roll up your sleeves?' Coburg asked.

'Why?' demanded Watson warily, but Coburg could tell he already knew the reason.

'Because I'm a police officer and I'm empowered to ask you to,' said Coburg calmly.

Watson hesitated, then unbuttoned the cuffs of his rumpled shirt and rolled his sleeves up, exposing the needle marks on his forearms.

'I'm a diabetic,' he said defensively.

'Of course you are,' said Coburg blandly.

'Can I roll my sleeves down now?' asked Watson. He shivered. 'This place is cold. I get sick easily.'

Coburg nodded, and Watson rolled his sleeves down. Coburg asked Watson the same questions he'd asked Kepple, and got the same answers: Watson and Kepple meeting Benny in Archer Street and agreeing he'd join them for that night's gig at the Riff Club. When Coburg asked Watson if Benny had mentioned owing some heavy characters money, Watson shook his head and gave the same response that Kepple had given: 'He wouldn't bother asking us if he was in money trouble; he knows we're both flat broke.'

'When did you see him last that night?'

'We'd finished and packed up, and then Benny said in surprise: "What's she doing here?" It turned out he was talking about his sister. He couldn't understand it. She hates jazz,' he said.

'His sister, Alice?'

'Yeah, that's the name he said.' Watson nodded.

'What happened then?'

'I think he went looking for her. I didn't see him again that night; I had to go and see someone.'

Yes, a dealer, thought Coburg. Aloud, he said, 'What time was it when you last saw Benny?'

Watson shrugged. 'I've no idea. I don't have a watch. Time is meaningless.'

Coburg released Kepple and Watson with the

standard warning to keep themselves available in case they were needed later.

'Stay in London,' Coburg told them as they stood in Scotland Yard reception.

'You can count on that,' said Kepple. 'We can't afford to go anywhere, and all the best gigs for jazz are here in London.' He looked enquiringly at Coburg and asked, 'Are you the same Coburg that Rosa Weeks married a couple of months back? I remember the name because someone said she'd married a guy called Saxe-Coburg, and I thought, "Hey, a guy called Sax – very appropriate for a jazz musician."'

'Yes,' said Coburg. 'That was me.'

'How is she?' asked Kepple. 'I heard she got shot in the arm, which really put her out of the piano-playing business for a while.'

'She was shot, but she's recovered and doing well,' said Coburg. 'I'll tell her you asked after her.'

'Tell her if she ever wants a sax and drums duo to back her, we're available,' said Kepple.

'I'll do that,' said Coburg. He shook hands with both men, then they – in turn – shook hands with Lampson and left.

'Urgh.' Lampson grimaced in distaste, looking at his right hand. 'I'm going to have to wash this now. I hate junkies. They carry all sorts of diseases.'

'But I believe he's a good drummer,' said Coburg. He looked thoughtful as he added, 'So Alice Martin was there that night, despite telling us she hated jazz. And not just us – Benny said the same about her to Watson. What was she doing there?'

'There's only one way to find out,' said Lampson.

Alice Martin was still in her dressing gown when they called on her in her room. Coburg thought she looked like she'd been crying; her eyes were red-rimmed and the skin on her face was pale and blotchy.

'What do you want?' she demanded.

'We've been talking to some people about the last gig Benny did,' said Coburg. 'It was at the Riff Club in Soho.'

'So?' she said sullenly.

'They told us you were there that night.'

'So?' she repeated, even more sullenly.

'I thought you said you didn't like jazz,' said Coburg.

'I can take it or leave it.' She shrugged.

'Benny told his fellow musicians you hated it.'

'Yeah, well, what does he know.'

'So what made you go to the Riff Club?'

She hesitated, then said, 'I went there with a friend.'

'Who was the friend?'

Again, she hesitated, before saying, 'A man.'

'What's his name?'

'He said his name was Alan.'

'Second name?'

'I don't know.'

'Where did you meet him?'

'In a café. He came and sat down at my table and we got talking. He asked me if I'd like to go to this club with him.'

'Did you see Benny there? He went looking for you.'

'No,' she said. 'After the band finished, me and Alan left.'

'Where did you go?'

'To my room.'

'Did he stay?'

She nodded. 'Yes.' Then she looked at them defiantly. 'It's not illegal. There's a war on. It's what people do.'

Dan Reeves sat in the pub with a glass of beer and thought vengeful thoughts about Joe Barker, Ernie Morris, Billy Dodds and Alice Martin. Especially Joe Barker. To have gone into Alice's room and snatched the box of jewellery like that, it was . . . it was . . . words failed him. It was bare-faced theft. Joe knew that box was Dan's perks. Alright, Dan hadn't said as much to the others, but he was the one who did the hard work of breaking open the safes, and the one who sold the jewellery on to a fence; it was only right he kept a certain amount back. The cash they took was shared equally. And none of the others would know where to offload the jewels, not without getting almost nothing for it. It was only right that Dan got his proper share. And now that bastard Joe Barker had taken it.

How to get it back, that was the problem. Originally, as he'd told Alice, he'd thought of getting hold of a gun and forcing Joe to hand the box back. Dan would need a gun to make him do that, because Joe was armed. The trouble was, guns cost money, especially on the black market, and Dan was hard up for cash. The money they'd taken from the fire calls seemed to vanish like so much water, which was why the jewels had been important. It was like money in the bank.

Then a thought struck him. He knew a man with a gun, and this man owed Dan. Even better, Dan knew something about him that was worth money. Big money.

Yes, he thought, *the answer's been staring me in the face.* He finished his beer and made for the door.

Time to make the call and then he'd face Joe Barker down and get what was his back. And he'd finish Joe off for good measure, just to let Ernie and Billy know what would happen to them if they tried the same thing on him.

CHAPTER TWENTY-TWO

Friday 6th December 1940

Dr Welbourne, or one of his assistants, had acted with great efficiency, and Coburg looked at the photographs of the two dead men that had arrived from UCH.

'Right, Sergeant,' he said to Lampson, 'get a warrant for Shelley Buttons and bring him in. Better take a couple of uniforms with you in case he starts playing rough.' He passed a sheet of paper across to Lampson. 'There's the address of his Red Feather club, and also his home address if he's not at the club. Take him to the interview rooms and get the desk to let me know when he's arrived.'

'Right, guv,' said Lampson. 'Handcuffs?'

'Only if he plays up,' said Coburg.

An hour later, Coburg's phone rang.

'Desk sergeant here, sir,' said the voice. 'DS Lampson says to tell you he's got your Mr Buttons in Interview Room Two.'

'Thank you, Sergeant. I'll be right down.'

* * *

The man sitting at the bare wooden table in Interview Room Two opposite Sergeant Lampson was a large man, his bulk a combination of muscle and fat. He wore a white shirt, open at the collar, under a dark jacket. There was a flower in the buttonhole of the jacket, a pink rosebud. His fair hair was so thin and scraped back that at first sight he gave the impression of being bald. His chin and cheeks were stubbled, suggesting he hadn't shaved for at least a day. He gave a scowl as Coburg entered the interview room. He wasn't handcuffed, Coburg noticed, so he'd come in apparently willingly.

'Good afternoon, Mr Buttons,' said Coburg. 'I'm Detective Chief Inspector Coburg and I shall be interviewing you.'

Coburg took his place on the empty seat next to Lampson.

'What's all this about?' demanded Buttons. 'Barging into my place and dragging me in like I was some sort of lowlife.' Coburg pushed the photographs of the two dead men, Wally Maples and Henry Punt, across the table to Buttons.

'Do you know these men?'

Buttons shook his head. 'No,' he said, pushing the photos back. 'And I'm not likely to, either, going by those photos. They're dead, ain't they.'

'They are. Someone shot them.'

'What's it got to do with me?'

'They worked for Pat Riley at the Riff Club. He told me you've been leaning on him lately, trying to get him to sell his club to you at a knock-down price. Riley says he sent these two men to have a word with you. Warn you off. And lo and behold, they disappear and we fish them out of the canal, both shot dead.'

'That's complete cobblers,' said Buttons calmly.

'Which part? The accusation that they were shot after coming to warn you off?'

'All of it. They never came to have a word with me, friendly or otherwise. As for me wanting to buy Riley's club, yes, I made him an offer, but he turned me down. End of story.'

'What about Jake Pond?'

'Who?'

'He owned a club you had your eye on but he didn't want to sell. Next thing, he ends up dead. Run over, I'm told. And not just once but three times.'

Buttons grinned. 'I hope he was insured. That'd count as three lots of payouts.'

'You find it funny, a man being killed like that?'

'At this time with thousands being killed by bombing, you got to admit it makes you laugh a bit.'

'It didn't make me laugh,' said Coburg.

'Different people laugh at different things,' said Buttons. 'So, is that it? Can I go now?'

'No,' said Coburg. 'There are a few more questions we need to ask.'

'What about?'

'You'll see as we go along,' said Coburg.

Buttons scowled. 'In that case I want my solicitor with me.'

'Certainly,' said Coburg. 'If you write down his contact details, we'll get in touch with him. And while we wait for him to arrive, we'll take you to one of the remand cells.'

'You're locking me up?!' said Buttons, outraged. 'You can't do that!'

'I can,' said Coburg. 'How long for depends on your solicitor. If he's here within the hour, it'll just be for that long. But if he's not available and can't be here for a day or two . . .'

Buttons leapt to his feet, anger suffusing his face.

'You can't lock me up!' he snarled.

'Actually, I can, and I will. I'm sure your solicitor will explain why when he arrives.' He looked at Lampson. 'Sergeant, would you assist Mr Buttons in resuming his seat.'

Buttons turned and saw Lampson approaching, a look of grim delight on his face, and immediately sat down.

'You're gonna pay for this!' he growled.

'Is that a threat?' asked Coburg calmly. 'It certainly sounded like one to me. Did it to you, Sergeant?'

'It did, sir,' said Lampson.

'Threatening behaviour towards a police officer,' said Coburg. 'That's a charge that carries a conviction.'

'I demand my phone call,' grated Buttons. 'I'm allowed to make one.'

'Actually, you're allowed to request the police to make a phone call to a person you designate, and for the police to tell them whatever it is you wish to say to them.'

'I'm allowed to make the phone call, *personally*!' bellowed Buttons. 'That's the law.'

'That may have been the way it was done in Birmingham, but here in London we stick to the strict letter of the law, which I've just outlined to you. Again, your solicitor will clarify that for you when he arrives.' He paused, then added, '*If he arrives.*' He slid a piece of paper and a pencil across the desk to Buttons. 'If you'll write down his contact details, I'll get on to him. In the meantime' – and he looked at Lampson – 'would you take Mr Buttons to the remand suite, Sergeant.'

'He's a nasty piece of work,' said Lampson when he and Coburg were back in the office.

'I agree, but did he kill Punt and Maples, or have them killed, and was he behind Rosa being abducted?'

'No idea, guv,' said Lampson. 'One thing's for sure, he's going to be a hard nut to crack if he did do it. He's not going to give anything up, and it'll be even harder when his brief arrives.'

'Yes,' agreed Coburg. 'He's an old hand at this. If he was able to avoid being jailed in Birmingham, he'll know which strings to pull here. This isn't going to be a quick case unless we can find some strong evidence against him.' He held out the photographs of Maples and Punt to Lampson. 'In the meantime, can you get these copied. I want to send one of each to Rosa to make sure these are the two men who held her.'

'Right, guv,' said Lampson.

As the sergeant left, Coburg's phone rang.

'Sorry to trouble, you, sir,' said the desk sergeant, 'but we've just had a report of another dead body. A male. This one's been shot as well.'

'Where is it?'

'The same place that young man was found, sir. In the tunnel at Aldwych station.'

'Do they know who he is?'

'Not as far as I know, sir. All I've had from the constable is a man's been found shot dead there.'

'Right, Sergeant. I'll take this one.'

Coburg wrote Magnus's address on an envelope, adding a brief note, then took it along to the copy room where Sergeant Lampson was handing over the two photographs to a technician in a white coat.

'We've got to go, Sergeant,' he said. 'Another dead body at Aldwych. Shot.'

'Another?' said Lampson. 'Bloody hell, this is getting out of hand.'

Coburg handed the envelope to the technician.

'When you've made the copies, can you put one of each in this envelope and get it sent off,' he said. He wrote 'URGENT' on the envelope to hopefully ensure it wasn't delayed.

'What do we do if Buttons's brief arrives while we're out?' asked Lampson.

'I'll leave a message at the desk telling him to wait until we come back,' said Coburg.

'Buttons won't like that,' said Lampson.

'Good,' said Coburg. 'The edgier he gets, the more chance there is of him saying something that incriminates him.' He looked thoughtful. 'In fact, while Buttons is in custody, I think it might be a good idea to raid his clubs.'

'You're thinking about the drugs business in Birmingham.'

'I am, and if he's using his clubs in London to do the same, we can hang on to him over that while we investigate him in relation to the murders. Can I leave you to organise the raids while I go to Aldwych and look at this dead body? There are three clubs. Take one yourself and get some intelligent detective constables and some uniforms to do the other two.

The usual form: impound any drugs found and bring 'em back. Arrest anyone who tries to obstruct the raids, or seems suspicious.'

'Bring them back here?'

'The drugs, yes. The people arrested, no. There are four nicks in and around Soho; put them there under lock and key until we're ready to talk to them.'

'Right, guv. Leave it to me. I'll see you back here.'

CHAPTER TWENTY-THREE

Friday 6th December 1940

There was only a smattering of people on the platform at Aldwych when Coburg arrived, people who had decided that they didn't want to risk losing their place of safety to others who came later. A whole new species of humans was evolving, he thought as he walked past them. People who would spend most of their lives below ground, never seeing the light of day. At least miners who worked deep below the surface came up now and then for days off and saw the sunlight. Some of the people seeking refuge in the Tube stations never even ventured out to get food; they sent others to do their shopping. The majority of the people sitting in chairs or lying on mattresses on the platforms were old or infirm and were either unable to constantly go up the stairs to the outside world and then back down again, or didn't want to.

He dropped down to the railway track from the platform and began to walk towards where the Elgin Marbles and the other British Museum treasures were stored. He saw a young, uniformed constable was waiting for him at the barrier at the station end of the flatbed railway wagons bearing the enormous marble carvings. The constable was talking to the two guards from the British Museum keeping careful watch over their precious treasures and he left them as he saw Coburg approaching.

'The body's at the far end, sir, by the barrier at the other end,' said the constable. 'Shot, by the look of it.'

Coburg passed through the barrier, then he and the constable began the long walk past the wagons to the far end. In the same place where Benny Martin had been found, another man lay spreadeagled across the tracks.

'This is exactly how he was found, sir,' said the constable. He looked along the line and added, 'And here's the man who found him.'

Coburg looked up as Percy Wenlock, the maintenance man, came towards them from his little room.

'I was watching out in case it was you, Chief Inspector,' said Wenlock. 'Two of 'em, in the same place. That's weird, that is.'

'It certainly is,' agreed Coburg, looking down at the dead man. 'Now we've got to find out who he is.'

'Oh, I know who he is,' said Wenlock. 'I told the constable. Didn't he tell you?'

Coburg looked at the young constable, who looked

flustered. 'He . . . er . . . he did mention it, sir, but I thought it best to wait until you arrived,' he said awkwardly.

'Who is he?' Coburg asked.

'His name's Dan Reeves,' said Wenlock.

'And you knew him?'

Wenlock nodded. 'I did. He worked for the underground. He was a rail tapper.'

'What's a rail tapper?' asked Coburg.

'They walk along checking the rails, make sure there aren't any cracks in them. Even though this line's been turned off, it still needs to be checked.'

'So Reeves would have walked along the line tapping the rails.'

'That's right. And listening to them.' He pointed to a long metal tube lying between the tracks. 'That's his listening tube. He puts one end to his ear and the other to the rail. If there's anything not right in the metal, he'll hear it. The note is different if there's a flaw or a crack in it.' He frowned, puzzled. 'His listening tube's here, but not his hammer.'

'His hammer?'

'What he taps the rails with. But he had it with him when I saw him.'

'When was that?'

'When he turned up. I offered him a cup of tea and a biscuit, like I always do, so we sat in my hut and chatted a bit, then he went off to check the rails. He had his listening tube and his long-handled hammer with him, but the hammer's gone.'

'How often did Reeves do this?'

'This section, usually once a fortnight. There's a lot of track to check.'

'So he'd be familiar with this line and the tunnels.'

'Oh yes. The best way to learn about a place is to walk it.'

'Did he always come on the same day every time?'

'No, it depended on what had gone on the night before. He was a volunteer with the AFS, see, and often he'd be called out on a big fire.'

'Do you know which fire crew he was with?' asked Coburg.

Wenlock shook his head. 'Sorry. No idea.'

'Do you know who'd have an address for him? I assume that'd be the London Underground railway authority.'

'Actually, I've got his address in my hut,' said Wenlock. 'He gave it to me because he said if I found anything that I wasn't happy with about the tracks, it was quicker to drop him a note than go through all the bureaucracy, which could take forever. I'll go and get it for you.'

As Wenlock hurried towards his hut, a shout behind them caused them to turn. A man carrying a medical case had arrived.

'Scotland Yard?' he asked.

'Indeed, sir. DCI Coburg. I assume you are the medical man.'

'Guilty as charged,' said the man. 'Dr Ian Purkiss.'

He was in his early thirties, and seemed very much a man in a hurry, very different from Dr Welbourne. He bent down beside the body and began to examine it, checking the wound in the man's chest, the flexibility of his arms and legs and neck, muttering to himself as he did so. Finally, he got to his feet.

'Cause of death is pretty obvious,' he said. 'Shot at close range. Whoever did it didn't want to miss. I assume the bullet's in the heart because there's no sign of an exit wound, but I'll know more when I open him up.'

'Time of death?' asked Coburg.

'I'm guessing about two hours or so ago. Again, I'll know more when I open him up.' He gave a call, and two men carrying a stretcher appeared from the direction of Aldwych station.

'I'm taking him to the Middlesex,' said Purkiss. 'I'll send my report to you at Scotland Yard. If there's anything you're unsure of, just give me a ring at the hospital.'

With that, Dr Purkiss supervised the loading of Dan Reeves's body onto the stretcher, and then led the way towards Aldwych station.

Coburg turned to Percy Wenlock, who'd just returned with a piece of paper with Dan Reeves's address on, which he handed to Coburg.

'Thank you,' said Coburg, putting the paper in his pocket. 'I'll be back later to have a proper look at the scene of the crime.' He then turned to the constable. 'In the meantime, I look to you to secure the scene. Someone will be back as soon as we've got some urgent business back at the Yard wrapped up.' When he saw the unhappy look on the constable's face, he added, 'I'll arrange for someone to come and take over from you as soon as I get back to the Yard.'

'Thank you, sir,' said the constable. 'It's my daughter's birthday and I was keen to get home to see her.'

Coburg left Wenlock and the constable talking and made his way back to the station. It was time to talk to Shelley Buttons.

Lampson had ordered the driver of the police van to park around the corner from the Red Feather club in the heart of Soho. Here in this maze of narrow streets, the presence of a police van wasn't unusual. Every now and then there was a raid on a suspected brothel, or one of the many strip clubs in case any laws were being contravened. Usually the suspicion was prostitution, but there were also checks to make sure that if any of the clubs were presenting tableaux of nudes, that the nudes did not move. A moving nude was illegal; a static one was considered legitimate, artistic.

That had been the argument presented to the Lord Chamberlain by the Windmill Theatre in the 1930s when the theatre was being prosecuted for putting on obscene displays, namely tableaux of women in the nude in some alleged artistic setting – usually a Roman scene or some other historical period. The Windmill's defence had been that statues of nude women were on display in art galleries and other public places, and that if the nude woman was perfectly still there was no difference between her and a statue. Surprisingly, the Lord Chamberlain had agreed, and since that ruling not just the Windmill but other establishments, such as the clubs like the Red Feather in Soho, had done good business with their nude displays.

Lampson had little affection for Soho. To him it was a blot on the city: a seething den of vice, drugs and corruption, in many cases protected by corrupt police officers on the payroll of brothel-owners and drug-dealers like Shelley Buttons, not even pretending that their clubs were respectable places of entertainment. If Lampson had his way, he'd have the whole area closed down. The only upside to Soho was that it was where most of the real villains gathered, so if something happened a good policeman could usually find out who was behind it, and where they were.

Lampson led his raiding party of six uniformed officers and a detective constable along the short street to the entrance of the Red Feather. The large photographs of nude women on the wall outside the club, along with the sign that boasted 'The Fleshpots of Soho', told Lampson the place was brazenly promoting itself as a strip joint, with possibly an unofficial brothel in the background. The group stopped outside the entrance to the club.

'Right, lads,' Lampson said. He brandished the search warrant. 'We go in and go right through them. Start with the toilets and work backwards. Search everyone, staff and customers. Anything suspected of being drugs or drug-related, confiscate it.' He turned to two of the uniformed officers and said, 'You two stay by the door. Anyone tries to leave, turn 'em back inside. If they get difficult, arrest 'em and chuck 'em in the van.' He indicated the large black police van parked just along the road, then produced his police whistle and put it to his lips. 'Always start with something that upsets 'em,' he said with a wink, and he blew.

There was one elderly man on duty at the ticket office and he stared in bewilderment as the police burst in and past him, Lampson waving the warrant at him.

'Where's the manager?' demanded Lampson.

'He's not here,' said the doorman.

'Is there a performance going on?' demanded Lampson.

'Yeah, and it's all legal. The girls don't move.'

'They'll move now,' said Lampson. 'Go in and tell

everyone the show's over. Everyone's to stay right where they are.'

'What about the girls?' bleated the man. 'They've got nothing on. They'll catch cold.'

'You go and get their coats for them and they can put those on. But no one leaves the stage.'

As the doorman moved off, Lampson turned to the young detective constable. 'You start with the dressing rooms, and then do the offices. Check every drawer, filing cabinet, cupboard, everywhere.'

'Right, sir.' The constable nodded.

Lampson walked into the performance area. It was tiny, just a space with a slightly raised platform at one end, draped with red curtains, which at this moment were open. There were four rows of cinema seats, with just six men separate from one another in them.

A naked, middle-aged, blonde-haired woman was standing on the stage, looking in astonishment at the interruption. Another woman was peering round the curtain to see what was happening. At the sight of uniformed police officers spilling into the performance space, the men in the audience got to their feet and attempted to make a run for the entrance, but they were stopped by another blast on Lampson's whistle.

'Stay where you are!' ordered Lampson. 'This is an official raid on these premises being carried out by Scotland Yard. Anyone attempting to leave, or refusing to co-operate, will be arrested.'

Reluctantly, the six men sat down again. The doorman returned with four coats, which he began to pass to the naked woman onstage, her equally naked friend who had been peering round the curtain, and two other naked women who appeared from the back of the stage.

Lampson left the uniformed officers to search the men in the audience while he joined the detective constable in the office.

'I think we've got the goods, sarge,' said the constable, pointing to bags of white powder that he'd taken from the filing cabinet and put on the desk.

'Excellent,' said Lampson. 'Keep looking.'

He then joined the other officers in the toilets, the dressing rooms and the storeroom where the drinks were kept, all in bottles, along with some snacks. It was in the boxes of snacks they discovered more bags of white powder. There were also traces of drugs in the dressing rooms.

Only one of the men in the audience was found to have drugs on him, in his case a chunk of marijuana, but he also had a dangerous-looking knife in his pocket, so he was taken to the waiting police van.

Lampson decided to let the girls onstage go, after first taking their names and addresses. The employees of the club – doorman, barman, a bookkeeper, a cleaner – were arrested and also taken to the van, where they were put into the van's small cells.

CHAPTER TWENTY-FOUR

Friday 6th December 1940

Coburg found a very annoyed and impatient solicitor, Edwin Vickers, waiting for him when he got back to Scotland Yard.

'This is outrageous, Chief Inspector,' barked Vickers. 'My client has been waiting, as I have, for you to arrive in order for this ridiculous farrago to be over.'

'You should both be grateful for the delay. I have actually been out investigating another aspect of the case, which might have led to your client being exonerated.'

'And has it?'

'No,' said Coburg. 'But it could have, showing that we have made no prejudicial judgement against your client.'

Coburg and Vickers made their way down to one of the interview rooms in the basement, where a uniformed sergeant was already in place, standing against one wall and watching over the contents of the room, the bare wooden table and four chairs, with an eagle and protective eye.

'I've sent for the prisoner, sir,' the sergeant informed them.

'He's not a prisoner!' snapped Vickers. 'He's here for interview.'

'Technically, as he's been remanded in custody, he is a prisoner,' said Coburg. 'For the moment.'

The door opened and Shelley Buttons was escorted in by two constables. Buttons wore handcuffs. The constables escorted Buttons to the waiting chair, and he sat down.

'Why has my client been shackled in this way?' demanded Vickers.

'A precautionary procedure,' said Coburg. He looked at the constables. 'You may remove the handcuffs, Constable.'

The constable unlocked the handcuffs and clipped them to his belt. Buttons glared with barely suppressed anger at Coburg.

'To begin, Chief Inspector, what is my client charged with?'

'Your client has not been charged. He is here helping us with our enquiries into the murder of one Benjamin Martin, and the kidnap and attempted murder of one Rosa Coburg.'

'Your wife?' asked Vickers, surprised.

'The same,' said Coburg.

'In that case, Chief Inspector, I insist that you excuse yourself from this case. There is a conflict of interest here that precludes impartiality of an investigation.'

'Very well,' said Coburg calmly. 'Then, for the purposes of this interview, we shall limit ourselves to the murder of Benjamin Martin – although, as you will see, both cases are interconnected.'

'I've never heard of this Benjamin Martin,' grunted Buttons.

'What about Henry Punt and Wally Maples?' asked Coburg.

Vickers held up his hand. 'One moment, Chief Inspector, before my client answers that question, I demand to know who these people are and why you believe they have any connection with my client.'

'We have a statement from another party that he sent Mr Punt and Mr Maples to see Mr Buttons, and that Mr Buttons allegedly persuaded Mr Punt and Mr Maples to carry out some illegal acts for him. We believe these acts included kidnap, and also murder.'

'Who is this other party?' demanded Vickers.

'Pat Riley,' grunted Buttons. 'It's all crap, of course. He's just disgruntled because I tried to buy his club from him and he didn't like it.'

'Do you have any proof of the allegation made by this Pat Riley?' demanded Vickers.

'That is the purpose of this interview, along with other interviews we are conducting with other parties,' said Coburg.

'Are these other parties also being kept in custody?' demanded Vickers.

'That is information purely for members of the police investigation,' said Coburg.

'In other words, no,' snapped Vickers. 'Therefore I insist my client is released immediately.'

'At this moment—' began Coburg.

'At this moment you have no evidence, no proof, merely slanderous gossip by a disaffected business rival of Mr Buttons. Therefore I demand: on what possible grounds can you have for keeping my client in custody any longer?' He was interrupted by the door opening and Sergeant Lampson looking in.

'Sorry to disturb you, sir,' he said to Coburg, 'but I've got some important information for you.'

Vickers looked at Coburg and said curtly, 'If this information concerns my client, I insist we all hear it.'

'If it does, you will,' said Coburg, getting to his feet. 'Please excuse me for one moment.'

He left the room and joined Lampson outside in the corridor.

'We've got him, guv.' Lampson grinned triumphantly. 'Drugs at each of the clubs he owns. They're now under lock and key here at the Yard. We've taken his staff at the clubs into custody.'

'Well done,' said Coburg. 'You'd better join me in case Buttons's brief has any questions for you. We can't be seen as not being transparent.'

Coburg and Lampson went back into the interview room, Coburg resuming his seat and Lampson joining him at the table.

'You were asking on what grounds we could keep Mr Buttons in custody, Mr Vickers,' said Coburg. 'Well, the reason is supplying illicit drugs. We've just mounted a series of raids on the three clubs that Mr Buttons owns and manages. Large quantities of illegal drugs were found at each premises. We have taken the staff at each club into custody and they are currently being questioned.' He looked at Buttons, who sat staring at him in stunned incomprehension. 'Shelley Buttons, I am charging you with conspiracy to sell drugs. There may be further charges to be made, but for the moment this is enough for you to be remanded in custody.'

'You can't do this!' said Buttons hoarsely.

'I can,' said Coburg. 'Your solicitor will confirm that I can.' He looked at the uniformed sergeant. 'Sergeant, take Mr Buttons to the custody suite and arrange for him to be put in a cell until a place can be arranged for him to be held on remand at a prison.'

'No!' burst out Buttons, and he leapt to his feet.

'Sergeant,' said Coburg calmly, and the sergeant pushed Buttons back down on his chair.

'Mr Vickers, I would suggest you advise your client to curb his behaviour otherwise other charges will be forthcoming, namely resisting arrest.'

Buttons looked around at the other people in the

room, his eyes scanning the room itself, then he said urgently, 'I want to talk to my solicitor in private.'

Coburg studied him quietly, then said to Vickers, 'If I agree, your client's behaviour will be your responsibility. If he attempts any destruction of the furniture, or anything else, that will lead to further charges.'

'I ain't gonna smash the place up,' grated Buttons. 'I just need to talk to him in private.'

'That is a perfectly reasonable request, Chief Inspector,' said Vickers. 'And one that is allowable under the law.'

Coburg nodded, then got to his feet. 'I'll give you ten minutes,' he said.

'That may not be long enough,' objected Vickers.

'It will be,' said Buttons grimly. 'More than enough.'

Coburg ordered the other officers to leave the room. 'We shall be right outside,' he said. With that, he walked out of the room.

Buttons and Vickers heard the key turn in the lock.

Vickers turned to his client, concern on his face.

'This business of the drugs . . .' he began.

'Go to see a bloke called Gerald Atkinson at MI6. Tell him what's happened.'

Vickers looked at him, puzzled. 'Why MI6?' he asked.

'I'm not allowed to tell you,' said Buttons. 'Just get hold of Atkinson and tell him what's happened.'

CHAPTER TWENTY-FIVE

Saturday 7th December 1940

Rosa and Magnus sat at the long, cloth-covered table in the dining room at Dawlish Hall, tucking into the fried breakfast Mrs Hilton had provided.

'This is delicious,' she said. 'This is such a rarity. Real eggs, real bacon. In London it's powdered egg, which could be sawdust for all the taste it's got, and Spam, which is like some reconstituted odd bits of pig minced up and pressed.'

'Yes, I've had Spam and powdered egg,' said Magnus. 'Not the greatest of delicacies.' He pointed with his knife at the food on their plates. 'This is one of the advantages of living in the country. Most people have a few hens for the eggs, and there's always someone who's got a pig being fattened. Then there are cows for milk and butter and cheese, all locally produced. I had some of that margarine while I was in London. Ghastly stuff. They say it's made from whale blubber, and I could well believe it.

'There's also the positive side that we don't get subject to the same intensity of air raids you do in

London. Occasionally, a bomb drops, but usually it's the Germans jettisoning their load before heading home. There are no airfields near here. No major armaments depots.'

'But you still think if the Germans land it will be at a place like this?'

'It makes sense,' said Magnus. 'There's no major defensive force here, except the local Home Guard. The Germans could arrive here by parachute, take vehicles, and then drive into the nearest big town and take it over. Professional soldiers against a bunch of elderly reservists. They'd take what heavy armoured vehicles they could and make for London. Most of the defences are on the south coast, Kent and Sussex. The north of London is like an open door.' He gave a grim chuckle of satisfaction as he added, 'But if they land here and try anything at Dawlish Hall, they'll be in for a nasty surprise.'

'Yes, I've noticed the rifles and pistols dotted about the place by the windows and doors,' said Rosa. 'Shouldn't they be in a secure case, under lock and key?'

'No time for unlocking cases if they start arriving,' said Magnus. 'Malcolm and I need them to hand. Have you ever fired a gun?'

'No,' said Rosa. 'It's not something that's ever arisen.' She looked down at the scar left by the bullet in her left arm and said ruefully, 'Mind, after having been shot, perhaps it would have been a good idea to know how to defend myself. Although, in that case when I got shot, I wouldn't have had a chance even if I'd had a gun.'

'This is your chance to learn,' said Magnus. 'I suggested to Mrs Hilton that she ought to learn, but she's pig-headed about not wanting to handle a gun.'

'I heard that,' said Mrs Hilton, entering the room bearing a silver tray with an envelope on it. 'Guns are dangerous things. I'm not being forced into using one.'

'I wasn't forcing you,' protested Magnus. 'I was just suggesting it might be useful if we were invaded.'

'That's what the Home Guard are here for, and all those gamekeepers who are used to handling rifles and such,' said Mrs Hilton. 'Anyway, the postman has just been.' She walked round to Rosa and laid the tray beside her plate. 'Just this for you, Mrs Coburg. Nothing for you, Your Grace.'

Rosa took the envelope, and Mrs Hilton lifted the tray and left the room.

'I can't make that woman see the sense of it,' grumbled Magnus. 'If the Germans land, we're going to need everyone ready to fight. Man, woman, anyone.' He looked at Rosa as she opened the envelope. 'Who's it from?'

'From Edgar.' She took out the two photographs

and Coburg's note, looked at them, then passed them to Magnus. 'It's the two men who abducted me. They've been found, shot dead. Edgar asks if I'd confirm these are the two men who kidnapped me.'

'And are they?'

Rosa nodded. 'I'll phone Edgar after breakfast and tell him.'

'So you're safe?' asked Magnus.

'Not according to Edgar. He says they're still trying to find out who was behind the two men.'

'Good.' Magnus smiled. 'That means you'll be here a little longer. Malcolm will be pleased.'

Rosa looked at Magnus inquisitively and asked, 'Why doesn't Malcolm eat with us?'

Magnus gave a sigh. 'Because he's so impossibly hidebound about tradition. He believes a servant's place is in the kitchen, not – as he calls it – at top table with the gentry. I've tried pointing out to him that with the war on and most of the estate workers having gone off to join the forces, we don't have the same number of servants here at Dawlish Hall as we did. And he's more than a servant. We've known each other for twenty years. We were in the trenches together. He was my batman, and a better person I couldn't have had looking out for me. But he's got this old-fashioned idea about status. I'm an earl and master of this estate, and he's a worker.' He shook his head. 'Madness. There are just he and I rattling around in this place, with Mrs Hilton coming in from the village to cook and look after things.' He looked hopefully at Rosa. 'Perhaps you could have a word with him. Persuade him to join us for meals. He listens to you. He's got one of your records, you know.'

'Oh? Which one?'

'It's got "Stardust" on one side and "Summertime" on the other. He plays it on the gramophone when he thinks I'm not listening.' He shook his head. 'He can be so irritating. Trouble is, I don't know what I'd do without him.'

In London, Coburg and Lampson made their way to the address in Paddington that Percy Wenlock had given them for Dan Reeves. Coburg was glad to pass the driving over to Lampson, while he sat in the passenger seat and ran through recent events in his mind.

'Well done on those raids on Buttons's clubs, Sergeant,' he said. 'Whether or not he was guilty of the murders, and so far we've only got what Pat Riley says, the drugs bust will put Buttons behind bars and out of action for a good while. Which means that with Buttons in jail and Riley being kept a close watch on, both those two suspects in the murder of Benny Martin are where we want them. We now have to grasp the nettle of the other one who's been accused, Lord Colin Cuddington.'

'Accused?' asked Lampson.

Coburg told him about his meeting with Pamela Cuddington, and the stories she'd told him about her husband: his claim to have killed a former gay lover, and also that he'd been behind Benny's death.

'It may be just bluster to put the frighteners on her,' said Coburg. 'But we need to look into it, which means talking to Cuddington.'

'He's banging blokes as well as his wife?' said Lampson, shocked.

'Who knows what goes on in people's private lives behind closed doors,' said Coburg sagely.

'Well, I can tell you, nothing like that goes on behind my door,' said Lampson firmly.

'More importantly,' said Coburg thoughtfully, 'is the death of Dan Reeves connected with the other murders, of Benny, Punt and Maples, and also the attempt on Rosa? Or is it separate?'

'This case is getting more complicated with every passing day,' commented Lampson.

'Possibly because it's more cases than one, and they're all entwined,' said Coburg.

They arrived at a small, narrow terraced house in Paddington, the address for Dan Reeves. There was no answer to their knock, so – at a nod from Coburg – Lampson went to work with his lockpicks, and they were soon inside the small living room.

The décor inside the house was spartan, very bare.

'Doesn't look like there's a Mrs Reeves,' observed Lampson.

Coburg picked up a framed photograph from the dresser, which showed a young man and woman in front of the porch of a church. The couple were obviously just married, he in a dark suit and the young woman in a long white dress.

Coburg turned the photo over and saw written on the back: *Ellie and Dan, 3rd March 1930. Our day.*

'There was,' commented Coburg. 'Whether she's still around is another matter. My gut feeling is she died. If she'd run off, he wouldn't still have the photo on display.' They started to go through the contents of the dresser, turning out the papers and different documents in the drawers.

'Payment slips for volunteer fireman Daniel J. Reeves, Volunteer AFS crewman, Crew 127,' said Lampson.

'Crew 127,' mused Coburg. 'The looters. That's interesting.' He took a letter from the drawer he'd opened. 'And so is this.'

He passed a letter to Lampson. The letter was written in a barely literate hand, but there was no doubting the sentiments expressed. It was a love letter 'to my darling Dan' from Alice Martin.

'It could be the parts of the puzzle might be coming together,' mused Coburg. 'Benny Martin

217

is found dead, poisoned, his body dumped by someone who knows the tunnels around Aldwych station. Dan Reeves is also found dead there, shot, and he works in the tunnel as a rail tapper. 'Reeves's girlfriend is Alice Martin, Benny's sister. Reeves is a member of AFS Crew 127, suspected of looting when they're called to a shout.' He frowned. 'Lots of boxes ticked, but what's the actual connection? Did Dan Reeves kill Benny Martin? If so, why? And who shot him?'

'Maybe Benny found out about the looting and threatened to tell the law, so Crew 127 had to shut him up. Remember that jewellery box in Alice Martin's room? Maybe Benny found out about it from Alice.'

'Alice said she hadn't seen Benny, but Sam Watson said he saw them together at the Riff Club the night he died.'

'That box in her room says she's on the crook in some way,' said Lampson. 'Crooks lie.'

'Yes,' agreed Coburg. 'I think we need to call on Alice. Someone's got to tell her the bad news about Dan Reeves.'

In the barn at Dawlish Hall, Magnus had set up a row of targets printed on paper against a pile of straw bales stacked against one another to a depth of six feet. In his hand he held a revolver, which he'd just loaded with bullets, and he held it out to Rosa for her to look at it.

'The Enfield Number 2 Mark 1 pistol,' he told her. 'It saw me and many others safely through the First War. An excellent weapon. This is the modified version. The first Mark 1 had a longer hammer that was troublesome for the tank crews it was issued to. Kept getting caught in the internal workings of the tank, sometimes with dangerous results. This is known as the Mark 1 Star. Six bullets in a revolving chamber.'

He pointed it at the bales of straw, then lowered it. 'When it comes to being able to shoot, forget all that stuff you see on the pictures about cowboys being quick on the draw. You don't need that. Half the time people who try that shoot themselves in the foot. It's about taking aim at what you want to hit, holding the pistol firmly so it doesn't waggle all over the place, and squeezing the trigger gently. I suggest at first you use both hands to hold it to make sure it doesn't jump in your hand when you squeeze the trigger. When a pistol goes off there's a small explosion that causes the barrel to jerk upwards if you're not holding it firmly. If anything, aim it slightly downward from the centre of the target, so if it does jerk up a bit you won't miss what you're aiming at completely.

'Another thing, if you're aiming it at an enemy

who's armed, forget all that stuff about shooting their weapon out of their hand. It does happen, but mostly accidentally. The aim is to stop the person from shooting at you, so aim at the biggest part of the target. That's the body. When you get to be an expert you can go for the legs or an arm, or the head, but from a distance your best chance is aiming at the body, the chest down to the stomach. Like this.'

Magnus aimed the pistol at the target, holding the butt firmly in both hands. He put his forefinger on the trigger and gently pulled it back. There was a loud bang and the bullet flew from the gun and tore through the paper target and into the straw bales behind it.

Magnus held the pistol out to Rosa.

'You have a go,' he said. 'But make sure you hold it firmly, and expect it to kick upwards when it fires.'

Rosa imitated what she'd seen Magnus do, pointing the pistol at a target and gently squeezing the trigger. When it fired, she found herself stepping back in order to keep her balance as the barrel of the gun jerked upwards.

'Good,' Magnus complimented her.

'It's got some kick,' she said.

'Yes, but you held it firm.' He pointed at the target. 'Your shot hit the top of the target, which is good for first-time shooting. Most people it goes much higher when the gun kicks, sometimes ending up in the ceiling. Try again.'

This time, forewarned, Rosa was able to hold the pistol level when it fired, her bullet hitting the target.

'Excellent!' Magnus beamed. Then he added reflectively, 'There's a part of me hoping the Germans will try and come here. I want to pay them back for killing Charles that way. One dead German will go a way to achieving that.'

As Rosa lined up her next shot, Magnus said quietly, 'I've asked the War Office if they can arrange to bring Charles's body home. I'd like him to be buried here at Dawlish.'

'Do you think they'll be able to?' asked Rosa, temporarily lowering the pistol.

'It depends who's involved at the German end,' said Magnus. 'There are some good chaps among the Germans. There's a chap called Rommel I've heard decent things about. A pity he's on the other side, but by all accounts he's fair. Someone at the War Office knows him and said he'd make contact. It'd be the decent thing for them to do after the cowardly way they killed him.'

There was a noise outside the barn, then Malcolm appeared looking flustered.

'What's going on?' he demanded. 'I heard gunshots.'

'Magnus is teaching me how to use a pistol,' said Rosa.

Malcolm glared indignantly at Magnus. 'Without me?' he demanded. 'Who won the regimental pistol marksmanship medal?'

'And he'll never let anyone forget it,' groaned Magnus.

'Actually, Magnus is teaching me very well,' said Rosa.

'I'm hitting the target.'

'Of course you are, because the target's not moving,' said Malcolm with a snort of derision. 'The enemy doesn't do that. They come at you, zigzagging, diving for cover.'

'We'll be doing that later,' said Magnus. 'Right now Rosa needs to learn the basics, get to be comfortable with the weapon. Once she's done that, we can get on to more complicated stuff.'

'It's how I'd prefer it,' said Rosa to Malcolm with a friendly smile. 'This is all new to me.'

It was the smile that did the trick, taking the look of indignation off the face of the elderly Scot.

'Very well,' he said. 'But I hope there'll be no objection to my being here and watching these *basics*, as you call them. With perhaps the odd word of helpful advice, if you've got no objection.'

'If you think it's necessary,' said Magnus, his face showing his doubt.

'From my perspective, I feel I'm lucky to be learning from both of you,' said Rosa. 'Can I try another shot?'

Both men nodded. Rosa levelled the pistol, pulled the trigger, and the bullet sailed through the centre of the target. Magnus smiled at Malcolm.

'See?' he said. 'And that's only the third time she's fired a gun.'

'And under my tuition, she'll improve enormously,' said Malcolm smugly.

As had been the case with their visit to Dan Reeves's house, when they got to the house where Alice Martin lived there was no response to their ringing of the doorbell, so Lampson did his trick with his lockpicks on the front door, and then on the door to Alice Martin's room.

'I wonder where she is?' wondered Coburg, walking into the room. He stopped as he bumped into the bulky figure of Lampson, who was standing staring at something lying on the floor.

'There,' said Lampson grimly.

Alice Morgan lay on the threadbare carpet. She was in her dressing gown, which was spattered with blood. What remained of her face where she'd been bludgeoned was barely recognisable. Lampson hurried to her and knelt down beside her, even though he knew there was no chance of her being alive. He felt for a pulse, the lack of it confirming his fears.

'Dead,' he said. He got up, looked down at the battered body of the young woman and said, 'What bastard did this?'

CHAPTER TWENTY-SIX

Saturday 7th December 1940

Coburg and Lampson waited in Alice's room until the duty medical arrived at the scene. Coburg was relieved to see it was Dr Welbourne.

'Beaten to death,' said Welbourne, 'as you can see.'

'Anything more you can tell us?' asked Coburg.

'Not at this stage, but I'll be able to give you a report once I've taken a proper look. I'm taking her to UCH and I'll get onto it straight away. I guess you want this tout de suite?'

'As tout as you can would be greatly appreciated, Doctor,' said Coburg gratefully.

Once Welbourne and the stretcher bearers had removed Alice's body, Coburg and Lampson returned to Scotland Yard, where they got the message Rosa had left with the switchboard confirming that the two men in the photographs he'd sent her were the ones who'd abducted her. Coburg telephoned her at Dawlish Hall to tell her he and Lampson were still on the case and that they hoped to be able to get her back to London shortly.

'I'm afraid the case has got more complicated,' he admitted.

'In what way?' asked Rosa.

'In a way I can't say over the telephone,' apologised Coburg.

He then made his way to Superintendent Allison's office to report the latest murders. The superintendent stared at him, shocked.

'You're saying there are now *five* murders connected with this case? Five!'

'It looks that way, sir, though we have yet to confirm it. The fire crew that General Walters claims robbed him included a man called Reeves. Reeves was found today, shot dead, at the same spot in the tunnel at Aldwych where the young jazz guitarist, Benny Martin, was found dead, poisoned. Benny Martin's sister was called Alice. She was going out with Dan Reeves. We found her beaten to death today in the room where she lived. Henry Punt and Wally Maples were the two men who abducted Rosa and were told to kill her. Their bodies were pulled from the canal at King's Cross. They'd both been shot.'

'Have you got any idea what's behind it?'

'Punt and Maples grabbed Rosa after she started asking questions about Benny Martin's guitar. So the connection to all the deaths is Benny Martin.

'At the moment we have two men in the frame

as possible suspects, both club owners in Soho. A man called Pat Riley, and a gangster who used to dominate Birmingham called Shelley Buttons. We've had both of them in for questioning, but so far we've got no firm proof against either of them in relation to the murders, but we have got Buttons bang to rights over drug dealing. We've now got him on remand at Pentonville. Sergeant Lampson carried out a series of raids on his Soho clubs and found a large quantity of drugs and has made several arrests.'

'Excellent,' said Allison.

'We're also looking at a man called Lord Cuddington as a possible suspect.'

'Lord Cuddington?' queried Allison. 'He's some financier or something, isn't he? I often see him mentioned in the financial columns of the newspapers. How does he fit into this?'

'His wife, Lady Cuddington, was having an affair with Benny Martin. Lady Cuddington has accused her husband of killing Martin. Or, at least, of being involved in his death.'

'My God, this is a tangled web,' groaned Allison. 'Are there no pointers at all to who might be behind all of this?'

'We think a lot of this case may revolve around the fire crew who assaulted General Walters, so we're going to pull the remaining three members of the crew in for questioning.'

Allison nodded. 'Very well, Chief Inspector. I leave it to you, but keep me informed.'

Coburg left the superintendent's office feeling frustrated and angry. Yes, they'd pull in AFS Crew 127, but Coburg had a feeling this was just a minor part of the whole investigation. It was possible that they could be connected with the death of Dan Reeves, but he had a feeling that might be as far as it went. His only hope in pulling them in for questioning might be that one of them might say something that could give them a clue as to where Benny Martin, Henry Punt and Wally Maples fitted into it. Pat Riley seemed the most likely connection, but the regular report from the detective constables keeping watch on him indicated that he went nowhere except the Riff Club and his home, so he couldn't have shot Dan Reeves or beaten Alice Martin to death. But that wasn't to say that he hadn't hired someone else to do it.

Shelley Buttons seemed to be in the clear as he'd been under lock and key when Reeves had been shot and Alice Martin beaten to death. But, as with Riley, he could have got one of his gang to do both.

Coburg walked into the office and told Lampson, 'It's time to pull in the three remaining members of the fire crew: Ernie Morris, Joe Barker and Billy Dodds.'

'You reckon one of them did Reeves?' asked

Lampson. 'Maybe, or maybe they did it together. Or maybe they're not involved at all.' He sighed. 'The only way to find out is to talk to them. Have them picked up separately, but they're all to be lifted at the same time so one can't get a warning to the other two.'

'Leave it to me, guv,' said Lampson. 'I'll pick up Barker and arrange for a DS and a couple of uniforms to each bring in the other two.'

Joe Barker's reaction when Lampson arrived with a warrant and two constables was to try and slam the door in his face, but Lampson's large boot stopped that. Lampson then had the two constables handcuff Barker and stay with him while the sergeant began a search of Lampson's small terraced house. The first cupboard he opened revealed the jewellery box Lampson had previously seen in Alice Martin's flat.

'Well, well.' Lampson smiled, holding the box up.

'I've never seen that before,' said Barker defiantly.

'Well, I have,' said Lampson. 'In the room of Alice Martin, who's recently been beaten to death. And now, here it is in your house. Anything to say, Joe?'

Barker glared angrily at him, tight-lipped.

Lampson's next discovery was a pistol inside the drawer of a dresser. Lampson took it out carefully and wrapped it in a handkerchief.

'Better and better,' he said. 'We've just come from looking at the body of an old pal of yours, Dan Reeves. He'd been shot dead. And lo and behold, here's a gun. Are you going to say you've never seen that before as well, Joe? In which case it's unlikely we'll find your fingerprints on it, isn't it? Or will we?'

'I'm saying nothing till I've seen my solicitor,' said Barker.

CHAPTER TWENTY-SEVEN

Saturday 7th December 1940

With Morris, Dodds and Barker all under lock and key in separate cells in the basement of Scotland Yard, Lampson took the jewellery box and the pistol to Coburg in his office. 'It looks like we may have Barker bang to rights,' he said. 'We know Alice Martin had that jewellery box in her room. As for his gun, I'm going to get the technicians to check it against the bullets that killed Dan Reeves, and Punt and Maples.'

'How did they react when they were bought in?' asked Coburg.

'Barker, as expected. Bolshie. Aggressive. Says he's saying nothing till he's seen his solicitor. Ernie Morris is a bit on edge but trying to appear calm and innocent. Billy Dodds is the one who's most scared. Nervous.'

'In that case we'll start with Dodds,' said Coburg. 'Phone down and have him waiting for us in the interview room. We'll use what he gives us to open up Ernie Morris. If we can get some good evidence against Barker from them, we can nail him.'

'Do you think Barker killed them? Dan Reeves and Alice Martin?'

'I don't know,' admitted Coburg.

Coburg and Lampson took the gun Lampson had found at Barker's along to the technical department for testing against the bullets that had been taken from the dead bodies of Reeves, Punt and Maples; then they went down to the interview room where Billy Dodds was waiting for them.

Coburg spotted at once that Lampson was correct in his assessment of Billy Dodds. The man was jumpy, nervous, shifting about on the hard wooden chair. He also kept his head down, desperate not to look the two detectives in the eye.

'William Dodds,' said Coburg, 'you are charged with robbery and looting while carrying out your duties with Auxiliary Fire Crew 127. You are also a suspect in the murders of Daniel Reeves and Alice Martin.'

At the word 'murders', Dodds's head came up and he looked at the detectives, his face agonised.

'I never killed anyone,' he said.

'But you do admit to looting?' asked Coburg.

'No,' said Dodds, his voice almost a whisper, and he dropped his head again.

Coburg had brought a paper file with him, and he opened it now and read from the sheet of paper inside it.

'I have here six statements from the owners of premises that were attended by AFS Crew 127, all of which say valuables had been found missing when the owners returned to their properties. In five of the cases, a safe had been broken open by means of a heavy hammer.' He looked at the unhappy Dodds, still with his head bowed. 'Six statements, Dodds. That's not just casual theft, that's a conspiracy to rob, and looting is a hanging offence.'

Dodds's head jerked up and he appealed desperately, 'I never did anything. It was the others. I just went along with them. I couldn't say no or I'd have been in trouble.'

'You're in even bigger trouble now,' said Coburg. 'Who broke open the safes?'

Dodds dropped his head again and mumbled something inaudible.

'Speak up, please,' said Coburg.

'Dan,' muttered Dodds.

'Dan Reeves?' Dodds nodded.

'Why did you kill him?'

Dodds's head shot up and he burst out, 'I didn't!'

'Who did? I assume he was ripping you off. We found the box with the jewellery that he'd been creaming off. We saw it previously at Alice Martin's place, but today it was in Joe Barker's house. How did Barker get hold of it?'

Dodds hesitated, then said, 'He must have gone to

see her. Joe said that Dan was ripping us off. Dan was the one who sold the jewels. He knew a fence, but Joe found out that Dan was only giving us a share of part of the money he was getting for the jewels.'

'How did he find out?'

'Joe followed Dan and found out who his fence was, and he asked him how much he'd given Dan for the stuff.'

'Who was the fence?' asked Coburg.

'Joe never said. Then there was a row. After that general bloke reported us to the police, Ernie said we had to stop doing the safes. Dan got mad about it and said if that was the case he was quitting our crew.

'It was after he'd gone that Joe told us he'd been to see the fence, who told him what he'd really paid Dan for the jewels the last time. He said he stuck a gun in the fence's ear to make him talk. The fence said he'd given Dan six hundred quid more than Dan had told us he'd got. Joe said he was going to face Dan and get the money he'd cheated us out of.' He looked at them, a look of urgent appeal on his face again as he said, 'I didn't want any part of it. I didn't even want the money. I only took it because the others would get suspicious if I didn't.'

Ernie Morris was next, and as soon as Coburg told him that Billy Dodds had confessed to the looting of the premises they were called to, Morris folded.

'It didn't start out like that,' he said. 'We were doing it to put out fires and save people. It was Dan who said we weren't getting paid properly for what we were doing, just getting volunteer rates for putting our lives at risk while some of the places we went to had everything. Paintings on the walls, real paintings, not prints from Woolworths. Sometimes there'd be jewellery lying about. He said the rich people wouldn't miss it if we took the odd bit. After all, we'd rescued things. They would've burnt if we hadn't been there saving stuff.'

'How did you get on to opening the safes?'

'The first time it happened, the safe was already open. The people in the flat had left in such a rush they'd left the door of it ajar. There wasn't a lot of cash in it, mostly jewellery. It was Dan who said he knew someone who could turn it into cash for us, a fence.

'The next one we went to was in an expensive block of flats; this time Dan brought his heavy hammer with him. He opened it up, and again there wasn't a lot of cash but there were jewels and stuff. That's how it started.'

'But it went wrong when General Walters complained, didn't it,' said Coburg. 'You told the others you'd have to stop opening the safes. And Dan Reeves didn't like that.'

'No, he got shirty with us. Said in that case he

was going off to join another crew.'

'And Joe Barker found out that Dan had been short-changing you with what he got from the jewels?'

Morris nodded.

'Who was Dan's fence?' asked Coburg.

'He never said, and we never asked,' said Morris. 'Joe said we should go and face Dan over it, get the money he stole from us.'

'Which you'd stolen from other people.'

'Like I said, we didn't see it like that.'

'So you went to see Dan?'

Again, Morris nodded. 'But Dan wasn't at home. So Joe suggested going to see his girlfriend in case he was there.'

'His girlfriend being Alice Martin,' said Coburg.

'Yes,' said Morris. 'We went to the room she rents, but Dan wasn't there. So we came away again.'

'What about the jewellery box?' asked Coburg. 'Did you take it or did Joe?'

'Joe,' said Morris. 'I didn't want anything to do with it. To be honest, I didn't even want to go to her place, or to Dan's, because I knew it would be trouble.'

'What sort of trouble?'

'People getting hurt. Joe had a gun, and Dan had his hammer. I knew it would turn out bad.'

'But you went anyway.'

'I was scared,' said Morris. 'Scared of both of them.

Especially Joe. He's got a screw loose. The fact he has a gun shows that.'

Coburg had Morris taken back to his holding cell, just as he'd done with Billy Dodds, and then Barker was brought into the interview room. He stood across from the table from Coburg and Lampson, glaring at them. Coburg gestured at the chair in front of him.

'You can seat yourself or we can have a couple of constables assist you,' he said calmly.

Barker scowled, but sat down.

'We're investigating the murders of Dan Reeves and Alice Martin,' said Coburg.

'Don't know them,' grunted Barker. Coburg gave a weary sigh.

'We're not going to get anywhere if you're going to play this game, Joe,' he said. 'You and Reeves were both on AFS Crew 127. And that box of jewellery we found at your place we last saw in Alice Martin's room. So you took it from her. Did she try to stop you? Is that why you beat her to death?'

Barker glared at them. 'I never touched her,' he said. 'She gave it to me.'

Coburg and Lampson exchanged looks of amusement, which angered Barker.

'What's so funny? It's the truth!'

'Joe, we have you bang to rights. We know that you and your fire crew were looting, and that it was Dan Reeves who broke open the safes of the places you went to. Dan was ripping you off, taking the jewels and keeping them for himself, the box left at his girlfriend, Alice Martin's, place.

'You knew he'd been robbing you and you went to Alice Martin's place after the jewels. She was beaten to death and the box ends up with you.'

'She was alive when we left!' said Barker. 'Ask Ernie Morris. He was with me.'

'We have, and he admitted that. But who's to say you didn't go back and decide to silence her, to stop her telling Dan Reeves what you'd done. Dan's got a temper. He'd be coming after you.'

'I never went back!' shouted Barker, rising from his chair in anger and being pushed back down by the watching constable.

'Let's move on to Dan Reeves,' said Coburg. 'You wanted revenge on him for ripping you off. Next thing, he ends up shot dead in the tunnels at Aldwych station. And what do we find at your place? A pistol. Want to tell us what happened? Did he go for you in revenge for taking the jewels and scaring Alice out of her wits, and you shot him?'

'I never did!'

'Who was Dan's fence?' asked Coburg. 'We know you followed Reeves to find out who he was selling the jewels to.'

Barker looked at them sullenly. 'I'm not saying anything else until I have my solicitor with me.'

'Very well,' said Coburg. He pushed a piece of paper and a pencil across the table to Barker. 'If you write down your solicitor's contact details, we'll get in touch with him.'

Barker scowled and pushed the paper and pencil back towards Coburg.

'I don't have a solicitor of my own,' he said sourly. 'I'm not like one of these lucky rich bastards. You're supposed to provide me with one.'

'And we will,' said Coburg. He turned to the constables standing watching and said, 'Will you take Mr Barker to the custody suite and instruct the turnkey to put Mr Barker in a cell, pending the arrival of a solicitor.'

Barker sat stiffly on the chair, anger suffusing his face, and for a moment Coburg thought he was going to resist as the constables approached him, but then he stood up and allowed himself to be led out.

Lampson turned to Coburg.

'What do you think, guv?' he asked.

'I think we let Morris and Dodds go for the moment, but warn them to make themselves available to us. As for Barker, we keep him under lock and key until a duty solicitor arrives. We need the name of Reeves's fence, and it looks like Barker's the only one who can tell us. In the meantime, we'll wait to see what ballistics tell us about Barker's gun, and if it matches the bullets taken from Dan Reeves, Henry Punt and

Wally Maples.' He frowned thoughtfully as he added, 'The way Alice was killed worries me. Three men had been shot but she was beaten to death. Why didn't whoever killed Alice simply shoot her?'

'Worried about the gun making a noise?' wondered Lampson.

'Beating someone to death the way she was is just as noisy, if not more so,' said Coburg. 'And what was she beaten with?' He picked up the telephone and asked the operator to connect him to University College Hospital. Once through, he asked for Dr Welbourne.

'DCI Coburg,' came Welbourne's voice. 'What can I do for you?'

'The body of the young lady you took in. Have you had a chance to look at her yet?'

'There are still some tests I've got to do on the internal organs, but I can give you the broad picture,' said Welbourne. 'There were no injuries except for the ones to the head, so it was the battering that killed her.'

'Any idea what sort of weapon was involved?'

'From the injuries, I'd say something made of metal.'

'A pistol? A hammer?'

'No, something more like a small statuette. Not too small. I'd say something about twelve inches high and quite bulky to give weight to the blows.'

Coburg thanked Welbourne and hung up.

'A metal statuette about a foot long, quite bulky,' he told Lampson. 'It will also be covered in blood, bone and brains.'

'I can't see anyone carrying that around openly,' said Lampson.

'Nor can I,' agreed Coburg. 'There was a window in the back wall of Alice's room that overlooked the rear garden.'

'Yes, I looked out at it,' said Lampson. 'Not so much a garden as a rubbish patch. Weeds and nettles and Lord alone knows what else.'

Coburg got up. 'My guess is whoever did it threw the weapon out of the window. I'm going to instigate a search of the garden.'

'I can come with you if want,' offered Lampson. 'My parents won't mind if I'm late picking Terry up.'

Coburg shook his head. 'You don't get much time with your son. And tomorrow's your day off, so grab the chance to spend some time this evening with him, then Sunday. You deserve it, and so does Terry. With Rosa away I'm at a loose end, so this'll give me something to do.'

With daylight fading, and concerned in case the Luftwaffe began to attack once night fell, Coburg organised a party of uniformed officers to carry out the search with him in the overgrown garden at the rear of the house where Alice had lived. Coburg pointed out

241

the window of the room that had been Alice's.

'We're looking for something like a small statuette. Whatever it is, it'll be made of metal, about twelve inches tall, and quite bulky. The blood on it will have dried, but there could be bits of bone and brain on it. My guess is that the person who wielded it then chucked it out of that window, so if it's here it'll be somewhere below it. Start close to the wall, beneath the window, and work your way out. I'm afraid it means searching through nettles and lots of other junk. If you see anything likely, bag it, whatever it is, and I'll sort through it all later back at the Yard.'

Fortunately, whoever had beaten Alice to death had let the weapon drop straight down, rather than throwing it, so it took just fifteen minutes of searching before one of the constables called out, 'Found it, sir!'

Coburg hurried over and joined him. There, half hidden in the tall nettles, was a black statuette of a gorilla, arms akimbo. Smears of white matter and bits of bone were stuck to it.

Well done, *Dr Welbourne*, thought Coburg. First, he'd worked out from the grooves in Benny Martin's fingers that he was most likely a jazz guitarist, and now he'd correctly identified the murder weapon from the wounds on Alice's head. The doctor would make an excellent detective.

Carefully, using a handkerchief to avoid messing up

any possible fingerprints, Coburg popped the statuette into an evidence bag.

'Thanks, everyone,' he announced to the search party. 'A successful outcome.'

He drove back to Scotland Yard and took the evidence bag to the technical laboratory.

'This is a possible murder weapon,' he told the chief technician, John Wise. 'I'm hoping there might be fingerprints on it.'

'Leave it to us, Chief Inspector,' said Wise.

The sound of a gunshot exploding close by made Coburg jerk round in alarm. The chief technician smiled.

'Nothing to concern yourself about,' he said. 'We're carrying out ballistics tests on the gun you brought us. With luck, we'll have a report for you tomorrow.'

'Sunday?' queried Coburg.

'Crime doesn't take days off, Chief Inspector,' said Wise wryly.

CHAPTER TWENTY-EIGHT

Saturday 7th December 1940. 5 p.m.

Gerhard Schroeder piloted the Dornier Do 17 eastward, making for the English coast, and then home to Germany. It had been a good raid in that they'd survived the flak from the anti-aircraft guns. A raid in daylight was a rarity for them these days, now the Luftwaffe mainly bombed at night, but now and then a daylight raid was ordered to remind the British that the Luftwaffe could strike at any time, night or day.

On this raid, their target had been the railway lines to the north-west of London. They'd dropped their bombs, but how successful their attack had been was still to be assessed.

The voice of Groot, the Dornier's navigator, was heard in Schroeder's ear, giving him the course he was to take. Suddenly he heard Wurtz, the gunner, cut in with: 'Spitfires coming from the south.'

Schroeder looked to the south. He saw them, three Spitfires in formation.

'Fire when in range,' ordered Schroeder.

There was the sound of an explosion and a yell of pain in Schroeder's headphones, then the shocked voice of Groot: 'I've been hit. They came at me . . .'

His words were cut off by another burst of firing and a scream, and the sound of glass shattering.

Schroeder heard the sound of rapid return gunfire from the lower turret. A glance out of his window showed the three Spitfires leaping and spinning through the air, reminding him of trapeze artists he'd once seen at a circus in Berlin.

A Spitfire was coming at him head-on, bullets blazing, tearing through the thin fabric of the outer skin of the bomber. Schroeder saw the answering lines of tracer from the gun-turret in the Dornier's nose just below him, but the Spitfire seemed to somersault sideways and let off one last burst before skimming just over the bomber's cockpit.

Suddenly, Schroeder smelt smoke. He glanced quickly over his shoulder, and saw that the interior of the plane was enveloped in thick, oily, black smoke, which was belching towards the cockpit. The bullets from the Spitfire had cut through the hydraulic pipes that operated the turret. Flames could be seen licking at the narrow walkway that linked every position.

Out of the corner of his eye he saw Mertz, the bombardier, grab a fire extinguisher and advance towards the flames and the thick black smoke.

There was an explosion of bullets tearing through

the skin of the plane to his left, and he saw Groot slumped forward in his seat.

'Westermann!' he shouted. There was no answer.

He looked round and saw the wireless operator, Westermann sprawled, held to his seat by his safety belt. Westermann's mouth and eyes were open and there was blood running down his face from beneath his flying helmet. Groot gone. Wurtz gone. Now Westermann gone. Just himself and Mertz alive. What was worse, the bomber was dropping out of the sky. The controls had obviously been hit during the attack by the Spitfires.

He considered parachuting out, but they were now too close to the ground and there was the danger of his parachute getting caught in the plane's wings, or catching fire as the flames spread.

Fortunately, this part of England was mainly rolling flat green fields with very few buildings. He could crash land, skidding the plane along the grass, providing he could do that before the flames reached him.

Rosa, Magnus and Malcolm looked in horror as the burning German bomber came down on the field a couple of hundred yards away, flames leaping out from it. The plane crashed through a wooden fence and then slewed round, skidding on the grass before hitting a tree and grinding to a juddering halt a hundred yards away from the main house. As they watched, two men fell out of the burning bomber and began to run towards the house. Malcolm saw them change direction and shouted, 'They're making for the garage! They're going to steal the car!'

'Oh no they're not!' snapped Magnus.

He grabbed up a rifle and ran towards the main door. Malcolm picked up a pistol and a rifle and followed him. Rosa grabbed up a pistol and chased after them.

The two German airmen were almost at the garage with its door open, revealing the Bentley inside. Malcolm fired a shot over their heads and ran towards them, levelling the rifle at them. There was a shot, and then Malcolm toppled to the ground.

Magnus stopped, stunned, and turned towards his fallen friend. The German who'd shot Malcolm fired again, this time at Magnus, before rushing into the garage with his companion.

There was the sound of the car starting up, and Magnus cursed the fact that he'd insisted the keys be left in the car so they wouldn't get lost.

Magnus ran towards the garage, aiming his rifle and firing, just as the Bentley came hurtling out of the garage.

There was the sound of another shot and the windscreen of the Bentley splintered, then shattered and the car skidded and slid into a tree.

The passenger door of the car sprang open and one

of the German airmen fell out.

Magnus turned and saw Rosa standing, holding a pistol with both hands, pointing it at the car.

He looked back at the car and saw that the other German had appeared from the driver's side. Both Germans were holding their hands up in surrender.

Magnus scowled and ran towards them, stopping just short of them.

Rosa saw Magnus raise the rifle and aim it at the nearest German, and saw from the angry expression on his face that he intended to fire.

'No, Magnus!' she shouted. 'They're unarmed!'

'So was Charles!' Magnus shouted back.

'If you kill them, you'll be as bad as those who shot Charles,' Rosa begged him. 'You're a soldier, not an executioner.'

Magnus hesitated, his finger on the trigger, the young German nearest him in his rifle sights, then slowly, reluctantly he lowered his rifle.

'They still shot Malcolm!' he said angrily to Rosa.

Rosa looked at where Malcolm lay, and saw that he was struggling to his feet.

'You're alright!' shouted Rosa delightedly, running towards Malcolm while Magnus kept his rifle aimed at the two Germans.

Malcolm looked down at his left sleeve, where blood was staining it.

'Just a flesh wound,' he said. And then he fainted.

CHAPTER TWENTY-NINE

Saturday 7th December 1940

'Malcolm fainted?' smiled Coburg, amused.

'Shh,' Rosa hushed him. 'It wasn't a faint as such. I think it was loss of blood that caused it. The bullet had nicked a vein, or something. My St John training came in useful; I put a tourniquet on his arm, which kept him safe until the doctor arrived from the village, along with about fifty other people armed with pitchforks and all manner of agricultural instruments. They'd seen the plane come down in flames.'

It had been six o'clock when Coburg heard from Rosa over the phone about the incident at Dawlish Hall. He'd immediately telephoned Superintendent Allison at his home to tell him what had happened, and that he needed to drive to Dawlish Hall.

'I'll be back as early as I can tomorrow morning,' he said.

'That's not a problem,' said Allison. 'You spend as much time with your wife as you think you'll need. It must have been an awful experience for her.'

'She's quite strong, sir. And I need to check with

ballistics about the gun we took from Joe Barker tomorrow. I told Sergeant Lampson I'd deal with it. And we think we've found the weapon with which Alice Martin was killed. I've got the technical people checking for fingerprints.'

'Very well, I leave that to you, Chief Inspector.' The superintendent's voice sounded awed as he said, 'Astonishing! Your wife brought down a German bomber!'

'Er, no, sir, the Spitfires actually brought it down. Rosa helped take the surviving crew prisoner. She shot my brother's car, which they stole trying to get away, forcing them to get out with their hands up.'

'Your wife is some woman, Coburg,' said Allison, impressed.

'Yes, sir, she is,' agreed Coburg.

He packed an overnight bag and made the journey to Dawlish Hall in time to join Rosa and Magnus for a very late supper, where he was able to listen to the actual events from both of them.

'What a shot!' enthused Magnus. 'Smashed my windscreen, but got the Jerry who was driving in the shoulder. Bang, right into a tree. End of their escape.'

'And you're alright?' Coburg asked Rosa anxiously. 'No after-effects?'

'None,' she said, spooning up the soup Mrs Hilton had served.

'And Malcolm?' asked Coburg.

'Patched up and as irritating as ever,' said Magnus. 'He's claiming the credit for teaching Rosa to shoot. Absolute nonsense.'

'You both taught me to shoot,' said Rosa. She looked enquiringly at Coburg. 'Any news on who organised for me to be abducted? Is it safe for me to come back to London yet?'

'With German planes crash-landing right next to you, I was wondering on the way here if you might not be safer back in London. But then I thought: No, let's not take a chance.'

'Who's this other man you're suspicious of? You said you couldn't name him over the phone, but you're here now.'

'He's a man called Shelley Buttons,' said Coburg.

'Shelley Buttons?' said Magnus, his tone scoffing. 'What sort of name is that?'

'One that struck fear in the people of Birmingham, and is now striking fear into the demi-world of Soho club owners, if the stories are to be believed. He's a gangster, and quite ruthless.'

'What makes you think he's the one who had me lifted?' asked Rosa.

'The allegation was put forward by your friend Pat Riley. Riley claims that Buttons paid two of his men, the ones who took you prisoner, to do it to cover up Buttons's part in the murder of Benny Martin.'

'Why would this Shelley Buttons want to kill Benny?' asked Rosa.

'At the moment we have no idea if there was a motive. Buttons denies having anything to do with Benny, or with the two men who abducted you. If he's telling the truth, then the finger points back to Pat Riley.'

'And if Buttons is lying?'

'That's what we're trying to find out at the moment. The trouble is that Buttons operates by striking fear into people, which means there's a kind of wall of silence among people who know him.'

'It sounds like you're dealing with some pretty dangerous people,' observed Magnus.

'It goes with the job,' said Coburg. 'Among the things I haven't been able to tell you over the phone is that there have been two more murders.'

'More?' said Rosa. 'Since the two men who abducted me were shot?'

'Yes. Another man who worked as a volunteer fireman, Dan Reeves, and Benny's sister, Alice Martin. Ted Lampson and I found her beaten to death.'

'How horrible!' said Rosa. 'Do you know who did it? Was it the same person who killed Benny and those other two men, and this Dan Reeves?'

'I don't know,' admitted Coburg. 'I suspect it's someone different because of the way Alice was killed. I'm hoping we might find out who did quite quickly.

We found the murder weapon and I've asked our technical people to check it for fingerprints. We also have a man in custody as a suspect for the shootings. I'm waiting for a ballistics test back on a gun we found in his possession.' He gave Rosa an apologetic smile. 'I'm afraid that's why I have to return to London first thing tomorrow, to get the results of all these tests.'

'So this really *is* a flying visit,' said Rosa.

'I'm afraid so,' said Coburg. 'But if it means we can get you home quicker, I think it's worth it.'

'Do you really think that Pat Riley's behind all this?' asked Rosa. 'The murder of Benny, shooting dead these three men, and beating Benny's sister to death?'

'That's my gut feeling,' said Coburg. 'But at the moment I can't prove it, and I'm having difficulty finding out where the proof may be.'

'I still can't believe it,' said Rosa. 'I've known Pat for a couple of years. I've appeared at his club. He always struck me as honest and decent.'

'A lot of crooks do on face value. Con men and con women especially cultivate that, and get other people to believe that's who they are.' He shrugged. 'But I could be wrong about him. I've been wrong before.'

Magnus pushed his empty plate away, obviously satisfied with what he'd eaten.

'Mrs Hilton has done us proud at short notice,' he said. He looked enquiringly at Coburg. 'Edgar, do you fancy a game of billiards? It's been years since you and

I have played a frame, and you never get up here. And with his arm bandaged up, Malcolm is out of action for a game.' He looked at Rosa and added, 'With your permission, of course, my dear. I know you want to spend time with your husband on your own, but it's such a rarity to have my brother here at the Hall. If you wouldn't mind.'

Rosa smiled. 'You have my permission. Providing I can watch. I promise not to put you off. I know what a hallowed place a billiard room is; my father used to play at a billiard hall in Edinburgh and he had special dispensation to allow me to go in and watch him. While I was small, that is. Once I became a teenager, I was officially a woman and so barred.' She looked at them and asked, 'What is it about billiard halls that women aren't allowed in?'

'I don't know,' said Magnus. 'But I have to admit it was the same in the army: women weren't allowed in the billiard room. I remember my wife wanting to see me urgently and tried to come in, but she was refused entry.'

'What was the urgency?'

'Our mother was dying,' said Magnus. 'Fortunately, Estelle was made of strong stuff. Her father had been a brigadier so she knew how to handle people in the army. She simply pushed the man aside and stormed into the billiard room. She'd got a telegram urging me to come home at once.' He looked at Coburg. 'You weren't around that night, were you?'

'No. I was still at school.'

'Charles was here at the Hall,' said Magnus. 'It was he who'd sent the telegram.' He shook his head sadly. 'I'm afraid by the time I arrived, poor Mother had gone. Father was away somewhere abroad.'

'I remember I came up from Eton very early the next morning,' said Coburg. 'Charles sent a car that night for me, but the driver had difficulty in persuading the school authorities that I could leave. Fortunately, my housemaster stepped into the situation and got me an exeat.'

Magnus stood up. 'Come on, let's put these unhappy memories behind us for the moment and play on the baize. I'll set them up.'

As Magnus walked out of the room and headed for the billiard room, Rosa laid her hand gently on Coburg's. 'It sound ridiculous to say this when you grew up surrounded by all this luxury, but you had it tough as a kid, didn't you? You father away most of the time. Brought up at school rather than at home.'

'I was lucky in Charles,' said Coburg, squeezing her hand. 'He was five years older than me, but he became my father substitute. He really took care of me, as much as he could.' He got up. 'Come on, let's go and you can watch Magnus thrash me at billiards.'

'That's a defeatist attitude to start with,' said Rosa.

'You haven't seen Magnus at work with a cue,' said Coburg with a rueful smile.

Coburg's prediction about him losing to Magnus at billiards became evident during the frame, as Magnus – who won the toss to break – made a series of cannons off the red and Coburg's white ball, interspersed with potting the red and in-offs of both the red and Coburg's non-spot white. He'd run up a break of seventy-five before Coburg was able to get off the bench and approach the table. Coburg knew it was lost before he'd even addressed his first shot because they'd agreed before the game to limit the winning score to one hundred points, but he sat down pleased at having scored thirty, especially as it had been a very long time since he'd picked up a cue. Magnus then returned to the table and polished off the game with break of twenty-six.

'Another?' asked Magnus.

'No thanks.' Coburg smiled. 'One thrashing has been enough, and it's been a long and stressful day.'

As Coburg and Rosa made their way to bed, Rosa commented, 'Magnus is very good at billiards.'

'He ought to be,' said Coburg. 'He plays almost every other day, one of the advantages of having his own billiard table. But Charles was better.'

'Really?'

'Yes. Eight times out of ten, Charles would beat Magnus.'

'Did you ever play him?'

'Rarely. Whenever I did, he always won. Except once. But I'm pretty sure he let me win. The only time Charles ever made a foul was when he played me.'

'I wish I'd known him,' said Rosa. 'He meant a lot to you, didn't he?'

'He did,' said Coburg. He gave a sigh. 'I was looking forward to seeing him again when this was all over and introducing you to him.' He smiled at her. 'And that's the difference between Charles and Magnus. Charles would have let you beat him at billiards; Magnus, never.'

CHAPTER THIRTY

Sunday 8th December 1940

The following morning, Coburg enjoyed a hearty breakfast with Rosa and Magnus before leaving for London. He drove straight to Scotland Yard, arriving just after eleven, keen to get the reports on the gun and the murder weapon.

'Ah, you're here,' said John Wise when Coburg walked into the technical department. 'I wondered if you'd be in today.'

'Why wouldn't I be?' asked Coburg.

'Superintendent Allison phoned first thing this morning to tell me that your wife had been involved in shooting down a German bomber and you'd had to go and see her. He thought you might have to be with her, depending on her injuries.'

'She had no injuries,' said Coburg, doing his best to hide his annoyance at this wrong story circulating. 'A German bomber crashed near to where she was staying, that's all. Did you get any fingerprints from that statuette I brought in yesterday?'

'We found some partials, but it's taking us some

258

time to go through the records and find a match.' He gave Coburg a rueful look. 'If the person who wielded it has never been arrested, we may not find one.'

'See what you can do,' said Coburg. 'I'll keep my fingers crossed. So far most of the people we've come across in this case have been involved with the police in some way. What about the gun we brought in? Have you got the ballistics report on it?'

'It's already been taken,' said John Wise.

'Who by?' asked Coburg.

'Inspector Bedford. He's duty inspector for the day. He came and asked for it at ten o'clock this morning.'

'Why?'

'Apparently he had some solicitor on his back.'

'What did the report say? Were all the bullets from the same gun?'

'No,' said Wise. 'The bullets we took from the bodies of Punt, Maples and Reeves were from a different gun to the one that Sergeant Lampson and you brought in.'

Coburg made his way to Inspector Bedford's office. 'Coburg,' said Bedford in surprise. 'They told me you weren't coming in today. Something about your wife getting injured shooting down a German bomber.'

Coburg groaned. Where did these stories some

from? 'No, she wasn't injured, and she didn't shoot it down. But it crashed right by her and she shot one of the German pilots.'

'Good for her!' said Bedford approvingly.

'John Wise in ballistics said you came and took the report on the gun and the bullets.'

'Yes,' said Bedford. 'I had this solicitor in first thing demanding I let his client go. A Joe Barker. He said there was no evidence to keep him. I took a look at the file on Barker and it said you were waiting for the ballistics report. So I went to ballistics and got the report, and it said there was no match. So I had to let Barker go.'

Coburg groaned. 'I still had questions to ask him, the main one being: how did he know Reeves was cheating them?'

'Them?' Bedford frowned. Then his face cleared. 'Oh yeah, the auxiliary fire crew.'

'Yes,' said Coburg, frustrated. 'I needed to know who Dan Reeves's fence was, and Joe Barker seems to be the only one who knows.'

'There wasn't anything about that in the report,' said Bedford. 'Not that I saw, anyway. And this solicitor was talking about suing us for wrongful arrest and imprisonment.' He looked appealingly at Coburg. 'It was a Sunday morning. You weren't here, nor was DS Lampson. There were no senior officers in, no superintendents.'

'I said I'd be in later this morning,' persisted Coburg. 'Again, there was nothing to say that in the report. There was a note left in the file to say you'd been called away because your wife had been caught up in a bombing raid.' Coburg sighed. 'Okay,' he said, resigned. 'We can pick Barker up. We've got his address. I assume he went home?'

Bedford shrugged. 'I've no idea. I signed the forms and he went off with his solicitor.'

'Who was his solicitor?'

Bedford looked through the file and found the release documents. 'Peter Winstanley of Cooper and Lettice, solicitors, Fetter Lane.'

'Fetter Lane?' Coburg frowned. 'Barker told me he didn't have a solicitor of his own and we were arranging for a duty solicitor from the pool to come in and represent him. And now he's got a legal firm from the City of London representing him.'

'Which he did, arriving first thing this morning,' said Bedford. 'It's the luck of the draw with duty solicitors. He could have ended up with some lame duck from the back of beyond, but instead he gets a hotshot from the City.'

Coburg drove to the address they had for Joe Barker, but there was no answer to his knock. He tried a neighbour, who told him that – as far as he knew – Joe hadn't returned home. 'At least, I haven't seen him.'

Being a Sunday, Coburg knew it was a waste of time trying to make contact with Peter Winstanley or anyone at Cooper and Lettice; that would have to wait until Monday morning. Which left one option open to him: Lord Cuddington.

He returned to Scotland Yard and telephoned the Cuddingtons' home. The man who answered the phone identified himself simply as 'Cuddington' in a curt tone of voice. 'Lord Cuddington, my name is Detective Chief Inspector Coburg from Scotland Yard. We are currently investigating the murder of a young man called Benny Martin, and information we've received suggests that you may have some knowledge of the young man that may be of help to us in our enquiries.'

'I don't know him,' snapped Cuddington.

'Nevertheless, Lord Cuddington, I would like to call on you to discuss the situation.'

'On a Sunday?' barked Cuddington. 'Absolutely not.'

'You would prefer a weekday?' asked Coburg calmly.

'No. I would prefer not to be involved at all. Goodbye.' With that, the phone was hung up.

Coburg contacted the operator, and asked to be connected to the number again. When Cuddington picked up the phone and heard Coburg's voice, he snapped, 'Didn't you hear what I said?'

'I did, very clearly, and I wish to make clear to you that if you continue to refuse to meet with me it will result in a warrant being issued and you will be brought to Scotland Yard under police escort. The press, who are always here hanging around looking for stories, will undoubtedly be interested and will ask why you have been brought in, and they will be told it is part of an enquiry into the murder of a young man.'

'You . . . you dare to link my name with such a thing in the press!' burst out Cuddington.

'That is entirely up to you,' said Coburg. 'I can come and see you now and our meeting will be conducted out of the public gaze. Or you can refuse, and I'll send a police escort, with a warrant, to bring you to Scotland Yard.'

There was a pause, then the angry, strangled voice of Cuddington grated through clenched teeth, 'Alright, damn you. Come over. But this is a private meeting.'

'On the contrary, Lord Cuddington, although it may be conducted in private, it will be an official meeting.'

As Coburg drove to the Cuddingtons' residence in Knightsbridge, he wondered if Pamela would be there. He hoped not, but as nothing had happened between them at their last meeting, he felt it was something he could deal with. It was Cuddington himself who answered the door to Coburg's ringing of the doorbell, rather than a servant as Coburg had expected. Coburg followed Cuddington into a luxuriously furnished living room, where both men sat down.

'I know who you are.' Cuddington scowled. 'The former fiancé. War hero. My wife's first and only true love.' This last delivered with a sneer.

'Twenty years ago,' said Coburg quietly. 'We have not seen one another since.'

'Except at The Dorchester the other night,' said Cuddington with a smirk. 'I pay good money to keep an eye on her. Generous gratuities to the staff at The Dorchester, where she has a hidey hole.'

'I meant romantically,' said Coburg. 'That was the first time in twenty years we had met, and it was in a public tea room.'

'You mean you didn't shag her?' sneered Cuddington.

'There was no sexual contact between us at all,' said Coburg. 'I went there at her request over concerns she had about a murder case we are investigating.'

'The gigolo, Martin,' said Cuddington.

'The young jazz guitarist Benny Martin,' Coburg corrected him. 'Whether he was also a gigolo we have yet to establish.'

Cuddington scowled, then gestured for Coburg to sit down. 'Ask your questions,' he said surlily.

'Where were you on the night of Monday 2nd December?'

'I was here, at home.'

'Are there any witnesses who can support that?'

'Yes. Lord and Lady Winston. Sir Stamford Pereira. Mrs Edwina Brett. I had invited them to dinner. Nothing grand, just dinner for a few friends.'

'What time were they here from?'

'They arrived at about six. Dinner was served straight away in case we were interrupted by an air raid.'

'There was an air raid that night,' said Coburg. 'In fact, a series of raids.'

'There were,' said Cuddington.

'What time did your guests leave?'

'Lord and Lady Winston left about eight o'clock, along with Sir Stamford. Although the cellar here has been reinforced to withstand bombing, they preferred to go to their own houses.'

'And Mrs Brett?'

Cuddington smirked. 'She decided to stay. She left the following morning at approximately eleven.' His smirk grew even broader as he added, 'She's a widow. And a very attractive one.'

'I assume your wife wasn't here?'

'You assume correctly.'

'Do you know where she was?'

'I have no idea.'

'You said you pay good money to be kept informed of her movements.'

'True, and I can tell you she was not at The Dorchester that night.'

'What was your opinion of Benny Martin?'

'He was a money-grabbing gigolo who'd attached himself to my wife. Or, my wife had attached herself to him.'

'Your wife told me you threatened to kill him.'

'Why on earth would I do that?' asked Cuddington. 'If I killed every man my wife has been shagging, the streets of London would be deep in dead bodies.'

'You're saying your wife lied?'

'Of course she lied. She always lies. Whatever she's told you, I'd take with a very large pinch of salt.'

'So you had no part in the death of Benny Martin?'

'None at all.'

'We have reports of you getting into a fight with him at a jazz club.'

'Oh that!' he said dismissively. 'I forget what it was about, just that the little weasel and her Whoreness had gone too far. I was provoked. That's all. There wasn't even a fight, just raised voices and a flapping of hands.' He looked at his watch. 'Is that all? Only I'm meeting someone shortly.'

'Almost,' said Coburg. 'We've also received information suggesting that some of your activities are in breach of the Criminal Law Amendment Act 1885.'

Cuddington stared at him. 'What on earth are you talking about? What activities?'

'Relations with other men.'

Cuddington stared at him, then rose to his feet. 'How dare you?!' he said, outraged.

'May I take that as a denial?' asked Coburg.

'You bloody may!' burst out Cuddington. 'Where did you get this filth from?' Then his eyes narrowed and he said, 'This is from Pamela, isn't it? That lying bitch trying to stitch me up. Well, if she's using that tactic to try to get a divorce, she's barking up the wrong tree.'

'If things are as bad between you as you both claim, why don't you divorce?' asked Coburg, curious.

'And give that bitch half of everything I own?' said Cuddington. 'Along with having our private lives splashed all over the common press. Not a chance!'

CHAPTER THIRTY-ONE

Sunday 8th December 1940

When Coburg got back to the Yard, he found a note waiting for him on his desk from John Wise: *Fingerprints identified*, it said. *I'll be in the lab with the results*.

Coburg hurried along to the technical lab, full of expectation. At last, they had a breakthrough!

'I got your note,' he said when he entered the lab. 'Who is it?'

'A Lady Pamela Cuddington,' said Wise.

Coburg stared at him, stunned. 'Are you sure?' he asked.

'I am,' said Wise. 'The search took longer than we hoped because although she'd been arrested a few times, she'd never actually been charged with a crime. But the fingerprints on that statuette are definitely hers.'

Coburg returned to his office, his mind in a whirl at this revelation, and telephoned The Dorchester.

'It's DCI Coburg from Scotland Yard,' he told the receptionist. 'Is Lady Cuddington still resident there at this moment?'

'She is indeed, sir,' said the receptionist. 'Do you wish to be put through to her suite?'

'No thank you. However, if she prepares to leave for any reason, even for just a short time, would you mind asking her to stay for a few moments. Tell her DCI Coburg needs to talk to her urgently.'

'Certainly, Mr Coburg.'

Coburg made out the arrest warrant, then went to the duty office and arranged for a couple of WPCs to accompany him. A short, tough-looking woman in her forties, WPC Amanda Barclay, and a tall younger woman in her twenties, WPC Marion Daly, were assigned to him.

'Good to meet you, ladies,' said Coburg after he'd been introduced to them by the duty sergeant. 'We've never worked together before.'

'No, sir, but we know who you are,' said Barclay.

'We are going to The Dorchester hotel to make an arrest,' said Coburg. 'The person we are arresting is a Lady Pamela Cuddington.'

'On what charge, sir?' asked Daly.

'Murder. She is accused of beating another woman to death. We have strong evidence that points to her as the culprit. She is quite a volatile person, so she might resist. If she does, I want you to be prepared to join me in subduing her.'

'Yes, sir.' Barclay patted the truncheon fixed to her belt. 'I'm ready.'

'I'm hoping it won't be necessary to hit her,' said Coburg. 'If you have to, concentrate on her arms. Do your best to avoid her head. We don't want a situation where she suffers severe brain damage during the arrest.'

'Don't worry, sir,' said Barclay grimly. 'I've had to deal with a few tough people in my time. And not just women.' She flexed her clenched right fist at him. 'There are a few people who've had this in their gut and given up. And Daly here knows her way around a mêlée.'

'Good,' said Coburg. 'Let's go.'

On their arrival at The Dorchester, Coburg enquired if Lady Cuddington was still in. On being told she was, he and the two women police constables took the lift up to the second floor and made their way to her suite.

Coburg knocked at the door. When Pamela Cuddington opened it and saw Coburg standing there, her face lit up with delight.

'Edgar, darling!' she exclaimed. Then she saw the two uniformed women police constables standing behind him and she looked at Coburg in bewilderment.

'What's happening?' she asked. 'What's going on?'

'Lady Cuddington, I am arresting you for the murder of Alice Martin. You do not have to say anything, but anything you do say—'

Before he could finish, she attempted to kick the

door shut in his face, but Coburg had anticipated this and blocked it with his foot.

Pamela ran into the suite and picked up a rolled umbrella, which she brandished at them, point first.

'Constables,' said Coburg, 'do your duty.'

Barclay and Daly entered the suite, Barclay taking the truncheon from her belt, and Daly a pair of handcuffs from hers. Pamela rushed at them, levelling the umbrella like a sword. Barclay stepped to the side and smashed her truncheon down on the umbrella. The force of the blow not only knocked the umbrella from Pamela's grasp, it caused her to stumble and fall to the carpet. The two WPCs moved in on her, but she rolled away and, snatching up a heavy brass ornament from beside the dresser, she scrambled to her feet and launched an attack on them with it, swinging it wildly. Again, Barclay dodged nimbly to one side, then sank a fierce punch into Pamela's stomach.

Pamela tumbled to the floor, doubled up and gasping for breath. Immediately, the two WPCs fell on her and twisted her arms behind her back, where Daly snapped the handcuffs on her.

'Shall we tie her ankles together, sir?' asked Barclay.

Coburg looked at Pamela, sitting on the floor, her face twisted in rage.

That depends on you, Lady Cuddington,' said Coburg. 'Do you wish to be tied up and carried through the lobby for everyone to see, or will you walk between the two constables out of the hotel and to the car?'

'With these bloody things on?!' spat Pamela.

'A necessity, I'm afraid, in view of your reaction,' said Coburg. 'But we can avoid tying your ankles together and lugging you out if you agree to offer no further resistance. It's up to you.'

Pamela struggled to her feet, her face still contorted with rage.

'You bastard!' she shouted at Coburg. She turned to the two WPCs, who were waiting silently, watching her alertly for any sudden movements. 'And you two are a pair of . . . !'

'Abusing the officers will only make your situation worse,' said Coburg. He turned to the WPCs. 'Tie her ankles together.'

'No!' shouted Pamela. 'I'll walk, damn you! And may you all rot in hell.'

On their arrival at Scotland Yard, Coburg led the way down to an interview room in the basement, Pamela Cuddington following between the two watchful WPCs, who each held on to one of her arms to stop her making a run for it, or attacking Coburg from behind. Once they were in the interview room, with Coburg and Pamela facing one another across a bare wooden table, with the two WPCs taking their places immediately behind Pamela's chair, Coburg took a statement form from a drawer in the table and set it out before him.

'Lady Pamela Cuddington,' he said, 'you are charged with the murder of Alice Martin in that you beat her to death with a metal statuette in the room where she lived. You are entitled to a solicitor to represent you. If you give me the name of your solicitor, I will remand you to a custody cell and await your solicitor's arrival before continuing this interview.'

She looked at him and sneered. 'You think that's supposed to frighten me? You think it's the first time I've been held in a police cell?' Then she gave him a wicked smile as she said, 'This is a lovely table, Edgar. It reminds me of the one we had sex on at my parents' house. Do you remember? Not actual penetration, you were too conventional for that, but your fingers, my darling! And mine on you!'

Coburg glanced at the two WPCs, who were standing like two statues, their faces inscrutable, although the blush that came to Amanda Daly's cheeks showed her discomfort and embarrassment.

'If you persist in this line of talk about any prior personal contact we may have had, I shall arrange for my detective sergeant to take over the interview,' said Coburg calmly. 'He will not be in until tomorrow, so I shall have you locked up on remand until then.'

Pamela scowled. 'Ask your bloody questions,' she growled.

'Did you kill Alice Martin?' he asked. 'And, before you answer, I have to tell you that we found the murder weapon, a metal statuette of a gorilla, in the garden directly beneath the window in Alice's room. It had her blood, brains and bone on it, as well as your fingerprints.'

She glowered sullenly at him, then said, 'Yes. I killed the bitch.'

'Why?'

'Because she killed Benny. I went to the Riff Club to find out what had happened, and I learnt he'd met his sister there and had a blazing row with her.'

'What about?'

'I don't know. All I know is that she suggested they go somewhere else and sort things out. And that was the last anyone saw of him.' She glared at them. 'She must have poisoned his drink.'

'Was she alone with Benny when they left the club?'

'I was told there was a man with them.'

'Who was the man?'

'I don't know.'

'Who told you this?'

'Pat.'

'Pat Riley?' She nodded. 'He saw them?'

'No, he told me one of his men did.'

'You said before that your husband was the one who killed Benny.'

'That was before I talked to Pat.'

'How did it happen? You killing Alice?'

'I didn't go there intending to kill her,' said Pamela, suddenly aggressively defiant. 'So it wasn't murder. It was self-defence. The proof is that the gorilla statue was in her room. I didn't go there with any weapon. The worst you can get me for is manslaughter.' She gave a sly smile. 'But I won't even get that. Like I said, it was self-defence, and I'll have the best barrister there is when it comes to court. *If* it comes to court.'

'What happened?' Coburg asked again.

'I went to where she lived, his sister, some scummy bedsit in a hovel of a house. I told her she'd been seen leaving the Riff Club with Benny and a man, and that they were the last people to see him alive. I wanted to know what happened.' She looked at Coburg with pursed lips and added, 'I was perfectly polite. Not threatening her in any way.

'She denied it. She admitted she'd seen Benny that night and they'd had a bit of a row, but she said it was over nothing important. She denied leaving the club with him. She said he went off on his own. I asked her who the man was she was with and she said it was none of my business. She then told me to get out.

'I told her I wasn't going until she'd told me who the man was. She started swearing at me, telling me it was nothing to do with me. She called me an old tart. She said I was disgusting, and a lot worse. She then threatened me.'

'How?'

'She said her boyfriend would be coming at any moment, and he'd beat me up and throw me out. So I told her in that case I was going to the police and I'd bring them back with me and they'd pick up both her and this boyfriend of hers. As I was making for the door, she suddenly came at me. She'd picked up this gorilla statuette from somewhere in her room and she swung it at me. She missed and it dropped out of her hand. She went to grab it up, but I beat her to it. Then she came for me again, trying to get hold of it, trying to scratch at my eyes. So I hit her with it.

'She went down, but then pushed herself up and came for me again. She was like a madwoman, so I had to hit her again. This time I carried on hitting her; I was terrified she'd get up and come for me again. Then I realised . . .' She stopped and lowered her head, before mumbling, 'I realised she wasn't moving any more.'

'You realised she was dead?' asked Coburg.

Pamela looked up at him with anger glaring in her eyes. 'No! I just knew I'd stopped her killing me. I thought she might be . . . badly injured. The statuette was covered in blood and bits of brain and bone. It was disgusting. I opened the window and threw it out, shut the window again, and then I left.' She looked at him defiantly. 'So, it wasn't murder. It was self-defence.'

* * *

Coburg arranged for Pamela to be taken to Holloway prison to be held on remand, and he also arranged for a duty solicitor to attend her. 'Although I expect she'll appoint someone she chooses,' he told the legal duty office. 'But we need to be seen to go through the motions.'

After Pamela had been taken away, Coburg turned to the two WPCs, Barclay and Daly, who he'd asked to stay behind.

'Good work today, both of you,' he said. 'I shall put in a report recommending both of you.'

'Thank you, sir,' said Barclay.

Coburg hesitated, then added, 'The suspect said some things of a personal nature that were inappropriate. They may or may not come up in court as evidence, depending on her solicitor. I'd appreciate it if you'd keep those comments she made to yourselves unless you are asked in court about them. In which case, obviously, you have a duty to report what was said.'

'You can rely on us, sir,' said Barclay firmly. 'We didn't hear anything,' added Daly.

Oh yes you did, thought Coburg wryly, *and you'll be telling your pals what she said. That's what I would have done when I was a young beat copper.*

CHAPTER THIRTY-TWO

Sunday 8th December 1940

Coburg's next move, following Lady Pamela Cuddington being taken to Holloway prison to be held on remand, was a return visit to Lord Cuddington's house. This time the butler answered his pressing the doorbell.

'Detective Chief Inspector Coburg from Scotland Yard,' said Coburg. 'I'd like to see Lord Cuddington.'

'If you wait here, I'll see if His Lordship is available,' said the butler.

Coburg put his foot in the doorway to stop the butler shutting the door on him.

'Would you tell him it's very important?' he said.

The butler didn't reply, just gave him an icy look, then disappeared into the house. A couple of minutes later, Cuddington appeared.

'What the hell do you want?' he demanded. 'I thought we'd finished our business.'

'I'm here to tell you that your wife has been arrested for murder,' said Coburg.

Cuddington stared at him, stunned, his mouth

opening and closing silently like a fish.

'M . . . murder?' he stammered. 'Who is she supposed to have murdered?' Then his gaze hardened as he said, 'That gigolo? The guitarist?'

'His sister,' said Coburg.

'Oh my God,' said Cuddington, obviously shaken. 'This will ruin me!'

'I doubt if it will do your wife's reputation much good,' commented Coburg drily. He looked along the street towards a couple who were walking towards them, then asked, 'Do you want to talk about it here, in public, where everyone can hear, or would you prefer to discuss it inside?'

Cuddington stood aside, growling, 'Come in, if you must, goddammit.'

Coburg entered the house and followed Cuddington along the corridor, then into the living room where the two men had been earlier. Cuddington gestured for Coburg to take a seat, then walked to the sideboard where he poured himself a generous measure of whisky.

'Do you want one?' he asked Coburg.

'No thank you,' replied Coburg.

Cuddington sat down, nursing the glass of whisky. 'This is a disaster,' he groaned. 'Will it be in the papers?'

'That depends on you,' said Coburg.

'What do you mean?' asked Cuddington

suspiciously. 'I have no intention of contacting the press with this story. If you have a good solicitor to represent her, he might be able to block any such attempts to publish it, claiming the matter is *sub judice* as it might prejudice a trial.'

'What about her own solicitor?' asked Cuddington.

'I asked her about that, but she refused to have me contact one for her.'

'Yes, she would,' said Cuddington bitterly. 'Anything to make me look bad in the eyes of my business associates.'

'Does she have a solicitor of her own?' asked Coburg. 'I've no idea,' said Cuddington. He gave a rueful sigh.

'But they'll all come crawling out of the woodwork once word about this gets around. They can scent money, those bloody parasites.' Then a thought struck him, and he said, 'If she's found guilty, I'll be able to divorce her, won't I? And without paying her a penny!'

'That depends on the solicitor she chooses,' said Coburg. 'Now, if you instructed your own solicitor to defend her, you might benefit.'

Cuddington regarded Coburg with wary suspicion. 'Whose side are you on?' he demanded. 'I would have thought you'd be on her side.'

'I'm on the side of justice,' said Coburg. 'In this case, seeing that your wife gets a fair trial. I've arranged for a duty solicitor to call on her at Holloway prison, but, in my opinion, she'll be better represented by your family solicitor.'

'Yes, good point,' mused Cuddington thoughtfully.

'You haven't asked me how she came to be charged,' Coburg pointed out.

This remark made Cuddington startle. 'How did she?' he asked. 'Did someone say she ought to be a suspect?'

'Benny Martin's sister, Alice, was beaten to death in the room where she lived,' said Coburg. 'The weapon, a metal statuette, was found beneath the window of Alice Martin's room. Our forensic experts found your wife's fingerprints on it, along with Alice Martin's blood, brains and bone. Your wife confessed to killing Alice but claimed it was in self-defence. That Alice was trying to kill her with the same weapon.' He stood up. 'That's what I came to tell you, Lord Cuddington. I will leave it to you how you act in this matter. If you choose not to, the duty solicitor, whoever it is, will proceed with her defence.'

'I'll get hold of my man and send him along to Holloway,' said Cuddington. 'Can you pull this duty solicitor character off?'

'If you'll allow me to use your telephone, I'll make contact with the office now and prevent him going.'

'The phone's in the hall,' said Cuddington.

Coburg followed Cuddington out to the hallway,

where he picked up the phone and asked to be connected to Scotland Yard's duty solicitor's office. He knew that as it was a Sunday, the duty solicitor wouldn't be heading for Holloway until the next day, but the sooner he could stop the machinery working, the better. Like Cuddington, he didn't want this story finding its way into the newspapers, especially with Pamela very capable of gleefully telling the reporters about her engagement to Coburg and her sex life with him. In truth, their teenage sexual activity of what was called 'petting' would make very tame reading, but as he was a senior Scotland Yard detective the reporters would turn it into something almost pornographic, especially in the salacious columns of the *News of the World*.

Coburg's final visit of the day was to the Riff Club. The forlorn figure of DC Pritchard was on duty at the end of Wardour Mews, obviously fed up.

'This is a waste of time, sir,' he told Coburg. 'He goes in and he doesn't come out except to go home. He doesn't use his car, which is parked outside his house. He walks from his club to Charing Cross Road, where he catches a bus to Warren Street and walks to his house in Fitzroy Square. Once he's in there, he doesn't come out. We've got a room arranged in a house opposite, so one of us is there all the time. We've got three of us working eight-hour shifts so we're keeping watch on him twenty-four hours, day and night.'

'Companions?' asked Coburg.

'Sometimes a taxi arrives with a young woman who goes into the house. She stays there for a couple of hours, then a taxi arrives to pick her up and take her away again. She never stays the night. No one stays the night.' Pritchard gestured towards the door of the Riff Club. 'That's the only way in or out. The club backs onto other buildings, so there's no rear entrance.'

'And he doesn't come out once he's gone into the club?'

'Only to go round the corner to that coffee bar, Di Angelo's. He sits and has his coffee and reads the paper, then he comes back here.' He gave Coburg a look of appeal. 'It's a dead end, sir.'

'I know, and I sympathise,' said Coburg. 'But I've got a gut feeling about Riley. He's involved in these murders in some way, if only we can find a way to prove it. You're still making a list of who else goes in and out of the club?'

'Yes, sir. It's always in the report we put in.'

'Then keep it up. I know it's frustrating for you and the rest of your team, but sooner or later I feel he's going to make a slip. I'm about to go and see him now, Constable, so I expect to see my name on that list when it lands on my desk tomorrow.'

'It'll be there, sir,' Pritchard assured him.

Coburg made his way to the Riff Club, where he descended to the club floor itself, and a few moments later was sitting in Riley's office with the club owner.

'Any developments, Chief Inspector?' asked Riley. 'Have you found out who killed Benny yet? Or Henry and Wally?'

'Those investigations are still ongoing,' said Coburg.

'How much longer are you going to keep your boys watching me?' asked Riley. 'They don't even hide. There's always one parking himself at the corner of the Mews, then one's on my tail following me home, and in the morning when I head for work there's another one trailing after me. Surely by now you must know that I'm not guilty of anything? I'm just a businessman going about his routine to earn a living.'

'You might call it protective duty,' said Coburg. 'Keeping you safe. You said yourself that Shelley Buttons was a dangerous man and he's been leaning on you.'

'I can look after myself when it comes to Buttons,' said Riley. 'I heard that you picked him up, but you let him go. Why?'

'Your information's wrong, he's still in custody', said Coburg. 'Have you heard about the other murders?'

'What other murders?' asked Riley. 'How would I? I'm either here or at home.'

'You heard about Shelley Buttons being lifted.'

'Well, yeah, I hear things, but only related to the club scene.'

'Another man has been found dead in the tunnels near Aldwych. He'd been shot.'

'Where Benny was found?'

Coburg nodded.

'Who was he? Anyone I know?'

'I don't know. His name was Dan Reeves.'

Riley shook his head. 'Doesn't ring any bells. Who was he?'

'He was an auxiliary fireman.'

Riley looked puzzled. 'Who'd want to shoot a fireman?'

'The other one who's been murdered recently is Alice Martin, Benny's sister. She was beaten to death.'

Riley stared at Coburg, stunned. 'Benny's sister?' When Coburg nodded, Riley asked, 'Is it connected to what happened to Benny?'

'That's what we're trying to find out. Lady Pamela Cuddington told us that you told her you saw Alice here at the club on the night he was killed, and he left the club that night with her and another man. You didn't tell us that when we talked to you.'

'I didn't know about it then,' said Riley. 'I didn't even know Benny's sister was here that night. It was Henry Punt who told me he saw Benny going off with his sister and some other bloke.'

'How did Punt know she was Benny's sister?'

'One of the other musicians told Henry. Apparently, Benny had told this other musician that Alice was his sister.'

'You didn't think to tell us this?'

'I didn't know how true it was. And by that time, Henry was dead.'

'But you told Pamela Cuddington.'

Riley gave him a rueful look. 'She was in here, bending my ear and demanding to know everything that happened that night. She was getting very uptight, and when she gets uptight things get thrown around. She's got a very short fuse. So I told her what Henry had told me.' He shrugged. 'That was it.'

Coburg left the club and commiserated with DC Pritchard, who was still at his post at the edge of Wardour Mews, then headed home.

Inside the flat, he made himself a sandwich and poured himself a drink of whiskey, choosing a smooth Irish to bring a little bit of Rosa into the otherwise empty flat. He then put on one of Rosa's records just to hear her voice, while he mulled over the events of the day. On one level it had been a successful day: the murder of Alice Martin had been solved and her murderess was under lock and key. But, overall, he felt it had been a failure. They were still no nearer to finding out who had killed Benny Martin, Henry Punt, Wally Maples and Dan Reeves. Punt and Maples had been found in the canal, but the bodies of Benny and Reeves had both been dumped at the same place, in the tunnel off Aldwych station. Whoever was doing it knew those tunnels like the back of their hand. For Coburg, this effectively eliminated Shelley Buttons. Buttons had arrived from Birmingham where Coburg was sure he knew every nook and cranny, tunnels, canals, back alleys and rat runs, but he wouldn't have an in-depth knowledge of the tunnels that ran beneath central London. By all accounts, Buttons's men were all people he'd brought with him from Birmingham, so the same would apply to them.

The only person they knew for certain had a real knowledge of the tunnel was Percy Wenlock, the maintenance man, but although Wenlock had admitted knowing Dan Reeves, they'd found no connection of any sort between Wenlock and Benny Martin.

The person who connected Benny Martin with Punt and Maples was, of course, Pat Riley. And it was now known that Alice Martin had been in Riley's club on the night that Benny was killed.

Alice had said she'd been in the club that night with a man called Alan, but Coburg had his doubts. There were the love letters she'd sent to Dan Reeves. Didn't that suggest that if she'd been there with a man that night, it could well have been Dan Reeves, but she wouldn't want to name him in case that got him into trouble with the police?

The record had stopped, but instead of putting on

another, Coburg ran through the scenario in his mind: Alice and a man had been at the Riff Club and Alice had got into a row with Benny, but later Alice, Benny and the man were reported to have left the club together, Benny leaving his guitar behind with Pat Riley as security for the loan of fifty pounds. Why had Alice gone to the club when she'd been firm that she didn't like jazz? Her dislike of jazz had been confirmed by Benny saying to Sam Watson: 'What's she doing here? She hates jazz.' So if Alice hadn't been there for the music, what was she doing at the club? The man had taken her there, and if this man had been Dan Reeves, then the glaringly obvious reason was to sell jewellery that AFS Crew 127 had stolen. Dan Reeves had been the fire crew's man who sold on the jewellery to a fence. So Reeves had been there that night to sell to his fence. But if his fence was just an ordinary customer of the club, there would be no guarantee that he would be there to do business with Reeves; that would mean the fence was someone who was there permanently and always available.

Pat Riley, thought Coburg. Everything pointed to Pat Riley, except for the fact that he had the perfect alibi for when the murder of Dan Reeves took place: he was under close watch by Coburg's own detectives. But that didn't stop Riley from being the one who arranged the murder, got the message out to someone. And whoever that person was, it was someone who had an in-depth knowledge of the tunnels around Aldwych.

CHAPTER THIRTY-THREE

Monday 9th December 1940

Monday morning found Lampson waiting for Coburg outside his terraced house in Somers Town, as was their regular routine. On this occasion, Lampson was keen to find out what had happened during the weekend, and asked, 'Is everything alright, guv?'

'I think we're closing in on our murderer,' replied Coburg. 'All we need is the proof.'

'I meant with your missus,' said Lampson.

'With Rosa?' asked Coburg, puzzled.

'There's this pal of mine at Somers Town nick, and he had to take some stuff to Scotland Yard yesterday, and he heard that your missus had shot down a German bomber and you'd had to go to her.'

'This is unbelievable,' Coburg groaned.

'So she didn't?'

'Rosa was involved in a situation with a German bomber crash-landing next to Dawlish Hall on Saturday evening. Two of the Germans attempted to escape from the crashed plane, shooting at my brother and his butler, before they took Magnus's Bentley from his garage. Rosa shot the windscreen out and hit one of the Germans, and they were both arrested. She phoned me to tell me what had happened, and I had the superintendent's permission to go to Dawlish on Saturday night to make sure she was alright. She was, and I came back to London yesterday morning and spent the day working on the case.'

'She shot them?' said Lampson, awed.

'She shot the car and wounded one of them. She did *not* shoot down a German bomber.'

'Bloody hell, guv, your wife is some woman. She gets shot taking on some spies. She stops your brother being killed by beating up his would-be assassins. And now she captures some Nazi pilots.'

'She *helped* capture them,' Coburg corrected him.

'But still . . .' said Lampson, still awed. 'She shot the windscreen. Of a moving car! What is she, some Dead-Eye Dick?'

'It was a lucky shot,' said Coburg. 'Anyway, how was your Sunday with Terry?'

'Not as exciting as yours. We went to the park for a kickabout with the football team. Next Saturday's my Saturday off and we've got a match lined up with the boys from King's Cross Methodist Chapel. We're getting quite a bit of interest from other boys' organisations: Scouts, Cubs, church choirs. We might even be able to get a league going. Somers Town District.'

'And is Miss Bradley still able to help?'

Lampson chuckled. 'She's great. She keeps the boys in line. No one messes about when she's around.'

'Any romantic interest there?' asked Coburg.

Lampson hesitated before answering with an awkward, 'Maybe. Maybe not.'

'You haven't asked her out, then?'

'It's difficult, with her being Terry's teacher. You can imagine the ribbing he'd get from the other boys if they thought his dad was going out with his teacher. I thought I'd wait and see how it goes.'

'What, until the war's over?' Coburg asked with a smile.

'In a year's time, Terry will be moving up to the big school. That might be the time.'

Coburg shook his head. 'Don't wait, Ted,' he advised. 'There's a war on. Anything could happen in a year. She might meet someone else who hasn't got the same reservations you have and be gone.'

'Yes, well, I'm going to see how it goes,' said Lampson. 'Anyway, how did you get on yesterday? You said you were busy on the case.'

'The big news is that we found the murder weapon that Alice Martin was beaten to death with, and there were fingerprints on it.'

'Whose?'

'Lady Pamela Cuddington.'

'Blimey!' exclaimed Lampson. 'Where is she?'

'In Holloway, on remand. I've charged her.'

'Did she say why she did it?'

'She thinks Alice killed Benny so she went round to Alice's to confront her. According to Lady Pamela, Alice attacked her with a metal statuette, so she took it off Alice and beat her to stop her.'

Lampson scoffed. 'Do you believe that?'

'It's not up to us to believe it,' said Coburg. 'We'll charge her with murder and she'll stand trial, but it's what her barrister gets a jury to believe. And, knowing the sort of barrister her husband can afford, it wouldn't surprise me to find she either gets off, or is found guilty of manslaughter.'

'And they say you can't buy justice,' snorted Lampson cynically.

'The other thing is that Joe Barker was released yesterday before I got back to the Yard, so he's back on the street.'

'Released?' said Lampson, outraged. 'Without consulting us?'

'Barker's solicitor put pressure on the duty inspector, and unfortunately I wasn't there to stop it.'

'What about Shelley Buttons? Did his solicitor do the same, move in as soon as he knew you weren't there and get him out of jail?'

'As far as I know, Buttons is still in jail on remand. Then I went to see Lord Cuddington.'

'Was that before or after you arrested his missus?'

'Before *and* after. He's got an alibi for the night Benny Martin was killed. He also strongly denied the allegation of being engaged in homosexual relationships.'

'Well, he would,' said Lampson.

'Yes, but I flatter myself with thinking I can read people, what's really going on inside them, and I got the impression he might be telling the truth about that. He said that Lady Cuddington is someone who lies all the time, so we might have to take everything she told us about him with a large pinch of salt.'

'The homosexual stuff? Him killing someone?'

'Yes. However, I did have a feeling that Cuddington is hiding something. It was in his attitude towards me when I first got to his house, and when I phoned to arrange to see him. Defensive. Worried what I was going to ask.'

'About him banging blokes?'

'No, he simply dismissed that as a vicious lie by his wife. But by the end he had relaxed. It was as if the thing he was worried I was going to ask him about, I hadn't done so.' He frowned. 'I think I'm going to look a bit further into Lord Cuddington, see if we can work out what it is he's worried about.' He grinned. 'Mind, he wasn't so relaxed when I went back later and told him his wife had been charged with murder. He thinks that could be the ruin of him with his business associates.'

'Good,' said Lampson. 'Serve him right.'

When they arrived at Scotland Yard, they found a report from the detective constables who'd been tailing Pat Riley. 'Riley's actions are as before,' Coburg told Lampson. 'He goes to the club and he goes home. He goes nowhere else.'

'So, if he was under watch all the time, it wasn't him who shot Dan Reeves,' said Lampson ruefully. 'Shall I go and get us a cup of tea, guv?'

'Thanks,' said Coburg. 'I've had an idea and we can discuss it over a cuppa.'

Lampson left and Coburg put through a phone call to Peter Winstanley at Cooper and Lettice.

'Mr Winstanley isn't in yet,' the receptionist at the solicitors' informed him.

'Would you ask him to call me when he gets in?' said Coburg. 'Detective Chief Inspector Coburg at Scotland Yard. It's concerning his client Joseph Barker.'

That done, he began doodling names on a piece of paper. The victims: Benny Martin, Alice Martin, Henry Punt, Wally Maples, Dan Reeves.

Then he started another, listing probable suspects: Pat Riley, Shelly Buttons, Joe Barker and Lord Cuddington.

There was a knock at his door, which opened and the glowering figure of Gerald Atkinson entered. Coburg looked at him in surprise. What was the MI6 man doing here?

'Chief Inspector,' said Atkinson curtly. 'I'm here

with instructions for you to release Shelley Buttons from custody.'

'On what grounds?' demanded Coburg. 'He's under investigation for murder, not to mention various other criminal activities. He's a gangster.'

'Perhaps, but he's *our* gangster. This is a matter of national security.'

'I don't understand.'

'You don't have to understand, you just have to release him.'

'If he's so important to you, you release him. Raise an official notice for his release, or whatever it is you people do.'

'We can't do that because it will show our hand to the enemy.'

'What enemy?'

'The Germans, of course!'

'You're telling me that Shelley Buttons is working for the government?' said Coburg in surprise.

'I'm not telling you anything, except to release him from custody. The reasons are governed by the Official Secrets Act. He needs to be released, and with the minimum of fuss and publicity. If you won't do this, I shall give Superintendent Allison the same orders, and warn him of the consequences if he fails to do it. The only reason I'm doing it this way, talking to you rather than him, is because the fewer people who know about the situation, the better.'

Coburg seethed as he looked at Atkinson. 'You want me to not investigate his role in a possible murder. What about his drug dealing?'

'You're not to touch that,' said Atkinson sharply.

'You condone his drug dealing?'

'That is no business of yours.'

The door opened and Lampson appeared, carrying two cups of tea. He stopped when he saw that Coburg had a visitor, one he'd encountered before in unpleasant circumstances. Lampson put one of the cups down on Coburg's desk, then said coldly, 'I didn't realise you had company, sir. I'll come back later.'

'No need, Sergeant,' snapped Atkinson curtly. 'I'm just leaving.'

With that, he left. Lampson scowled after him as the door shut.

'That was that snooty MI6 bloke, wasn't it? The one who was here before?'

'Gerald Atkinson,' confirmed Coburg sourly. 'He came to order me to release Shelley Buttons.'

Lampson stared at Coburg, shocked. 'Release him?'

'It seems that Buttons is working for the Secret Services.'

'What about his drug dealing?'

'I get the impression that's part of it.'

Lampson shook his head in angry bewilderment. 'I don't believe it. What are you going to do? Release him?'

'No,' said Coburg, getting up. 'I'm going to see

Superintendent Allison and see if there's a way round it.'

Superintendent Allison shook his head reluctantly when Coburg raised the subject with him. He proffered a sheet of paper to Coburg.

'This is from Atkinson to me confirming what he's told you. Shelley Buttons is to be released.'

'On what grounds?' demanded Coburg.

'There's no reason given. MI6 don't have to declare the grounds for any decisions they take,' said Allison. 'Where is Buttons?'

'He's on remand in Pentonville,' said Coburg.

'You'd better go over there and authorise his release,' said Allison. 'I'm sorry, Coburg, but our hands are tied here. We have to do as we've been ordered.'

No I don't, thought Coburg angrily as he drove to Pentonville prison. *I will not let gangsters like Shelley Buttons have a free hand in doing whatever they like in this city*.

Coburg arrived at Pentonville prison, showed his warrant card, and told the duty guards he was there to see the prisoner Shelley Buttons. Coburg was escorted to one of the interview rooms, and shortly afterwards the figure of Shelley Buttons swaggered into the room.

'Inspector Coburg.' He smiled. 'To what do I owe the pleasure of your company?'

'I've been told by MI6 to release you,' Coburg told him.

Buttons smirked. 'Yes, I thought that might happen

once they knew what was happening.'

'It seems your drug activities are too important to them to have you taken out of circulation.'

Buttons looked surprised. 'They told you?'

'Enough. They said you'd tell me the rest. The details.'

Buttons chuckled. 'Have you got that in writing?' he asked.

'There is nothing specific in writing,' said Coburg. 'Just instructions for you to be released. Just as there'll be no written report about this meeting. Now we can play games over this, you saying you'll only tell me if I get them to tell you it's okay, which is something we know will take a long time, time I don't have. In that event, I shall put you back in a cell and tell them you'll be released when they decide to authorise you to tell me the details. Or, to speed things up, you can tell me, and you walk.'

Buttons weighed this up, then he smiled at Coburg. 'This must get right up your nose, copper.' He grinned. 'Illegality going on right under your nose, and there's nothing you can do about it because it's sanctioned by the government and the security services. I am a hero. I might even get a medal at the end of it, though at the moment I'll take the money.' He shook his head. 'Put me back in the cell. But you're making a lot of trouble for yourself. This could be the moment your career goes down the drain.'

CHAPTER THIRTY-FOUR

Monday 9th December 1940

I refuse to allow myself to be ordered about by a gangster like Shelley Buttons, fumed Coburg as he drove away from Pentonville prison. Instead of heading back to Scotland Yard, he made for MI6's headquarters at 54 The Broadway, close to the Houses of Parliament and St James's Park. By the entrance to the tall building that housed MI6 was a brass plaque stating that the building housed the Minimax Fire Extinguisher Company, a ruse that Coburg felt fooled no one except the general public. Every international spy operating in Britain knew that this nine-storey-high building was the home of MI6, also known as SIS, the Secret Intelligence Service. MI6's sister organisation, and most bitter rival, MI5, had been based at Thames House in nearby Millbank until the start of the war, when it had been temporarily housed at Wormwood Scrubs prison. Two months before, MI5 had moved its headquarters to Blenheim Palace at Woodstock in Oxfordshire, although it still retained space at Wormwood Scrubs, where Coburg's colleague, Inspector Hibbert, had his office.

Coburg showed his warrant card to the security men at the door, and again at the reception desk, where he asked to speak to Gerald Atkinson. The receptionist picked up the telephone and made a call. Coburg half-expected to be told that Mr Atkinson was not available, but he was surprised to be told that Mr Atkinson would see him. Coburg was issued with a visitor's pass to be clipped to his jacket lapel and directed towards the lift. 'Mr Atkinson's office is on the seventh floor,' he was told. 'Someone will be waiting for you as you exit the lift.'

Coburg made his way to the ancient lift, which was being operated by an equally ancient lift attendant. When the lift stopped at the seventh floor and the door opened, Coburg was surprised to see Atkinson himself waiting for him.

'I'm hoping your visit is to confirm that you've released Buttons?' said Atkinson.

'Not yet,' said Coburg. 'I'm waiting.'

'What for, for God's sake!' exploded Atkinson. 'You've had your orders. Now carry them out, unless you want to face disciplinary action. Even worse, a charge of conspiring with the enemy.'

Coburg laughed. 'Come off it, Atkinson. That won't wash. I'm ready to release Buttons, against my better judgement, but before I do I want to know how his drug dealing is in the nation's interest.'

'That's not your business,' snapped Atkinson. 'This is a need-to-know situation.'

'And I'll tell you why I need to know,' said Coburg. 'To protect whatever is going on. You see, now the Soho police know about the drugs found on his different premises, they won't turn a blind eye to it. They're coppers, and they're not privy to the inside information about why Buttons and his drugs racket is untouchable. As far as they're concerned, a criminal activity is going on, and they'll be on to him, pulling him in time and time again, along with his confederates.

'Now, there's two ways to stop that happening. You can issue a statement to the Soho police station, and the other stations that border it, telling them that they're not to touch Buttons and his drug racket. But if you do that you'll have to explain why, otherwise sooner or later, one of them, very disgruntled, is going to the papers to express their disgust, and the press are going to start digging. And the exposure will blow Buttons's drug web wide open, and whatever your scheme with him is along with it. Or you can tell me, and I can tell them to lay off, but for reasons I'm not allowed to say. National security. The war effort. The difference between you telling them officially, and me telling them my way, is they know me. I'm one of them, a copper. They trust me. They don't know you, and if they meet you they won't trust you, I can assure you of that.

'So either you tell me what's going on, or I release Buttons and let the coppers in Soho crawl all over him, confiscating his drugs, making his life a misery. And a misery for some of his customers, which is what I think this is all about.'

Atkinson stood silent during this tirade, obviously seething with anger, and for a moment Coburg thought Atkinson was going to call security to have him removed from the building. But then the MI6 man decided to weigh up just how much trouble the police could cause in this situation if not kept in check, and he grunted, 'Follow me.'

Coburg followed Atkinson along a corridor, past a series of wooden partitions with frosted glass windows, until they came to Atkinson's own small office.

Inside, the room was spartan: a desk with a telephone on it, and two chairs. Atkinson took one of the chairs, and gestured towards the other.

'Sit,' he said. 'And let me say here and now that if you repeat anything of what I'm about to tell you, not only shall I deny this conversation ever happened, but I'll have you jailed for breach of the Official Secrets Act, which you have signed.'

Coburg nodded and sat down.

'What do you know about the drug business?' asked Atkinson.

'I've been a copper for twenty years,' said Coburg. 'Plenty of the cases I've dealt with, drugs are at the root of it. Usually the harder ones, heroin and cocaine. Along with amphetamines and crystal meth. In my experience, people who smoke marijuana are too stoned to do anything active.' Atkins nodded.

'Since the war began there's been a shortage of most of those drugs because they were usually smuggled in from abroad, and the U-boat blockade of this island has put a stop to that. I assume you know that Buttons ran drugs in his clubs in Birmingham?'

'Yes,' said Coburg. 'And he's doing it in his London clubs, so he's been able to get supplies.'

'We arranged it,' said Atkinson.

Coburg stared at him, incredulous. 'MI6 arranged for him to get drugs?'

'In our business we use everything at our disposal. We knew that drugs were in short supply in this country, and there was a big demand for them. There always is at time of war.

'Shelley Buttons came to our attention because of his activities in Birmingham. Soon after the war started, we had him arrested on some spurious charge, but one that had a death penalty attached, and offered him a deal. We could ensure a supply of drugs that he could trade in his clubs. We knew that in many places in Soho there are enemy agents operating, hanging around these low clubs to get information from the people who go to them: military people on leave, politicians, businesspeople who trade internationally, prostitutes whose clients include some very influential and important people. We told Buttons that we could arrange a good and constant supply of whatever drugs he wanted, providing that he identified possible enemy agents, and fed them misinformation about what we were doing in the war. We'd pass on to him what we wanted the enemy to think was happening, or about to happen. As a scheme it's worked; the false information we passed has led to the Germans bombing empty, redundant buildings because they'd been told that secret weapons development was going on there, and they also sent large numbers of troops to parts of the French and Belgian coasts where they'd been told we were about to launch an attack. The fact the attacks never materialised we later put down to bad weather on the English coast.'

'I see,' said Coburg. 'It's clever. But, if as you say there's a shortage of drugs coming into this country, where does Buttons get his supplies from?'

'From the Germans. Most, heroin, morphine, amphetamines, they synthesise themselves. Others, like marijuana and cocaine, come from North Africa into Italy and then into Germany.'

'But how do they get into England?'

'Courtesy of the Luftwaffe. Every now and then amongst the bombers that come over will be a plane carrying drugs. They will be dropped at a certain place, and Buttons's men will collect them. It seems the

Germans are very happy to do this because they believe the drugs will undermine the British population, and in return they get inside information.'

'But surely the German who was the initial provider must have been suspicious?'

'He already knew of Buttons's reputation as a drug dealer when he was in Birmingham, so he knew Buttons was authentic. They also knew how dangerous he was. Ruthless.'

'A killer,' said Coburg sourly.

'It helps his cover,' said Atkinson. 'You see now why we have to protect him?'

'I see it, but I don't like it,' said Coburg unhappily. 'I know what drugs do. They destroy people's lives.'

'No one wins a war by fighting cleanly,' said Atkinson. 'In the end it's the dirty work that wins the day.' He looked at Coburg enquiringly. 'So, you'll let Buttons go and drop the investigation into drugs at his clubs?'

Coburg nodded. 'I suppose I don't have much choice, do I?' he said unhappily.

'No,' said Atkinson. 'Not unless you want the War Office on your back.' He picked up the telephone and handed it to Coburg. He also passed a piece of paper across to him, on which was written the telephone number of Pentonville prison. 'The authorisation has to come from you,' Atkinson said.

Coburg scowled, but asked the operator to connect

him to the governor at Pentonville prison. When his authority had been accepted, and Buttons was ready to be released, Coburg returned the receiver to Atkinson, who hung it up. 'What happens if it's proved that Buttons is behind the murders we're investigating?' Coburg asked. 'Do we just let him off with a slap over the wrist? We're talking *five murders*.'

'We'll have to assess the situation when we come to it,' said Atkinson.

'So he could get away with it?'

Atkinson shrugged. 'Yes and no,' he said.

'What does that mean?'

'It means that if he's responsible for those killings, then perhaps we might need to replace him as the owner and manager of his clubs. It's a pity, but accidents happen. And there's always someone waiting in the wings.'

CHAPTER THIRTY-FIVE

Monday 9th December 1940

As Coburg returned to his car, he heard the car radio broadcasting: 'Control to Echo Seven. Urgent. Control to Echo Seven.'

He picked up the microphone and said, 'Echo Seven to Control, reading you.'

'Echo Seven. Message for DCI Coburg from DS Lampson. Dead male found in tunnel at Aldwych Station. DS Lampson attending. Awaits your arrival.'

'Echo Seven to Control. Message received and understood. If DS Lampson is in further contact, advise him I am on my way.'

Six murders! thought Coburg, aghast at the thought. *This is becoming a nightmare.*

The body was in the same place they'd found Benny Martin and Dan Reeves.

'It's Joe Barker,' Lampson told Coburg when he arrived. 'Shot, but not here. His body's been dumped, just like the other two.' He shook his head. 'What is it about this place that people keep dumping dead bodies here?'

'Someone who knows these tunnels,' said Coburg. 'He knows this place and how to get here without being seen. We're talking someone who works in the tunnels and knows their way around.'

'Percy Wenlock?' suggested Lampson.

Coburg looked doubtful. 'I can't see it,' he said. 'He knew Dan Reeves, but as far as we know he had no connection with Benny Martin or Joe Barker. And I can't see that he'd dump the bodies on his own doorstep. But we'll go along and talk to him.' He looked along the tunnel. 'To be honest, I'm surprised he hasn't come to see us.'

They walked along the tunnel to Percy Wenlock's small room, and found it locked. They returned to the dead body of Joe Barker and the constable standing guard over it, just as Dr Welbourne and two ambulance men arrived.

'This is getting to be a regular occurrence,' said Welbourne. 'Have London's criminals suddenly decided this is an ideal place to dump their victims?'

He knelt down and examined the dead man. 'Shot,' he said.

'The same as the other one, Dan Reeves,' said Coburg. 'Though that wasn't you, that was Dr Purkiss who examined him.'

'But I heard about it,' said Welbourne. 'This death occurred about ten hours ago, though whether he was dumped soon after I don't know.

You'd need to talk to whoever found him.'

'The British Museum guards,' said Lampson. 'They've been at the other barrier at the end nearest the station platform during the night and this morning. They came to this barrier to stretch their legs about an hour or so ago and that's when they spotted him.'

Welbourne got up and gestured to the ambulance men to put the body on the stretcher.

'I'll let you have my report as soon as I've taken a look at him,' Welbourne said to Coburg, then he and the ambulance men left with the body.

Coburg and Lampson went in search of the British Museum guards, who'd now moved back to the barrier near the platform. 'Have you seen Percy Wenlock?' asked Coburg. 'The maintenance man?'

'Not since Saturday,' said one of the guards. 'He told us Sunday and Monday would be his days off. He'll be in again tomorrow.'

'Let's take a look along the tunnel,' Coburg said to Lampson. 'See if we can spot where they came into this tunnel. Wenlock said there are lots of connecting tunnels.'

'It's not going to be easy, guv,' said Lampson. He kicked at the gravel between the tracks. 'This stuff doesn't leave footprints like earth does. And even if we find the one they came out of, from what Wenlock said there's bound to be a maze of tunnels going off it.'

'Finding the one they emerged from will be a start,' said Coburg.

They walked along the tunnel in the direction of High Holborn and discovered various smaller tunnels going off the main tunnel. There were no illuminations in these smaller tunnels.

'We'll need torches,' said Lampson.

'We'll also need Percy Wenlock, or someone who knows where these different tunnels go,' said Coburg.

As they walked back towards Aldwych station, Coburg commented, 'Everyone who's been killed is connected to the others in some way. Benny was the brother of Alice. Alice was the girlfriend of Dan Reeves. Reeves was on the same fire crew as Joe Barker. Henry Punt and Wally Maples were told to watch out for anyone asking about Benny's guitar, suggesting they were involved in his murder.'

Which means that Rosa is still at risk, thought Coburg, worried. She'd been picked up by Punt and Maples because she asked about Benny's guitar. Reasonably, she should be safe: she had nothing to do with any of the others. But she'd known Benny and been picked up by Punt and Maples, all three now dead. It was tenuous, but right now she was safer at Dawlish Hall than back here in London.

Coburg and Lampson returned to Scotland Yard, where Coburg telephoned Peter Winstanley. This time the solicitor was in. 'I understand you had Joe

Barker released yesterday,' said Coburg.

'I did, I'm proud to say,' said Winstanley. 'He was being kept in prison without any evidence against him.'

'He was being kept in protective custody,' said Coburg.

'That wasn't what I understood,' countered Winstanley.

'Protective custody against who?'

'Against people who might want him dead,' said Coburg.

Winstanley scoffed. 'Honestly, Chief Inspector, that's an old and well-worn ruse to justify illegal detention.'

'I doubt if Joe Barker will agree with you,' said Coburg.

'You think so?' chuckled Winstanley. 'I beg to differ, and so will Joe Barker when you talk to him next.'

'That's going to be difficult,' said Coburg. 'He was shot dead on his release from prison.'

There was a silence from the other end of the telephone, then Winstanley stammered, 'Sh . . . shot?'

'Yes,' said Coburg. 'To prevent him answering the questions we intended to ask him.'

'But . . . how was I to know?' demanded Winstanley. Then he added with a blustering, 'You weren't around. Neither was your sergeant. Nor your superintendent.'

'If you had put in a telephone call to Superintendent

Allison at his home, he would have told you that I was on my way to Scotland Yard.'

'That's irrelevant,' said Winstanley. 'I refuse to be blamed for the death of Mr Barker.'

'He would still be alive if he'd remained in custody,' said Coburg. 'But you can help me in trying to identify his murderer. I assume he was released into your custody. Your name is on the release form.'

'Yes,' said Winstanley warily. 'Where did he go?'

'I assume he went home.'

'You didn't accompany him?'

'No. My job, which was to get him released from custody, and that had been done.'

'Did you make arrangements to see him again?'

'Of course,' said Winstanley. 'I gave him the telephone number of our office and asked him to call on Monday to make an appointment to see me.'

'Is there anything else you can tell me?' asked Coburg. 'Anything he said to you that might throw a light on who might want him dead.'

'No,' said Winstanley. 'He gave no impression that he was in any danger. If he had, I might have been more circumspect about obtaining his release. As far as I'm concerned, my conscience is clear.'

Lampson looked at Coburg sympathetically as the chief inspector hung up the phone. 'We're getting nowhere, guv,' he said.

'I feel we are,' said Coburg. 'Before I got sidetracked

with Atkinson and the business over Shelley Buttons, I'd come to what I think could be the right conclusion: Pat Riley.'

'But he's been under close watch,' Lampson pointed out.

'That doesn't stop him hiring someone else for the actual killing, and if we want the proof we'll find it at the Riff Club. The Riff Club is the key to what's going on. Benny was playing there the night he died. Punt and Maples worked for him there. That's half the victims. Alice was there that night, and I believe she was there with Dan Reeves.'

He went on to explain his theory that Pat Riley was Dan Reeves's fence. 'Which links us to AFS Crew 127. Joe Barker told the rest of the crew he'd been to see Reeves's fence. If Riley was that fence, then that was a good reason for Riley to kill Barker to shut him up.'

'What about Shelley Buttons?' asked Lampson. 'Do you think he's involved in some way?'

'I'm having my doubts ever since Atkinson turned up with his story about Buttons,' admitted Coburg. 'For one thing, I'm surer than ever that whoever has been dumping the bodies at Aldwych has a serious knowledge of the tunnels around there. For me, that raises questions about Buttons: he's only fairly recently arrived from Birmingham. He wouldn't know about the extent of the tunnels in this part of London and how they connect.'

'He might have someone on his crew who knows,' offered Lampson.

'Buttons brought most of his crew of thugs and crooks with him from Birmingham,' said Coburg. 'They might know about the maze of tunnels, but not be able to find their way around them. Dan Reeves knew his way around them, and so does Percy Wenlock.'

'Do you think we ought to look into Wenlock?' asked Lampson. 'As you say, he knew Reeves, and he knows his way around the tunnels. That's two ticks against him.'

'But does he have any connection to Benny or the Riff Club?'

'We can ask him,' said Lampson. 'Maybe he didn't do any of the actual killings, just helped dispose of the bodies.'

'Why? And then get involved telling us about the tunnels?' He sat, thoughtful, then said, 'We need to take a different tack. Dig into Pat Riley and the Riff Club. The trouble is we have no proof, and he's been very careful to stay shut up inside his club or his home while all the other murders were taking place. But it's Riley, I'm, sure of it. I'd like you to go along to the Riff Club and start asking questions of the staff. Tell Riley I've sent you to talk to the staff to see what they remember about the last night Benny was there, the night he was killed. Anyone who may have been there who looked suspicious.'

'They're not gonna tell me, guv,' Lampson pointed out.

'No, I know, but the purpose of the exercise is for you to see if anyone says anything that might point us in the right direction. Something chatty that doesn't sound like they're grassing on anyone.'

Lampson nodded. 'Right, guv. Are you sure you don't want to do it? You're good at reading people.'

'So are you, Ted. For my part, I'm going to dig into Lord Cuddington.'

'Why? We know he didn't kill Alice; that was his missus.'

'He might have a connection with Riley. Money makes strange bedfellows. For one thing, I'm convinced that Cuddington is into something crooked. Pamela Cuddington told me that her husband had Benny killed. I want to find out if that's just her making waves, or if there might be something in it. According to her, Cuddington did it to stop Benny blabbing about his homosexual activities. When I saw him and asked him about those, he denied it. As you said, he would do. But there's still something there. So I'm going to spend some time talking to people who know them.'

'Ah, the old Etonian crowd?' Lampson grinned.

'Actually, I think Cuddington was at Harrow. No, I'm going to have a word with Jack Harkness. He's the DI at Vice who was very helpful about that order of nuns when we were investigating the Savoy business. Jack seems to know what's going on, especially when it concerns Soho.'

'Anyway, we've got Lady Cuddington for Alice's murder,' said Lampson. 'That's one result. Punt, Maples, Reeves and Barker were all shot, and likely with the same gun, but not the gun that Barker had. The odd one out is Benny, poisoned. That could still be Lady Cuddington if Benny gave her the elbow as Riley said.'

Coburg shook his head. 'No, that's not her way. She loses her temper. She'd have beaten him to death, the same as she did with Alice. And I don't put a lot of stock by what Riley says. He's lying, but there's no way to get evidence against him. Not at the moment.'

Lampson took his overcoat from the hat rack and was just about to leave, when he stopped.

'I was thinking, guv. It's twenty to three now, which doesn't give me a lot of time to have an in-depth look at the people in the Riff Club. Will it be alright if I go along there as well first thing tomorrow morning? For one thing, there'll be a different set of people there then, cleaners and such.'

'Yes, good idea,' said Coburg. 'I'm starting to think the key to everything is there, so the more time you take on it the better. I'll see you here some time tomorrow morning.'

CHAPTER THIRTY-SIX

Monday 9th December 1940

After Lampson had gone, Coburg put a call through to DCI Jack Harkness at the Vice Squad.

'Jack, it's Edgar Coburg,' he said.

Harkness chuckled. 'I wondered if you might be in touch,' he said. 'By all accounts the body count is mounting up in your latest case – the Bodies in the Tunnel, the boys here are calling it – and the word is, in some way the thing's connected to a couple of club owners in Soho.'

'Indeed,' admitted Coburg. 'Pat Riley at the Riff Club and Shelley Buttons.'

'Riley I haven't heard much about,' said Harkness. 'He seems to run a clean ship. But Buttons, now there's a villain and a half. What do you want to know?'

'Actually, it's not about either of those. It's about the pink list.'

'Which officially doesn't exist,' said Harkness. 'If we did have such a list, we'd be condoning a criminal offence by not arresting them.'

'Understood,' said Coburg. 'The name I'm

interested in is Lord Colin Cuddington.'

'A lord, eh,' chuckled Harkness. 'Well, we've got quite a few of them on the list, along with an admiral or two and a couple of generals and Members of Parliament. Which is why we can't admit to having such a list. It'd mean all these top nobs being sent to chokey, which would do no good for public morale at time like this. I'll have a look at the list, and also have a word with some of the other blokes, see if they know anything. There are plenty of people we know about but it'd be too dangerous to keep a record of them, just in case anyone got nosy.'

'Very important people?' asked Coburg.

'You'd be surprised,' said Harkness. Then he chuckled again. 'But, knowing you and your background, I doubt if you would. A large number of them are old boys of public schools, quite a few of them from your old educational establishment.'

Coburg hung up the receiver and sat looking at the paper with the list of names he'd written. Jack Harkness hadn't immediately recognised the name of Lord Cuddington, but it didn't mean he wasn't involved with the homosexual world. Pamela Cuddington had been very firm in her assertion that he was part of it, to the extent that he'd killed one of his male lovers. But how much of what she said could be taken as truth? On an impulse, he picked up the phone and asked the operator to put him through to Dawlish Hall. To his

318

pleasure, it was Rosa who answered. 'Dawlish Hall,' she said.

'Rosa, it's Edgar.'

'Edgar! Every time the phone rings, I pick it up in case it might be you. I think Malcolm is a bit peeved by me doing that; he sees answering the phone as his job. I'm hoping you're phoning to tell me it's safe for me to come back home.'

'I was hoping I'd be able to do that as well, but at the moment things are still a bit risky. I'm hoping to get hold of the proof I need to wrap the case up very shortly.'

'What sort of proof?'

'Again, I can't say over the phone. It really could be careless talk costs lives if the person we're after gets to hear about it. Actually, I wanted to speak to Magnus.'

'So, you're not just phoning because you love me and miss me desperately.'

'Yes, I am, all of that, but I'm hoping that Magnus might have some information to help close the case.'

'In that case I'll get him.' There was a brief pause, then he heard the sound of a kiss, and Rosa adding, 'I love you, Edgar.'

'I love you too, my love.' There was a rattling sound as she put the receiver down, then after a short delay Magnus's voice was heard.

'Edgar,' said Magnus. 'What news? Have you caught the miscreant yet?'

'Alas no,' said Coburg. 'But the question I'm about to ask is related to the case. You're involved with the business community.'

'I'd hardly call it that. I'm on the boards of a couple of companies.'

'Which means you know some of your fellow company directors, and possibly the directors of other companies.'

'Where's this leading to?'

'Have you ever had anything to do with a man called Colin Cuddington? Lord Cuddington?'

There was a pause, then Magnus asked carefully, 'Why do you ask?'

'I assume from that you have. His name has come up in the investigation.'

'This jazz guitarist fellow?'

'Yes. I'm curious to know if Cuddington is involved in anything. Underhand, that is?'

There was another pause before Magnus said guardedly, 'It depends what you mean by underhand.'

'It would help me if you could enlarge on that,' said Coburg.

There was another pause, then Magnus said, 'Not over the telephone. Could you come here?'

'That's difficult at the moment. We've had more murders.'

'I see. At the moment I'm not keen to leave Rosa here on her own. I'll tell you what, we could always meet in London. I can catch a train at Great Missenden into Marylebone. That should be enough time for the return train.'

'Yes, that would be very helpful. I'd appreciate that. When do you suggest?'

'It's three o'clock now. I can be there at five, if that suits you.'

'That suits me very well indeed. Thank you, Magnus. I'll see you at Marylebone at five.'

Rosa stood on the porch and watched as the Bentley, driven by Malcolm, left Dawlish Hall to take Magnus to Great Missenden station to meet with Edgar at Marylebone station. *I wish I'd gone with Magnus*, she thought. *I really miss Edgar.* It was lovely being here at Dawlish Hall, with its open spaces, the paddock where Mip the old horse grazed and trotted over to the fence when she came to give him an apple, or just to stroke his mane. It was idyllic, apart from being parted from Edgar.

She turned and walked back into the mansion. With Mrs Hilton returned to her cottage in the village until it was time for her to return to prepare the evening meal, the house was deserted.

She walked into the large drawing room and sat down at the piano. A Steinway, for God's sake! How many houses in Britain had their own Steinway? And why? Edgar didn't play, nor, as far as she knew, did Magnus. There'd been no talk about Charles playing. Magnus had mentioned that their mother played, but he also mentioned that the piano had barely been used since she died and he would appreciate it if Rosa would play it while she was here.

Her first attempts at playing it had told her that the piano needed tuning. She'd mentioned that to Magnus, but not pressed the issue because she thought it would be unfair to put him to the expense of bringing in a piano tuner when she might only be at Dawlish Hall for a day or so more.

As her fingers caressed the piano keys, she reflected that, out of tune or not, the instrument had a beautiful tone. It was a privilege to play it. The pianos she'd played during her career had varied, from beautiful Steinways at the top concert halls or hotels, and at the BBC, to upright barrel house pianos suitable for little more than boogie-woogie.

Seven years earlier, when she was beginning to build a reputation among jazz aficionados, and had made successful appearances across the continent, Berlin, Paris, Rome, there'd been talk of her going to appear in America. She'd been filled with huge excitement at the prospect, not so much at appearing there – which would be a dream come true – but to see and hear in real life the people she admired, especially the pianists: Duke Ellington, Count Basie, Art Tatum, each one a master. She'd actually seen Ellington with his orchestra when he came to London in 1933 and thought she'd never heard such a wonderful sound with so many virtuoso players. She remembered Ellington announcing, 'I hope this will be an annual event because I love coming to Britain.' As it turned out, that had been his last visit; the British Musicians' Union had placed a ban on American musicians coming to Britain to play, especially jazz musicians, claiming they were protecting the jobs of British musicians. The American Federation of Musicians reciprocated with a ban on British musicians appearing in America, and Rosa's dream of crossing the Atlantic disappeared.

At that time, although she'd been disappointed for herself that the prospects of playing in famous New York jazz clubs would now not materialise, her biggest disappointment was that she'd never see live the American musicians she loved, Ella Fitzgerald, Hoagy Carmichael, Ellington, Basie, Tatum, Louis Armstrong. All of them were banned from coming to Britain. The only way she could get to see them was if she could get to America, but she couldn't afford it. She'd told Edgar about this once, and he'd told her, 'When this war is over, I'll take you to America.'

The trouble was, this war seemed like it was never going to end.

She let her fingers run through Carmichael's 'Georgia on My Mind'. Out of tune or not, the music took her there, to America.

As Lampson walked through Soho, making for the Riff Club, he thought about the advice the guv'nor had given him about Eve Bradley. About putting off something that could be good.

Yes, Terry would be upset if it was known that his dad was going out with his teacher, but he'd get over it. At least, Lampson hoped so. The boss was right, life was too short, and especially in time of war, with the country under constant bombing. Who's to say how long any of them would survive. He remembered seeing the statistics in some official report: in October and November alone, thirteen thousand people had been killed by the bombing in London, with another twenty thousand seriously injured. The German bombing campaign had begun in September, and was still going on, every day more and more people being killed. It was all very well telling people to be careful, but being careful wouldn't keep you alive if a bomb dropped on your home, or a school, or a factory.

The problem was, he wasn't sure if Eve Bradley was interested in him in that way. She seemed to like his company when they were together, talking about the football team, and as far as he knew she didn't have a boyfriend, but what would her reaction be if he asked her out? Might she be frightened off? And where could he take her? Not to the pub. The pictures leapt into his mind. After all, everyone went to the pictures. When the war started, all the cinemas had been shut, but during the past year they'd been allowed to open again, with their hours gradually extended until now they were allowed to stay open until eleven o'clock at night, although most people went during the afternoons.

Saturday afternoons were difficult for him; he only had every other Saturday off work, and that was given over to the football team he'd started up.

I'll ask her if she'd like to go to the pictures, he decided. *She can only say no. If she does, at least I'll know where I stand. But what picture?*

He thought of the pictures that were currently the most popular. Lampson liked Westerns and thrillers, and there were two such films out at the moment that he wanted to see: the Western adventure *Stagecoach* starring John Wayne, and Basil Rathbone as Sherlock Holmes in *The Hound of the Baskervilles*. However, he doubted if either would tempt Eve Bradley. The big film at the moment, and one he felt she might go for, was *Gone with the Wind*, the epic set during the American Civil War with a love story at its heart, with Clark Gable and Vivien Leigh as the star-crossed lovers.

It suddenly struck him that his way out of his dilemma over Terry would be to ask Terry if he'd like to go to the pictures to see *Gone with the Wind*. He knew Terry would know it was a love story because Lampson's mother regularly got the film magazines to find out what was going on in the world of cinema, and Terry's response would be 'No. It's a soppy romance film.' So Lampson would offer for them to go and see *Stagecoach*, which Terry would go for. After that, Lampson would tell Terry he and Miss Bradley were going to see *Gone with the Wind*, because he, Lampson, wanted to see it and Terry didn't want to.

That, of course, all depended on Eve agreeing to go to the pictures with him, which was by no means guaranteed.

Still, whatever happened, at least he'd see *Stagecoach* and spend valuable time with Terry.

When he walked into the Riff Club, it was busy with the staff arranging the tables for the evening. The club was small; a narrow stage protruded from the back wall with the tables arranged around it in a semi-circle, this semi-circle pattern being repeated to the entrance to the performance space itself, where a small table marked where the ticket collector checked the tickets of the audience as they entered. At the moment, this small table was unoccupied.

The tables themselves were covered with white linen tablecloths ready for the customers. A man in a dinner jacket and bow tie appeared from the back of the small stage and approached Lampson.

'I recognise you,' he said. 'You're the copper who accompanied DCI Coburg when he called to talk to Pat. I'm Eddie Mars, the concierge, maître d', whatever you want to call me.' He held out his hand and Lampson shook it. 'I introduce the acts, but we don't start until eight.' He smiled. 'Luckily we're well below ground so this is as good as any bomb shelter.'

'I expect you get some people stay all night when there's a raid on,' said Lampson.

'We do indeed.' Mars grinned. 'Luckily, we're a club, so licensing hours don't apply. And around midnight and the early hours is when we make our money.' He gestured towards the bar, which ran along one wall. 'Can I get you anything?'

'No thanks,' said Lampson. 'We're still looking into the death of Benny Martin.'

'What a terrible thing!' said Mars with a heavy sigh. 'Such a nice guy.'

'Were you here the night he was killed?' asked Lampson.

'I'm always here,' said Mars.

'We're trying to recreate what happened to him,'

said Lampson. 'We heard that he had a row with his sister that night.'

'I knew there was a bit of a row, but I didn't think much of it,' said Mars. 'To be honest, I didn't even know she was his sister until the drummer told me. Sam Watson.'

'How did that come about?'

'I saw Benny and this girl having a go at each other, and Sam said to me: "That's his sister." I'd never seen her before.'

'Do you know what they were rowing about?'

'No, I had more important things to do. Once the band's finished, there are the bar bills to check, the money to sort out, all the paperwork.'

'You stay open all night?'

'We do.'

'But Pat Riley doesn't stay?'

'No. He's here during the day and for the evening performance, then he goes home.'

'Who does stay?'

'I do, usually, until about one o'clock. Then Jim Bridger comes in and looks after the place until it gets to about six o'clock. That's when we close to the public.'

'Who else is here from one o'clock?'

'The bar staff, the waiting staff, the cooks. Although at that hour we just do sandwiches. We only do meals – and then only small meals – from half past seven to ten.'

'If the band leave at about midnight, what's the entertainment until six?'

'Records, mostly,' said Mars. 'Though sometimes we get keen would-be musicians here and we give them a spot in the early hours. If they're any good, we let them play on. If they're no good, we gently ease them off and carry on with the records.'

'Is there anyone here now who was working at the club that particular night?'

Mars thought it over. 'There's Jerry George, the chief barman. He was here. The other two barmen don't come in until seven.'

'Can I talk to Jerry?'

'Sure. He's in the washroom having a smoke at the moment; I'll bring him in.'

'What about Pat Riley?'

Mars pointed at the entrance. 'His office is just out there, by the stairs as you came down.'

'Yeah, I remember from when we came before. I meant, is he in at the moment?'

'Pat's always here. At the moment he's busy going through the accounts. He does that at a quiet time before the musicians and the audience arrive. If you like, I'll see if he's free.'

'If you would,' said Lampson. 'It's only courtesy to let him know I'm here in his club, asking questions.'

'Sure,' said Mars. 'Wait here. I'll get Jerry to come and talk to you while I go and tell Pat you're here.'

Jerry George was in his fifties, and from the broken red veins in his nose and cheeks, Lampson guessed he was a great guzzler of the liquid he served. When Lampson asked him what he remembered about Benny and who he was with that night, he said regretfully, 'Nothing at all, I'm afraid. I was rushed off my feet serving drinks, bringing more stock from the storeroom, and making sure that all the money crossing the bar went into the till.' He gave a wink as he said, 'That night we had a new barman helping out, and I noticed he kept trying to manipulate the change, so I had to keep a close eye on him.' He chuckled. 'That was the last night he worked here. I need to trust the people who work with me.' Aware that George had little information of any use about that evening as far as Benny Martin was concerned, Lampson let him go, and then made for Pat Riley's office.

He got there just as Eddie Mars was coming out. 'Pat's on the phone at the moment,' said Mars. 'He's talking to his accountant and it's quite involved. He asks if you wouldn't mind waiting, or maybe you can come back again tomorrow.'

Lampson looked at his watch, then said, 'Tell him tomorrow will be fine. I'll be back then.'

As he made for the stairs up to the street, he reflected that the visit had been pretty useless as far as throwing any new light on who had killed Benny

Martin. Maybe they were on the wrong track. Maybe the answer wasn't here at the Riff Club at all, but in trying to find out the identity of the heavies that Pat Riley had told them Benny was due to meet. If they even existed. So far all attempts to find out anything about them had failed. The question was, where had Benny gone to after he left the club? So far the last sighting had been that of the late Henry Punt, who had said he saw Benny leave with his sister, Alice, and a man, who they suspected had been Dan Reeves. The problem was that all of them, Punt, Alice and Dan Reeves, were dead. The whole thing looked like a dead end.

CHAPTER THIRTY-SEVEN

Coburg stood by the barrier at Marylebone station, watching for Magnus amongst the crowds getting off the train, many of them young men in uniform carrying kitbags, obviously on their way to join their various units. It was very different from his time during the First War, reflected Coburg. Then, if you were in uniform you were generally heading for France. Some, like Superintendent Allison, had been sent further afield, to Turkey. In this war, these young soldiers could be heading for the Mediterranean or Africa, even the Far East ever since Japan had signed the Tripartite Pact in September to ally themselves with Germany and Italy.

Coburg spotted Magnus handing his ticket to the inspector before passing through the barrier and joining the milling throng in the railway station, and smiling in greeting when he saw his younger brother. They shook hands and Coburg asked, 'Would you like to go and talk somewhere over tea? There are plenty of cafés around here.'

'The station buffet will be fine,' said Magnus.

'Everyone saying goodbye or thinking about their journeys will be too wrapped up in their own affairs to want to eavesdrop on two men talking.'

They made their way to the buffet, where they ordered two teas and a bun each, then managed to find a free table. 'Rosa was keen to come with me,' said Magnus. 'But I put her off, just in case London was still a dangerous place for her.' He sipped at his tea and said, 'You wanted to know about Collin Cuddington.'

'Yes,' said Coburg.

'Why?'

'There's something about him that makes me suspicious,' said Coburg. 'I'm not sure if it's to do with this case I'm on. Or something else entirely. Someone suggested it may be . . .' He hesitated, then said in a low voice: 'unorthodox sexual activity.'

'Men?' asked Magnus, his lips barely moving.

Coburg looked around the buffet to see if anyone had caught the word. Then, relieved, that no one had, he said, 'Yes. Someone mentioned it as a possibility.'

'Not as far as I know,' said Magnus. 'But you're right, there's something underhand about him. He sells inside information.'

'What sort of information?'

'About the companies he's involved with. Knowledge that is very useful to a speculator or investor. Buy at the right time before a company is about to announce a major deal and you can make a lot of money. Equally, sell if you know the company's in dire straits and could go bust and you save yourself a lot of money. I'm not sure if it's actually illegal, but it wouldn't go down well with the companies whose boards he sits on if they found out about it.'

'How do you know about this?'

'He'd offered information for sale to one of my fellow directors, who asked me if I wanted to come in on it with him. Put up half the money. I declined. I don't do business that way.' He looked enquiringly at his brother. 'Does that help?'

'It helps to ease my mind, that I was right. I knew there was something wrong about him, but I didn't know what. Now, thanks to you, I can dismiss it from my thinking.'

'So you don't think he's involved in these murders you're looking into.'

'No, but you can tell Rosa that his wife is.'

'Pamela? The one you were engaged to?'

'Twenty years ago,' Coburg reminded him. 'And yes, it turns out that she killed Benny Martin's sister, Alice.'

'What's happened to her?'

'I arrested her yesterday. She's currently on remand at Holloway prison.'

CHAPTER THIRTY-EIGHT

Tuesday 10th December 1940

It was nine o'clock when Lampson made his return to the Riff Club the following morning. His hope was that this morning he'd be talking to a different lot of people than he'd spoken to the previous afternoon, cleaners, delivery people, people who looked after the storage of drinks and other stuff. However, the downside of this was that most of the people he'd be talking to would most likely not have been working on the night that Benny Martin was performing at the club. As Lampson walked into the cul-de-sac that was Wardour Mews, he spotted DC Pritchard lingering by the entrance to the Mews.

'Morning, Constable,' he said. 'Anything to report?'

'Only that I'm convinced we're wasting our time,' said Pritchard gloomily.

'Has Riley arrived?' asked Lampson.

'No. He generally comes about half past nine, sometimes ten. One of us is usually here early to watch him go in. Today, it's my turn.' Plaintively, he added,

'How much longer are we going to be doing this, sir?'

'I don't know, Constable,' admitted Lampson. 'Hopefully not for much longer.'

He walked into the Mews and then to the Riff Club. The door was shut and locked. Lampson rang the doorbell. A middle-aged man in shirtsleeves, unshaven and wearing a stained shirt, opened the door and looked out at him.

'We ain't open to the public yet,' he said.

'I know,' said Lampson. He showed the man his warrant card. 'DS Lampson. I was here yesterday afternoon. Your boss, Pat Riley, said I could come back and talk to the staff this morning.'

'This is about Benny Martin? The kid who was killed?'

'It is,' said Lampson. 'We're just trying to get a picture of who was here on the night he was appearing here.'

'Last Monday night,' said the man. 'I wasn't here. I only do mornings, keeping an eye on the cleaners and seeing what we need to re-order in the way of drinks and such.' He held out his hand. 'Len Peters. I'm happy to talk.'

Lampson shook Peters's hand, then walked into the club as Peters stood back for him. Peters locked the door then led the way down the two flights of stairs to the club itself. Three women cleaners were at work, sweeping and wiping down the bar and tables.

'I'll introduce you to them,' said Peters, and he hailed the three women.

'Dolly, Molly and Polly,' he said. 'Girls, this here is DS Lampson from Scotland Yard. He's asking about the night when Benny Martin was here.'

'The kid who got killed?' said one. She shook her head. 'None of us know anything about that; we weren't here that night. We do mornings.'

'I'd like to talk to you about the morning after, the Tuesday, 3rd December,' said Lampson. 'Did you notice anything unusual?'

'What d'you mean, unusual?' asked one of the other women.

'Anything out of the ordinary from any other morning,' said Lampson.

The women looked at one another quizzically, then shook their heads.

'No,' said one, who seemed to be the spokesperson for them.

'Except for Henry Punt,' put in one of the others.

The leader nodded. 'Yes,' she said. 'I'd forgotten about him.' She gave a heavy sigh. 'Poor Henry, getting shot like that. Him and Wally. Terrible.'

'What about him?' asked Lampson.

'Well, as I guess you know, Henry and Wally acted as doormen and also ran errands for Mr Riley, so they're never usually in until late in the morning, if at all. But that morning, Henry was here

337

talking to Chuck Wheeler. Chuck's another one who does errands for Mr Riley. Chuck's usually here in the morning, sorting out breakages and things. Sometimes things get a bit hectic at night and stuff gets broken.'

'What were they talking about?' asked Lampson. 'Henry and Chuck?'

'About a guitar,' said the woman. 'Henry told Chuck that Mr Riley wanted him to sell it.'

'No, that was Mr Riley himself who said that,' said the third woman. 'Remember, he came in early as well.'

'You're right, Polly,' said the first woman. 'He did. It was just after nine. It was Mr Riley who told Chuck to take the guitar. Henry went with Chuck and they went out carrying this guitar.'

'You're sure of the time?' asked Lampson. 'Just after nine on the Tuesday morning?'

The three women nodded in unison.

'Thanks,' said Lampson. 'I might need to talk to you later.'

'You'll always find us here from eight o'clock in the morning,' said the leader.

As Lampson went in search of Len Peters, he weighed up what he'd just learnt: Henry Punt and Chuck Wheeler had been sent by Pat Riley to get rid of the guitar just after nine o'clock on the Tuesday morning. But Coburg and Lampson hadn't identified the body as being of Benny Martin until the following day, the Wednesday. Yet Pat Riley had told them that he had only told his man to sell the guitar after they heard that the body in the tunnel was Benny's. So Riley had lied.

Lampson found Len Peters in the storeroom behind the bar. 'Just a quick question about the Tuesday morning,' Lampson said. 'Benny Martin's guitar. I understand that Chuck Wheeler and Henry Punt took the guitar for sale on Mr Riley's instructions that Tuesday morning. Is that right?'

'I wouldn't know,' said Peters. 'I wasn't in that Tuesday morning. I had a terrible cough and cold and a bit of a fever. I could hardly get out of bed. I phoned the club and told Mr Riley I was sick and said I'd be in later that afternoon if I felt better. He told me not to bother, just stay at home and take some stuff and get well.' He smiled. 'He's a good bloke like that, is Pat. Caring. Great man to work for. He's not stuck-up like some bosses. But then, he came up the hard way, didn't have money in his background. He was a worker. A real worker.'

'What sort of work?'

'Labouring,' said Peterson. 'You wouldn't think it to look at him now, the smart suits, the easy-going air, but when he was younger he worked at some of the hardest jobs there were. Tunnelling, for example. That's hard. Always the risk of cave-ins.'

'What sort of tunnels?' asked Lampson, suddenly alert.

'The Kingsway tunnel, for one. That's where I first met him. We both worked on it.'

'You can't have,' said Lampson. 'That tunnel opened in 1906, thirty-five years ago. Anyone who worked on it would be in their late fifties now. Riley's in his forties.'

'I'm talking about when they did the extra work to allow double-decker trams,' said Peterson. 'In 1930. The people in charge realised they weren't making the money they'd hoped for, so they came up with the idea of putting in double-decker trams to replace the single-decker ones. That meant lowering the trackbed and raising the roof of the tunnels. It took nearly a year. February 1930 till January 1931. During that time, the tunnel was closed to the public. That's where me and Pat first met. And later, when he opened this club, he remembered me and offered me a job here. Like I say, a good bloke.'

'A good bloke indeed,' agreed Lampson.

'Who is?' asked a voice.

Lampson turned and saw that Pat Riley had arrived. He gave a wry grin when he saw Lampson. 'You again?' he said, but he added a friendly chuckle.

'I was just telling the sergeant what a good bloke you are,' said Peters, 'and how you never had it easy. I was telling him about us meeting when we both worked on the Kingsway tunnel.'

Lampson thought he detected a look of alarm cross Riley's face, then it had gone to be replaced by his familiar friendly smile.

'Long time ago, Len,' he said. 'So long ago I'd almost forgotten about it.' He turned back to Lampson and asked, 'Is there anything you need me for today, Sergeant? Only I've got to meet someone. Business, you know.'

'You go ahead, Mr Riley,' said Lampson. 'I've just got a couple more people to talk to, then I'll be off.'

'I can't think of anyone else who could help you,' said Peters. 'You've talked to Dolly, Molly and Polly. There's really only us in the club around this time.'

'In that case, I guess I'm finished,' said Lampson. 'Thank you again for your time, Mr Riley.'

He made for the stairs that would take him up to street level, and Riley headed for the three cleaners.

'So, what did the copper want to know?' he asked.

'He was just asking about the night that poor young kid was killed,' said Dolly. 'We told him we weren't here that night. We only come in to clean in the mornings.'

'He seemed interested in the guitar,' added Molly.

'In what way?' asked Riley.

'He wanted to know what time Henry Punt and Chuck took it to sell. I remember hearing Henry and Chuck talking about it.'

'And you told him?'

'Well, we didn't know exactly. It was some time that Tuesday morning,' said Dolly. She looked at Riley, concerned. 'It was alright to tell him that, wasn't it?'

Riley gave her a reassuring smile. 'Of course it was, Dolly. We've got no secrets from the police.'

With that he made for his office, his mind in a whirl. In just a few seconds, everything had gone completely pear-shaped and fallen apart. Now they'd be coming for him. He had to get away before that happened and work out a plan. One thing was sure, he wasn't going to hang around and put his head in a noose.

CHAPTER THIRTY-NINE

Tuesday 10th December 1940

'It's Riley,' announced Lampson grimly when he got back to the office at Scotland Yard. He told Coburg what he'd learnt from the cleaners, and from Len Peters.

'So Riley sent his men to sell the guitar first thing the following morning, before he was supposed to have known that Benny was dead.'

'We should have gone nosing around the club in the mornings before,' said Lampson, annoyed. 'If we had, we've have found that out sooner.'

'That's my fault,' said Coburg. 'I should have thought of it. The clincher is discovering that Riley worked in the tunnels around Kingsway.' He got up and pulled on his overcoat. 'Right, let's pull him in.'

'I told DC Pritchard to tail him if he left the club,' said Lampson.

'I'm not sure if that was a good idea,' said Coburg, concerned. 'We now know that Riley's our killer, which means Pritchard's at risk if Riley spots him.'

'I think he'll be alright,' said Lampson. 'It struck

me yesterday that things might turn out to be a bit dodgy, so I signed out a pistol, just in case. I passed it on to Pritchard when I left the club.'

'How did he react?'

'Pleased. Soho's a dodgy place at the best of times.'

'Let's hope he hasn't had to use it,' said Coburg as he made for the door.

DC Pritchard was still on watching duty at the corner of Wardour Mews when Coburg and Lampson pulled up in their car.

'So far, so good,' said Coburg. He gestured at the constable, who came hurrying over. 'Any sign of Pat Riley?'

'No, sir,' said Pritchard. 'He's still in there. Three women left, though, about half an hour ago.'

'The cleaners,' said Lampson.

'In that case, you can return the pistol to Sergeant Lampson,' said Coburg.

Pritchard handed the pistol back to Lampson, who slipped it into his pocket.

'Keep an eye on the car, Constable,' said Coburg as he and Lampson got out of the car and made for the Riff Club. Coburg tapped his own pocket where the pistol he'd taken out from the weapons store felt heavy.

'You're sure we don't need back-up?' asked Lampson.

'We'd need to arm them all, and there's always a danger of someone getting shot by accident,' said Coburg. 'You said there was only Riley, this Len Peters, and the three cleaners in the place. With the cleaners out of the way, you and I should be able to deal with Riley and Peters.'

The door to the club was shut but unlocked. Coburg and Lampson made their way downstairs and found Len Peters carrying boxes of drinks to the shelves behind the bar.

'Hello again,' said Peters to Lampson. 'Forgotten something?'

'We need to have a word with Pat,' said Lampson. 'Is he in his office?'

At this, Peters looked uncomfortable. 'Well, he is and he isn't,' he said awkwardly.

'What do you mean?' asked Coburg.

'Sometimes he nips out for a minute,' said Peters.

'We've got someone watching the door, and he reports that no one has left except the cleaners.'

At this, Peters looked really unhappy. 'Sometimes he uses the rear entrance,' he muttered.

'What rear entrance?' demanded Coburg.

'Most people don't know about it,' said Peters. 'I do, because he trusts me. And some of the other blokes do.'

'Show me this rear entrance,' said Coburg, doing his best to contain his anger. A rear entrance! Riley had been playing them for fools all this time!

Reluctantly, Peters led them into Riley's office. At the back wall was a tall open cupboard whose shelves were filled with books and paper files. Peters gave the cupboard a push, and it rolled to one side to reveal an open doorway behind it.

Coburg pulled the pistol from his pocket and aimed it at the open doorway.

'Walk,' he snapped at Peters.

Peters looked at the pistol in Coburg's hand in horror. 'There's no need for that,' he protested.

'Walk,' repeated Coburg.

Peters stepped through the doorway and he must have pressed a switch, because lights came on in what was a low-ceiling, brick-walled tunnel. Peters began to walk into the tunnel, which twisted and turned a bit, before they reached a door, by which Peters hesitated.

'Open it,' ordered Coburg.

Peters pulled the door open, and they stepped into a storeroom in which boxes of coffee, tea and sugar were stacked. The smell of coffee permeated from upstairs.

'Di Angelo's,' said Coburg as he realised where they were. He waved the pistol at Peters and said, 'Upstairs.'

Peters gave a sigh of resignation, then stepped out of the storeroom and began to mount the steps that led up to the coffee shop itself. Coburg slipped the pistol into his pocket, and he and Lampson followed Peters.

Peters opened a door at the top of the stairs and they found themselves behind the counter of the coffee shop. Julia di Angelo, who was at the coffee machine, looked at Peters in surprise.

'Mr Peters?' she said.

Then she saw the two police detectives behind him and her eyes widened and her mouth fell open in alarm.

'Good morning,' said Coburg.

Coburg and Lampson returned to Scotland Yard, taking Len Peters and Julia di Angelo with them. Once at the Yard, Coburg took di Angelo into one interview room, while Lampson took Peters into another.

'Pat found that tunnel a couple of years ago, when he was having his office done up,' said Peters. 'He was having a storage cupboard put in, when the builder reported the space behind the wall was hollow. So the builder broke a hole in the wall to make like a doorway into it. Me and Pat then explored the tunnel. He took me with him because we'd both worked on the Kingsway tunnel, so we knew about tunnels. This tunnel wasn't long, but it was old, and we found there was a doorway at the far end. The door was locked, but Pat got the builder to break in, and that's when he found out it came out in the storeroom of Di Angelo's coffee bar. While we were in there, Pietro di Angelo came down from the shop to see what all the noise was about and found us there. He was shocked because as far as he was concerned that door was permanently shut. He knew it went into a tunnel but he'd never explored it. There was no lighting in it then, just a dark passage. Pietro had decided to shut the door permanently to keep out rats from his storeroom. There are rats in every tunnel in London.

'Even in those days, Pat had trouble with certain people. Dodgy people, as well as the police. With Wardour Mews being a dead end, if there was any trouble coming for him there was no way he could get out. So he suggested a deal to Pietro. He'd pay him so much a year if he allowed him to use the tunnel to go from the Riff Club and out through the coffee bar, if it was needed for any reason. Pat also said he'd have lighting put along the length of the tunnel with a switch at each end, so Pietro could use it to get to Pat's end unseen, if he wanted to, and Pat could do the same from the club.

'As far as Pietro was concerned, it was a good deal. He'd be getting money for something that he knew Pat would use only rarely, in an emergency, or something. And it also gave Pietro an escape route if things ever got nasty for him at the coffee bar. Don't forget, there was a time when Italians weren't popular with some people and Pietro had had threats.

'So that was it. The tunnel was made good. After Pietro was taken away for internment, Pat and Pietro's missus, Julia, kept the same deal. To be honest, it's hardly been used, except for lately. When Pat realised he was being watched by your blokes, twenty-four hours a day, he'd use it to disappear for a bit.'

'What did he do when he disappeared?' asked Lampson.

'I don't know,' said Peters. 'I never enquired. It doesn't do to ask questions.'

'Does Riley have a gun?'

Peters hesitated before answering, 'Yes. Most people in Soho have got a shooter of some sort. It's that kind of area. There are some very dangerous people around. You never know when you'll need to defend yourself.'

'Have you got a gun?'

'Me? No.' This said very emphatically. 'No one's after me. I ain't important.'

In the other interview room, Coburg listened as Julia di Angelo told him the same story about the discovery and renovation of the tunnel.

'Pietro, my husband, wasn't going to do it, but then these thugs arrived one day and started a fight

349

in the coffee bar. It was all about protection. Pay us and your coffee bar won't have any trouble. Don't pay, and you will have trouble. They also threatened me and the kids we had working for us. That made Pietro think: at the moment it's just fights, but he knew how dangerous these people were and it could get worse. He was worried they might turn up with guns or knives, and if they did the only way out was through the front door into the street. With the tunnel we could lock and bar the café door and then get away through Pat's club. And Pat was going to pay for it. It wouldn't cost us a penny. So Pietro said yes.'

She looked at Coburg and he could see the pain in her face as she said bitterly, 'You know where he is? That prison camp at Ascot. Have you seen it? Barbed wire on the high fences, big lights, armed guards.'

'Yes, I've been there,' said Coburg.

He'd visited the internment camp a couple of months earlier when he needed to talk to one of the internees. The winter quarters for Bertram Mills Circus had been taken over by the government, the animals dispersed and a high double fence of barbed wite erected, along with machine gun posts and watchtowers. The area still had tents, but these were enormous canvas bell tents rather than the circus variety. The internees were housed in single-storey brick buildings divided into soulless dormitories.

Thousands of Germans and Italians who had been living for many years in Britain had been rounded up and brought to the site as enemy aliens. Coburg knew that what Julia said was true: the vast majority of them had come to England as refugees from Nazi Germany or Fascist Italy, and now they were imprisoned alongside those few Germans who were Nazis, and those few Italians who supported Mussolini. The result was that most of the best Italian restaurants in London had had their chefs taken away, and London's top hotels had lost their best waiters when the Germans and Italians had been taken away. The site at Ascot was just one of the many internment sites that had been set up. Coburg had been told that the one on the Isle of Man now had the best meals of anywhere in Britain, such was the number of Italian and German chefs who'd been sent there.

'It is so cruel!' Julia burst out angrily. 'Pietro was never a fascist! He hates that kind of thing. That was why we came here to England. The land of the free,' she said, her voice heavy with angry sarcasm.

'How often did Pat Riley use the tunnels to come through your coffee shop?' asked Coburg.

'Until a week ago, hardly ever. And then he comes to me and tells me that the police are watching him. And not just the police, there are dangerous people also watching his club. He needs to use the tunnel to avoid them for his safety.'

'How often?' asked Coburg.

'Two, three times a day,' said Julia. 'He would appear and go out into Berwick Street, and then come back an hour, maybe two, later. I didn't keep a note of how often or for how long; it was none of my business.'

CHAPTER FORTY

Tuesday 10th December 1940

Coburg released Len Peters and Julia di Angelo, with a warning to both that he'd need to talk to them again so neither was allowed to leave London. When he and Lampson got back to their office, they found DC Pritchard waiting for them. Pritchard looked shamefaced.

'I'm sorry, sir,' he said, 'it never occurred to me he might have another way out.'

'It never occurred to me either, Constable,' said Coburg. 'He fooled all of us.'

'I've come to report that he's gone. From his home, I mean. And his car's not there.'

'Do you have details of the car?'

'Yes, sir. It's a red Austin 7.' He then gave them the registration number, which he obviously knew by heart, having spent so much time in the house opposite Riley's house looking at it and the car parked outside it.

Coburg picked up the telephone and put out an alert for the car, and for Riley. 'We'll let you have a photo of Riley and his description straight away,' he told the organiser of the search. 'Sergeant Lampson will bring it to you for distribution.'

He hung up, and Lampson made for the door, saying, 'I'm on it, guv.' Lampson added to the unhappy-looking DC Pritchard, 'You come along with me, Constable. Think of it as another bit of learning about police procedural action.'

They had barely gone, when Coburg's phone rang. It was Jack Harkness from Vice.

'You wanted to know if we had anything on Lord Cuddington,' he said.

'Yes, thanks,' said Coburg. He picked up a pencil. 'What have you got?'

'Nothing on Lord Cuddington, but there's gossip about his wife, Lady Pamela.'

'What about?'

'Male prostitutes, gigolos, whatever you like to call them. And drugs.'

'Drugs?'

'Yeh. She hangs around with some shady characters. Including a gangster called Shelley Buttons.' Harkness chuckled. 'The word is that you had Shelley Buttons lifted and put away.'

'I did.'

He laughed. 'I'd like to have seen his face. We wanted to move on him because we heard what was going on at his clubs, but we were warned off. Top-level government stuff. "Stay away from Shelley Buttons. The man knows some important people."'

'Yes, so I gather.'

'I also heard that you'd had Lady C arrested for murder,' said Harkness.

'Yes,' said Coburg. 'Where did you hear about it?'

'You know what this place is like,' chuckled Harkness. 'Gossip spreads faster than rabies. I even heard that your missus had shot down a German bomber. Now that one can't be right, surely?'

'No, it isn't,' said Coburg. 'But one thing is that you might be able to help us with: we've put out an alert for Pat Riley.'

'The owner of the Riff Club?'

'Yes. He's wanted for the murder of five people.'

'Five?! This is the same Pat Riley we're talking about? Mr Friendly, smiles all the time? Never causes any trouble?'

'That's him,' said Coburg.

'Bloody hell,' said Harkness. 'Of all the club owners in Soho, he's the last one I'd have thought of as being a killer.'

'I guess that's how he's got away with it,' said Coburg.

He hung up, and looked at the phone, considering whether to telephone Rosa and tell her the news, then thought against it. He decided to concentrate his energies on finding Riley. The fact he'd taken his car meant that he was definitely on the run. The thing now was to find out if Riley had contacts outside London, people he could run to. Coburg needed to delve into Riley's record, find out what other places apart from London he'd lived. He got up and headed for the office where the files on all those with a criminal record were kept.

Pat Riley pulled the car to a halt in the shadow of the high brick wall that surrounded the vast estate of Dawlish Hall. Aware that the police would most likely have circulated details of his red Austin 7, along with its registration number, he'd left the Austin in the garage of an old friend and exchanged it for a pale blue Triumph Dolomite. It had taken him what seemed like hours of scouring the country roads to find the place because all the direction signs had been removed in an attempt to foil the Germans if they invaded. Finally, he'd gone into the shop in the small village of Dawlish and asked the way to the Hall. The woman behind the counter had looked at him quizzically, then asked: 'What do you want them for?'

What is it about country people? Riley thought in annoyance. He forced a smile and said, 'I have something to deliver there.'

This seemed to satisfy the woman, who then gave him directions, which seemed to involve various crossroads and places that used to exist but weren't there any longer: 'Then you turn left at what used to be Abbott's Farm but is now just a tumbledown old cottage with an old apple tree in front of it,' was just one example.

Finally, Riley thanked her and left, doing his best to keep the puzzling directions in his head as he drove out of the village in what he hoped was the right direction. By driving slowly and remembering everything the woman in the shop had told him, he finally found the high brick wall. He parked on the grass verge, took a pair of binoculars from his car and climbed onto the bonnet, supporting himself against the top of the wall while he aimed the binoculars at the large white mansion. He wondered how many people were inside it. A house that big would need a large staff.

He tried to remember what he'd read in the papers about Coburg's family. Coburg's eldest brother, Magnus, was the Earl of Dawlish.

Riley knew he was taking a gamble. It was known that Rosa had left London after the attempt on her, but no one in London appeared to know where she'd gone. It was only Riley's guess that she'd come here, but it made sense. Far from London and the bombing, and with the protection of Coburg's brother and his staff. The question was: would he be able to find her in a place as large as this? She could be anywhere.

And then, unbelievably, he saw her. She came out of the main entrance to the house and was walking towards a paddock where an elderly horse grazed. In her hand she held what looked like an apple.

Riley dropped down from the car bonnet and hurriedly climbed back into his car, started it up, and then drove on the road beside the high wall until he came to the two tall stone pillars with a statue of a winged horse atop each. The gates were open, and Riley drove in and made for the paddock and Rosa, pulling up beside her just before she reached the paddock and the horse.

'Rosa!' he called cheerily.

Rosa looked at him in surprise. 'Pat! What are you doing here?'

'Edgar sent me. He asked me to take you back to London.'

Rosa looked at him suspiciously. 'Why?' she asked.

'He'll tell you that himself,' said Pat with what he hoped was a friendly grin. 'Come on, hop in.'

She shook her head.

'I'd better phone him first,' she said.

She was about to walk away, when she saw the pistol that had appeared in his hand and which he was aiming at her.

'Get in the car,' he said, and now all friendliness had vanished from him.

'But . . .' began Rosa.

'Get in the car,' snapped Riley, 'or I'll shoot you here and now.'

Rosa threw a look towards the house, wondering where Magnus and Malcolm were.

'In the car!' barked Riley, angry now, and he pushed the passenger door open.

Reluctantly, Rosa got into the passenger seat.

'I can drive one-handed,' said Riley, 'so don't try anything or this pistol will punch a very big hole in that pretty head of yours.'

With that, he started the car up and drove along the drive and out through the gates, pulling up on the grass verge after a few hundred yards. He reached to the back seat and produced two short lengths of rope, which he dropped in her lap.

'Tie one around your ankles, then the other around one of your wrists,' he ordered.

'Why?' asked Rosa. 'Isn't the gun enough?'

'Not with you,' said Riley. 'I know what you're capable of. Do it.'

Slowly, trying to give herself time in the hope that Magnus or Malcolm or somebody else from the Hall would appear, Rosa tied the length of rope around her ankles.

'Now the wrist,' barked Riley. 'And hurry it up.'

Rosa tied the rope around one of her wrists. Riley held the gun on her while, with one hand, he took the loose end of the rope and looped it around her other wrist, then pulled it tight and tied it. That done, he set the car in motion again. He drove until they came to a telephone box. He stopped the car and got out, holding the gun on her the whole time as he walked around to the passenger door and opened it.

'Hop to the phone box,' he ordered Rosa.

Rosa hopped and shuffled her way to the phone box. Riley dialled the number for Scotland Yard, pushing button A when the operator answered. The coins he'd put into the slot tumbled down into the box.

'DCI Coburg, please,' he said.

'Who's calling?' asked the operator.

'Someone with urgent information about his wife,' said Riley.

There was a series of clicks, and then he heard Coburg's voice asking, 'Who are you, and what's this about my wife?' Riley held the receiver to Rosa's mouth. Rosa said:

'Edgar, it's Rosa.'

'Rosa!' exclaimed Coburg.

Riley took the receiver back. 'As you heard, I've got her. She'll be safe so long as you do as I say. I want you to call off the search for me. I want to hear an announcement to that effect on the wireless, saying, "The police are no longer searching for Mr Patrick Riley." It's now eleven o'clock. I shall be making a phone call at one o'clock to a friend to hear if that

360

message has gone out. If it hasn't, I'll shoot her. And you know I will.'

With that, he hung up.

Coburg sat looking at the receiver in his hand, his mind in a tormented whirl. Lampson, who'd just returned to the office and saw the worried look on his boss's face, asked, 'What was that about, guv?'

'That was Pat Riley. He's gone to Dawlish Hall and he's got Rosa. He threatens to shoot her if we don't put out a message on the wireless that we're no longer looking for him.'

'Shoot her?' said Lampson, shocked.

Coburg gave the operator the number of Dawlish Hall and asked her to connect him.

'Master Edgar,' came Malcolm's cheery voice when the connection was made. 'How are you today?'

'In big trouble,' said Coburg. 'Is Magnus there?'

'What sort of trouble?' asked Malcolm, worried. Coburg heard him shout, 'Your Grace. It's Master Edgar! In trouble!' Then Magnus was on the phone.

'What's happened?' asked Magnus.

'The person who's killed all those people, a man called Pat Riley, has just kidnapped Rosa.'

'Kidnapped?' said Magnus, bewildered. 'That's impossible! She was going out to give an apple to Mip, which she's taken to doing every day.'

'I've just heard her voice on the phone,' said

Coburg. 'With him telling me he's got her and he's going to shoot her if I don't put an announcement out on the wireless by one o'clock today that says we're no longer looking for him. He can't be far away from you.'

'Leave it to me,' said Magnus. 'We'll go out and find her and get her back. Do you know what car he's driving?'

'He was driving a red Austin 7, but my guess is he'll have switched to another car, although I have no idea what. Something very different, I'm sure. Be careful, Magnus. This man is very dangerous, and he's already killed five people. He'll have no qualms about killing Rosa.'

'I'll bring in our local policeman.'

'He won't be much use against Riley. And the sight of a police uniform could well make things worse. If he feels trapped, he'll shoot, and Rosa will be the first to be shot. I'm going to come up and see what I can do.'

'If he's as edgy as you say, the sight of a police car up here won't help,' said Magnus.

'I'll borrow a private car,' said Coburg. 'If anything happens, call Sergeant Lampson, here at Scotland Yard.'

Coburg hung up and said to Lampson, 'You got all that?'

Lampson nodded. 'Shall I come with you?'

'No, I need you here to co-ordinate things.' He scribbled the telephone number of Dawlish Hall on a piece of paper and passed it to him. 'That's my brother's number if anything happens.'

'Do you want me to scramble the local police up there?' asked Lampson. 'Get some armed units out?'

'Yes, prepare them,' said Coburg. 'But tell them to take no action without consulting Magnus. Rosa's life is at stake.'

CHAPTER FORTY-ONE

Tuesday 10th December 1940

Malcolm drove the Bentley through the gates while Magnus in the back checked the pistols and rifles they'd brought with them.

'We have no idea if he's even still around here,' said Malcolm. 'He could be miles away.'

'My guess is he's tied Rosa up. She'd never sit still and let herself be taken away without putting up a fight. He wouldn't want to be caught driving around somewhere busy with a woman tied up. I believe he'll still be somewhere around here.'

'Even if you're right, we have no idea what car he'll be driving,' said Malcolm.

'I'm hoping Mrs Wimbell might be able to help us,' said Magnus.

'Excellent thinking,' exclaimed Malcolm, and he put his foot on the accelerator and hastened towards the village. 'People new to this area are always getting lost, and where do they go to for directions? The village shop.'

The village was quiet when they arrived. Malcolm

parked outside the village shop and kept the engine ticking over while Magnus went in.

'Good morning, Your Grace,' said Mrs Wimbell. 'What can I do for you?'

'I was wondering if anyone called in today to ask for directions to the Hall?' asked Magnus.

'Yes,' said Mrs Wimbell. 'A man. He seemed pleasant enough, He said he was delivering something. Did he find you alright?'

'I'm not sure,' said Magnus. 'Do you know what sort of car he was driving?'

Mrs Wimbell gave him an apologetic look. 'I'm sorry, I didn't see it. And even if I had, I'm not sure if it'd know what it is. I'm not very good on cars.'

Magnus's heart sank, but he gave her a grateful smile. 'Not to worry,' he said. 'I'll ask next door. They might have seen it.'

'Seen what?' asked a small boy who appeared from the back of the shop.

'A car,' said Magnus. 'The man who was driving it came in this morning to ask the way to the Hall.'

'Oh yes!' said the boy. 'It was a Triumph Dolomite. Pale blue.'

Mrs Wimbell gave the boy a fond look. 'That's my William,' she said proudly. 'He loves cars.'

'Did you happen to get the registration number, by any chance?' asked Magnus.

'I did,' said William proudly. 'I collect car

numbers. I wrote it down in my book.'

With that, he disappeared back into the storeroom and emerged a moment later holding a small notebook, which he had opened and was thumbing through.

'Here it is,' he said, and he read out the number. Magnus scribbled it down on the pad that Mrs Wimbell kept on her counter, tore off the page and tucked it into his pocket.

'You are a most excellent boy, William,' he said, 'and when this is over, I shall recompense you.'

With that, he hurried out of the shop.

'What's recompense?' William asked his mother.

'It means payment.'

William's face lit up. 'He's going to pay me for writing down the car number? Wow! I'm going to get some more.'

Magnus and Malcolm spotted the car, half-hidden in a small copse not far from a tumbledown, semi-derelict wooden barn.

'A pale blue Triumph Dolomite,' said Malcolm.

Magnus took out the scrap of paper with the registration number written on it. 'That's the one,' he said. 'We've got to be careful. If we go blundering in, he's just as likely to shoot her. And us. We have to treat it the way we did in the First War when we were sneaking into no man's land towards the German lines.'

'That was usually at night,' said Malcolm. 'If he's

looking out for anyone, he'll see us as we cross the open ground around the barn. He'll also be watching the door. It looks like the only way in.'

'The door doesn't look very secure,' noted Magnus. 'It's hanging on one hinge. One hard kick and it'll go in.'

'And the bullets will start flying,' said Malcolm. 'I think it's worth looking round the back and seeing if there might be a window we can peer through.'

'And if there isn't?'

'We look for a weak spot in the woodwork and kick it in.'

'We don't know where he is in the barn. Or Rosa, come to that. We go in with guns blazing, we could hit her.' Malcolm nodded. 'Let's creep round the back anyway, using those trees as cover. I suggest on our hands and knees, like we used to in the First War.'

'I didn't have arthritis in the First War,' said Magnus. 'Once I get down, I can't get up easily.'

'For God's sake, you're acting like an old woman.'

'No, I'm acting like a man of a certain age, which I am.'

'We'll crawl there. Once we're there, I'll lift you up.'

'For God's sake, Malcolm, this is starting to sound like *Laurel and Hardy Carry Out a Rescue*.'

'That may be,' said Malcolm primly. 'But I'm not going to let that young woman die if I can help it.'

* * *

Inside the barn Riley sat on a bale of straw, his pistol aimed at Rosa, sitting on another, near enough to her to be able to shoot her easily, but far enough away so that she wouldn't be able to launch a sudden attack on him.

'I don't want to hurt you, but your husband has given me no choice,' he said.

Rosa gave a bitter laugh. 'Really, Pat? It was you who ordered those two men to kill me.'

'I was out of my mind with worry,' Riley defended himself. 'I thought you might have found out the truth about Benny's guitar.'

'He didn't leave it with you as security,' said Rosa. 'You ended up with it in your hands after you killed him.'

'I had no choice. Benny was going to grass me up. Go to the police.'

'What do you mean, grass you up?' asked Rosa, thinking, *Keep him talking. Keep him interested. While he's talking, he won't be shooting me.*

'How do you think I make the club pay? Jazz? Jazz doesn't bring in that much money. So I operate a trading business. Dealing.'

'Dealing what?' asked Rosa, puzzled. Then her face cleared as the realisation hit her. 'You're the fence Edgar talks about! That fire crew who've been robbing safes and taking jewellery.'

'They came to me. Or, this one guy did. Dan Reeves.

What happened was he turned up that night at the club with a load of jewellery to offload, like he'd done before. But this time he was with his girlfriend. I'd never seen her before, but it turned out she was Benny's sister. Benny saw her and Reeves going into my office and put his head round the door to say hello to her, and he saw all the stuff on my desk and me handing some banknotes over to Reeves. He realised what was up straight away and got angry. Really angry. He threatened to go to the police unless they handed the jewels back to where they'd got them. He was so bloody straight it was unbelievable! I knew there was no way Dan Reeves was going to do that. To calm Benny down, I offered him a glass of whisky. I knew he liked a glass now and then.'

'Only you added strychnine to it,' said Rosa.

'I didn't have a choice!' insisted Riley. 'Dan suggested the best place to dump him was in the tunnel at Aldwych. He said it would confuse people. I knew the tunnels around there just like Dan did, so together we put his body there. Once I'd got rid of Benny's guitar to Izzy Morrant, I thought we were home free. And then you started asking questions. I'd asked Harry to keep his ears open for anyone asking questions, and when he told me it was you, I knew we were in trouble. If you found out anything, it would go straight back to your husband. As far as

I knew, you'd learnt something and when you came to see me you were just sounding me out.'

'So you put those two blokes onto me.'

'Yes, and a right mess they made of it,' said Riley bitterly.

'So you shot them?' Rosa hazarded a guess.

'Once they'd let me down like that, I couldn't trust them. What was worse, they knew I'd done Benny, and if the police got hold of them for lifting you, they were sure to talk. So they had to go.'

'And the others? Edgar said there were six people dead in all.'

Riley looked at her suspiciously. 'What is all this? You trying to keep me talking so I won't shoot you?'

'No,' lied Rosa. 'And you said you wouldn't shoot me if that announcement was made over the wireless.' She looked at Riley and said, 'There's no need to shoot me now. Edgar knows. He knows it was you, and if you shoot me, he'll hunt you down, and you won't die an easy death.'

'He may think he knows, but he's got no actual proof,' said Riley. 'All the people who knew anything are dead. All of them. There's no one alive who can testify against me, so it's all circumstantial. The only one who can is you.'

'You said you'd wait until one o'clock to see if the announcement is made on the wireless.'

'I said that to buy me time. Well, time's running

out. Any moment now, your husband will have this place crawling with coppers. I'm not going to wait here for that to happen. I didn't shoot you before because I needed you alive for him to hear your voice so he'd know I had you. More than that, I was genuinely trying to work out if there was a way not to kill you. I've always liked you, Rosa. But, like I said, you're the last one who can actually give evidence against me. I can't afford that.'

With that, he levelled the pistol at her head. The next second, a shot rang out.

CHAPTER FORTY-TWO

Tuesday 10th December 1940

Rosa stared in shock as Riley's head seemed to explode, blood, bone and brains bursting out, spraying over her, as his body tumbled to the ground.

'It's alright,' came a voice.

Rosa turned towards the door as Magnus entered, pistol in hand. Magnus hurried over to her and began to untie the ropes that bound her wrists and ankles.

'I'm sorry about the mess,' apologised Magnus. 'I told Malcolm it didn't need a gun that powerful.'

'I disagree,' said Malcolm, entering the barn, holding a large handgun that was still smoking. 'Use a popgun and there was still a chance he could have pulled the trigger. This is what was needed.'

'Where were you?' asked Rosa.

Malcolm pointed to the back wall where there was a small window, some of the glass of which was broken. 'I found that window at the back. It was out of his eyeline. So long as you kept him talking, I could line up my shot.'

Magnus looked at her, splattered with Riley's blood and brains.

'Malcolm will take you to the Hall,' he said. 'I'll stay here with the body in case anyone turns up and decides to nose around.' He looked at Rosa, relief writ large on his face. 'Thank God we found you.'

The first thing Rosa did when they arrived back at Dawlish Hall was telephone Scotland Yard. It was Lampson who answered the phone in Coburg's office.

'Mrs Coburg!' said Lampson. 'Where are you? What's happened?'

'I'm alright,' said Rosa. 'Pat Riley's dead. Is Edgar there?'

'He's on his way to you,' said Lampson. 'I can't get a message to him because he took a private car instead of our police one, so there's no radio.'

'At least he's on his way,' said Rosa.

'How did Riley die?' asked Lampson.

'I didn't shoot him, if that's what you're asking,' said Rosa. 'I'll let Edgar tell you when we get back. I'd rather not say what happened over the phone. But I am safe.'

Dusk was falling as Coburg drove. Five more miles to go and then he'd be at Dawlish. He'd borrowed an unmarked car from the police compound and felt frustrated at not having a radio in the car to make contact with Scotland Yard. A couple of times on the journey he'd considered pulling up at a telephone box and phoning Magnus to see what news there was, but he was fearful that it could be bad, and if that was the case, he didn't want to get that bad news over the phone.

I should have worked it out before, he berated himself. *Or at least taken Riley into custody.* If he had, then Rosa's life wouldn't be in danger as it was now. Because there was no doubt that Riley would kill her. He'd tried previously when he'd given the orders to Punt and Maples, but fortunately she'd got away from them. And Punt and Maples had paid the price for that. Riley had killed both of them, and blaming Shelley Buttons had been a clever smokescreen. Buttons was such a despicable character with a really bad record that the suggestion that he'd been responsible for both the abduction of Rosa and killing Punt and Maples had been very plausible. And then those other deaths while the very watchful eyes of the detectives were keeping a twenty-four-hour tab on Riley, establishing that Riley was either at the club or at his home, so he couldn't have been responsible for shooting Reeves and Barker and dumping their bodies in the Aldwych tunnel.

I should have conducted a search into Riley's earlier life, before he became a club owner, Coburg cursed himself. *Then I would have found out about him working on the Kingsway tunnel.* Wenlock had given him the answer when he'd told him and Lampson about central London being riddled with tunnels, created over hundreds of years. Almost two thousand years, since Roman times. Soho was old and had been a sanctuary for refugees to London for hundreds of years. Refugees always built tunnels so they could escape from their persecutors. He should have examined the interior of the Riff Club right at the start. And, because of his laxness, Rosa was at the mercy of Riley. Coburg had arranged for the announcement to go out on the wireless, as Riley had demanded, but he knew it wouldn't guarantee Rosa's safety. Riley had got away with it because he'd killed everyone who knew what he was up to, starting with Benny.

Alice Martin had gone to the Riff Club that night with her boyfriend, Dan Reeves. Dan had been taking stolen jewellery to Riley to sell. Riley was a fence. Benny must have gone into Riley's office to find out what his sister was doing at the club and discovered what was going on.

What had happened? Had Riley and Reeves offered him money for his silence? Or had they just killed him immediately?

Reeves worked in the tunnels in the Aldwych area and knew them like back of his hand. Together, Riley and Reeves must have transported Benny's body to a place where they could carry it through one of the many side tunnels and dump it.

Why had Riley killed Reeves? Because Reeves had walked away from AFS Crew 127, and as a result he needed money. He must have gone to Riley and threatened to grass Riley up unless he paid him.

And Joe Barker was the same. Barker had discovered that Riley was Reeves's fence. He'd also gone to see Riley to blackmail him, and got the same punishment. Coburg was sure that if Pamela Cuddington hadn't killed Alice, Riley would have got rid of her as well. All the witnesses who were a risk to him, dead. And now Rosa was facing the same fate.

By now, dusk had changed to night, and the car's shrouded blackout lights made very little impact on the darkness, especially on these minor winding country roads. *Slow down*, Coburg urged himself. *You can't see clearly; in this non-light, you're likely to crash into a hedge or a tree where the road bends.*

No, he argued with himself. *I need to get there quickly. I need to save Rosa!*

Straining his eyes, he didn't see the crossroads, nor the lorry coming at speed because its lights were off, the driver so familiar with this road that he wasn't expecting anything else to be on it now it was the blackout. All Coburg felt was the crash of metal on metal as the front of heavy lorry smashed into the side of his car, sending it careering out of control towards a hedge. The car ploughed through the hedge and then tipped and fell into the field beyond, rolling once, then twice before settling upside down. Coburg pushed at his door, but it was jammed shut. He tried to crawl to the passenger door, but he realised the front seats had become so twisted he was stuck upside down.

He could feel liquid trickling down his face and thought it must be blood, but then the smell struck him and he realised it was petrol.

Oh God, no! he thought. *It only needs one spark and I'll be burnt alive!*

And as he thought that, he saw a flame appear from beneath the upside-down bonnet of the car, and there was a mighty *woosh!* and the whole windscreen disappeared in a ball of fire.

CHAPTER FORTY-THREE

Wednesday 11th December 1940

'You were lucky,' said Magnus.

They were in a private room in the local cottage hospital, courtesy of His Grace, Magnus the Earl of Dawlish. Rosa sat in a chair beside Coburg's hospital bed; Magnus and Malcolm stood.

'The lorry driver had buckets of urine he was taking to make manure from, so he used them to put out the fire. You may have smelt, but at least you weren't roasted.'

Coburg's arms were bandaged, with another bandage across his chest from where the flames had singed his skin, but fortunately not burnt it too badly. And there were no bones broken. The doctor who'd examined him calculated he'd be able to be discharged on the morrow.

'Thank you, Malcolm. And you, too, Magnus,' said Coburg. 'If you hadn't intervened, I dread to think what would have happened.'

'We know what would have happened,' said Magnus angrily. 'Luckily, Malcolm is a good shot.

Better than me,' he added. 'I might have shot Rosa.'

'No you wouldn't,' said Malcolm. 'Don't come on with this false modesty. You're as good as I am.'

'I called Ted Lampson and told him about the accident,' said Rosa. 'He said he'd tell Superintendent Allison that you were in hospital and that you'd need to take some time to recover.' She grinned. 'I might have made your condition sound worse than it is. After all, you don't have to rush back. Riley's dead, the murders have been solved. You've got Pamela Cuddington in custody.'

'I always knew that woman was trouble,' grumbled Magnus. 'I said so when you got engaged to her. She was wild. Wilful.' He turned to Malcolm and said, 'Come on, Malcolm. We'll leave these two together.' To Rosa, he said, 'Telephone the Hall when you're ready to leave and Malcolm will come and collect you.'

The two men left, and Rosa leant forward and gently took hold of Coburg's bandaged hand.

'How are your burns?' she asked.

'Not as bad as they could have been,' said Coburg. 'It was my own fault for driving too fast in the dark.'

'Not the lorry driver's for not slowing down as he approached the crossroads?' asked Rosa.

'That man may have been partly responsible, but he saved my life,' pointed out Coburg.

She leant forward and kissed him gently.

'The cases have been solved,' she said. 'It would be lovely to take a couple of days away from London here at Dawlish. Away from the bombing. Just you and I relaxing in the country.'

'And Magnus and Malcolm.'

'They won't interfere with us,' she said. 'And anyway, I like them.'

'And they like you.' Coburg pulled her to him and kissed her again. 'Yes,' he said. 'Let's stay.'

ACKNOWLEDGMENTS

My grateful thanks for the creation of this first book in the London Underground Station Mysteries goes to Susie Dunlop and the team at Allison & Busby. After *Murder at Claridges*, the third in the Hotel Mysteries featuring DCI Edgar Saxe-Coburg, his wife, jazz-singer Rosa Weeks, and DS Ted Lampson, the question arose: what next? There were doubts expressed about how many more top-class London hotels we could feature without repeating ourselves, but A&B had had positive feedback about Coburg, Rosa and Lampson, and the London setting of the Second World War. At which point Susie said she had discovered there were a large number of disused and abandoned tube stations in London, many with their platforms and internal structures intact although in a bad state of repair. Some still had rail tracks connected to the underground network; some – like Aldwych – had had the electric supply to the rails switched off, but were now being put to other uses: in Aldwych's case for storing the Elgin Marbles and other treasures from the British Museum to keep them safe from air raids. Thanks to her stroke of genius this led me to research the world under London, not just the disused underground stations but the myriad lengths of tunnels that had been created beneath London since Roman days, and were still being dug up to the start of the Second World War. At times of war, sometimes an urban population goes underground, starting with the underground stations as shelters, and then moving further and further into deeper and older tunnels. Tunnels are places to hide things other than frightened people, they are places to secrete things some people don't wish to see the light of day . . . including dead bodies.

I hope you enjoy this trip underground.

JIM ELDRIDGE was born in central London in November 1944, on the same day as one of the deadliest V2 attacks on the city. He left school at sixteen and worked at a variety of jobs, including stoker at a blast furnace, before becoming a teacher. From 1975 to 1985 he taught in mostly disadvantaged areas of Luton. At the same time, he was writing comedy scripts for radio, and then television. As a scriptwriter he has had countless broadcast on television in the UK and internationally, as well as on the radio. Jim has also written over 100 children's books, before concentrating on historical crime fiction for adults.

jimeldridge.com